Praise for *A Room Away from the Wolves*

"Shiver-inducingly delicious."

—*The New York Times Book Review*

"[Suma's] narratives are subtle, quicksilver creatures, her language is elegant, and her characters keep more secrets than they reveal." —NPR

"Terrific . . . A gothic love letter to secret places of New York City and the runaway girls who find them."

—Kelly Link, author of *Get in Trouble*, 2016 Pulitzer Prize Finalist in Fiction

"This beautiful story is full of magical realism and luscious, lyrical writing." —*BuzzFeed*

"[Suma's] latest is another masterpiece from the haunting writer." —*Paste Magazine*

"Suma's dreamy prose builds suspense as she bends reality . . . Give this to readers who prefer their books dark with a hint of the supernatural." —*VOYA Magazine*

"Nova Ren Suma is a YA horror legend, and in her latest book, *A Room Away from the Wolves*, she proves her prowess at writing dark, unsettling, page-turning tales." —*Bustle*

"Nova Ren Suma's marvelous book is the thrilling and moving story of a young woman's escape to Gotham and the world she finds there." —*Flavorwire*

★ "A gorgeously written and evocative ghost tale . . . Perfect for fans of E. Lockhart's *We Were Liars* and Meg Wolitzer's *Belzhar.*" —*SLJ*, starred review

"Eerie and atmospheric as only Nova Ren Suma can write, *A Room Away from the Wolves* is a page-turning thrill. Gulp this one down and prepare to be left shivery and spooked and a little bit heartbroken."
—Emily X.R. Pan, *New York Times* bestselling author of *The Astonishing Color of After*

"Don't take a single word of this remarkable book for granted—Nova Ren Suma is a force to be reckoned with. Nobody writes like her."
—Courtney Summers, *New York Times* bestselling author of *Sadie*

"*A Room Away from the Wolves* is a beautifully tangled chain, a modern gothic haunting by one of our masters."
—Elana K. Arnold, author of *What Girls Are Made Of*

A ROOM AWAY FROM THE WOLVES

ALSO BY NOVA REN SUMA

Imaginary Girls

17 & Gone

The Walls Around Us

NOVA REN SUMA

A
ROOM
AWAY
FROM THE
WOLVES

Algonquin   2019

Published by
ALGONQUIN YOUNG READERS
an imprint of Algonquin Books of Chapel Hill
Post Office Box 2225
Chapel Hill, North Carolina 27515-2225

a division of
WORKMAN PUBLISHING
225 Varick Street
New York, New York 10014

First paperback edition, Algonquin Young Readers, September 2019. Originally
published in hardcover by Algonquin Young Readers in September 2018.
Printed in the United States of America.
Published simultaneously in Canada by Thomas Allen & Son Limited.
Design by Carla Weise.

LIBRARY OF CONGRESS CATALOGING-IN-PUBLICATION DATA
Names: Suma, Nova Ren, author.
Title: A room away from the wolves / Nova Ren Suma.
Description: First edition. | Chapel Hill, North Carolina : Algonquin Young
Readers, 2018. | Summary: Teenage Bina runs away to New York City's
Catherine House, a young women's residence in Greenwich Village with a
tragic history and dark secrets, where she is drawn to her mysterious
downstairs neighbor Monet.
Identifiers: LCCN 2018007016 | ISBN 9781616203733 (hardcover : alk. paper)
Subjects: | CYAC: Stepfamilies—Fiction. | Boardinghouses—Fiction. |
Runaways—Fiction. | New York (N.Y.)—Fiction. | LCGFT: Bildungsromans.
Classification: LCC PZ7.S95388 Ro 2018 | DDC [Fic]—dc23
LC record available at https://lccn.loc.gov/2018007016

ISBN 978-1-61620-984-1 (PB)

10 9 8 7 6 5 4 3 2 1
First Paperback Edition

For my mother's wild city—
the place that stole my heart,
broke me and made me broke,
and still somehow made my dreams come true

&

For E,
here with me through it all

A room is a place where you hide
from the wolves outside
and that's all any room is.

—Jean Rhys, *Good Morning, Midnight*

CONTENTS

PART ONE

In the Dark 3
Solid Ground 6

PART TWO: ONE MONTH BEFORE

Trouble 15
Vacancy 37
The Vow 60
The Wolves 90

PART THREE

The Welcome Party..103
Liars and Thieves..132
Dirt and Concrete...159
City of Strangers...183
Dawn 206

PART FOUR

Excavations...229
Fire Escapes 246
The Edge 270
Looking at the Sky 278

PART FIVE: SOMETIME AFTER

Through Glass 303
Passengers 310

PART ONE

IN THE DARK

WHEN THE GIRL WHO LIVED IN THE ROOM BELOW MINE disappeared into the darkness, she gave no warning, she showed no twitch of fear. She had her back to me, but I sensed her eyes were open, the city skyline bristling with attention, five stories above the street. It was how I imagined Catherine de Barra herself once stood at this edge almost a hundred years ago, when the smog was suffocating and the lights much more dim, when only one girl ever slept inside these walls of stacked red brick.

I was with my friend, if she could be called a friend, on the rooftop that night, close enough to pull her away or slip a word into her ear, close enough to push. I saw how far the gate was, how long the jump would be to reach it. I was there to witness how she flew.

It was dark, and I blamed the darkness. For those few moments, when she was midair and not even kicking, I practically became her. I grew her long legs and longer eye-lashes, I lost the jumble of knots in my hair, I let the mistakes spill out of my suitcase and scatter without a care into the wind. I was falling, and falling fast. There was a hum in my ears like a song leaking through floorboards. The windows on the way down were all lit up, every one, people I didn't know living their private lives inside as if no one could see. The sky-line above sparkled the way stars used to at home, and I didn't want to ever hit ground. I was someone here. I was someone.

Maybe that was what she saw, what she felt, what this house turned her into. She was out there beyond the ledge with nothing beneath her feet. She was high enough to clear the gate many times over. I swore she was out there. I swore the air had her, the night had her, the lights cast a ring all around her, and then the patch of darkness was empty.

I could see past where she'd been, as if I were sailing straight over buildings, beyond spires and scaffolding, past roof gardens and water towers, down through Lower Manhattan to the southern tip of the island, where the gleam-ing black bay took over. I saw the whole city spread out before me, sinister and strange and perfect. The air was clear, and she wasn't in it. No girl was falling or flying. Every window was dark. And how oddly quiet it became, like a patch of forest where no person had set foot for what felt like days upon days.

When I remembered where I was, I crept closer to the edge, gripping the bricks to stay steady, and I did what I knew she wanted.

I leaned out into the vacant night—the air boundless, feathery gray, and blooming with possibility—and I looked down.

SOLID GROUND

Monet Mathis, my downstairs neighbor and the first person on this patch of crowded earth who knew who I was and not who I tried to be, didn't disappear into thin air, not exactly. The night I lost her was clear and gray, hot and only faintly harsh-smelling. I couldn't tell where the tangles began and the stories took over, but I spotted her as soon as I looked down. She'd made it to the sidewalk. It was past midnight, and she was on the other side of the gate, on hard ground, beyond the limits of where I could even hope to reach her.

The story became that she fell out of the night sky without warning. According to some witnesses on the street, she came out of nowhere, dropping like debris from a passing plane. Others said they saw a figure on the rooftop, a figure flirting dangerously with the edge, and assumed she must have sent herself sailing. There were those who said she hurtled down from the sky howling, fighting the wind. Then there were those who said she dropped like a stone, knocked unconscious by the fall, that she didn't make a sound until the crack of impact when her body met sidewalk.

They didn't know a thing.

It was true Monet landed just outside the gated entry to Catherine House, where she had a room that faced east on the fourth floor. Passing strangers couldn't have known that this was a boardinghouse for young women, first opened in 1919 after a personal tragedy, and that it was the last remaining boardinghouse of its kind in Manhattan. In the gate's webbing of wrought iron, the words CATHERINE HOUSE could be made out, but the house's namesake was long gone and the gate itself secured for the night, as it was solidly past curfew. No girl was getting in or out, even if she banged on the bars. We all agreed to that rule when we moved in.

The girl who appeared from the sky—they didn't know her name, they didn't know her way of feeding on secrets while never offering any authentic ones of her own—narrowly avoided being skewered by one of the spiked posts gaping up at the darkness. The sidewalk fractured beneath her, hairlines skittering in all directions as if from a lightning strike. Belly down, arms reaching, cheek to pavement, she was the center. The sound of her landing practically popped eardrums. Then quiet, so much quiet the streetlights could be heard letting out their hum. The M20 bus could be made out careening along the nearest avenue, heading downtown through the Village, all the way to South Ferry. A car alarm bleated in the distance.

Though it was late, a small sleepless crowd gathered around to help, and to do a little gawking. A few people from the block came down from stoops, gripping house keys, searching out the source of the noise. The old lady in the basement apartment across the street came out clutching a squirming cat. The lady was threatening to call in another complaint to 311. A gaggle of tourists, who'd gotten turned around where Waverly Place met, somehow, impossibly, Waverly Place, paused to point. A man walking his tiny dog on a studded leather leash glanced at the body, then doubled back and took a detour around the block. They were all strangers to us. The house may have seemed like a magnet to tragedy, a patch of shrieking static in the otherwise calm. What went on inside they would never know.

To them, Monet was of another world, there on the sidewalk, caught and pinned to the page like a winged bug. She was illuminated in the glow of the streetlamp. Her short hair made an upward swoop at the back of her neck. She wore white, but the night turned it gray—the way ghosts are gray when they dissipate and can't be made out from the shadows. She was perfectly still, one foot shoeless, her mouth open. It wasn't clear if she was breathing.

Photographs were taken, filtered, captioned, shared. People shuffled around, waiting for an ambulance to arrive. A yellow cab screeched to a stop on the corner. The driver emerged and stepped out into the street, vacancy light still on so he could catch a fare. Someone poked the body. Someone said, "Don't move her, wait for the ambulance." Someone, out of sorts, hunched over and started to sob.

Stories swirled on the street about her possible motivations. Some were saying she jumped—she had the look of a jumper. Some assumed drunken accident or foul play. These were hunches. Guesses. Dangerous, dangling insinuations.

They were acting like they knew her, had seen her up close. But they weren't there. I was there.

I leaned out over the edge, but not one person noticed me up on the rooftop. The darkness, and a protruding drainpipe, shielded me from sight.

My bird's-eye view showed her on the sidewalk, a chalk outline all filled up. Her back was to me, as if she'd walked permanently out of the last known room. She wasn't moving.

Behind the drainpipe, in the deepest shadow I'd managed to find, I held my breath until I couldn't. What had she done? The sky was thick with dim haze. The wind was fierce. Why had she done it? She'd taken something from me, looted it right from my hands, and now I wouldn't get it back. Or her.

There was too much I didn't understand—it formed a curtain all around me, crawling with dust mites and reeking with near a century's worth of secrets. The curtain tightened, an uncomfortable cocoon, but I could stay there inside it so I wouldn't have to know.

I got to my feet. I was ready to go downstairs and return to the room I rented, which had been mine now for near an entire month. I was about to leave it be, to mourn her in private and wish things had gone another way, when I stopped. I felt the tug, as if she still had a part of me on a string. I went back and peered over, propelled to give it one last look.

And there.

Down on the sidewalk in the shadow of the tall iron gate that said CATHERINE.

Her foot was twitching.

At first it was a movement so subtle I might have missed it. Then the movement gained strength, traveling up her left leg and running through to the end of her right arm, where her five fingers spread open, clasping ground. She rolled over, curling up against the gate for a moment and then straightening, rising into a sitting position. She lunged forward, lifting herself to her feet, balancing her weight on both legs. She wobbled a bit. She held her hands to her head. As far as I could tell from this distance, she hadn't broken any bones.

She'd made it. She really had.

People down in the street were gasping, flinching, flinging themselves backward as if her miracle might infect them. They were so ordinary. No one seemed to know what to do. I could guess what they were all thinking: *Had she come plunging out of the sky at all?* Maybe they'd imagined it or got themselves fooled. Maybe I had along with them.

Monet gave no answers or excuses. She stood, wearing the one shoe, wavering in ghost gray on the other side of the gate.

I stayed locked in place. The ledge was narrow, and there was no guardrail to keep the night at bay—just a great wide emptiness that always got my legs shaking. Now, a rush of air prickled my arms as if a summer storm were coming through, but this was no weather.

She must have felt me looking.

That was when her chin angled for the rooftop. She put a hand above her eyes to see better, her gaze aimed right at me.

A few lurkers on the street were starting to follow her stare and lift their heads, and now I ducked down to avoid them, peeking out again from behind a small chimney.

I wondered what she was feeling, what she knew, what she saw from where she was standing. If there were colorful butterflies crowding through her brain right now, pulses of warm light rearranging the canals of her heart. If the darkness had a taste, if the impact unspooled every wrong thing inside her. All I knew was that her life would be forever different now. She wasn't here with us anymore. So what was she waiting for?

My ears filled with a dense, rumbling hum.

Down below, some onlookers were staring at her, shaking their heads.

"Hey, are you okay, sweetie?" some guy called.

She ignored him, as she'd ignore any man who called her "sweetie."

She searched the night, but the city sky was starless and the windows on the highest floors were black and I wasn't budging. An ambulance was on its way, but she wouldn't wait.

She headed for the gate, and I thought at first she was trying to get inside the house, but she came back carrying something. A suitcase. She'd had it waiting. She must have seen the glow of the taxi's light, because next she headed straight for it, and no one tried to stop her. The cabdriver didn't kick her from his back seat when she climbed in, throwing the suitcase in first and then herself. He only shrugged and got in to drive. The few remaining witnesses stood back. The noise hushed. The city went quiet in the way I was used to, as if instead of a maze of asphalt, concrete, and brick, all around me was a thick, tangled wood.

From up above on the rooftop, I watched. For a long moment, it felt like the night itself had swallowed Monet again, the way it seemed to when she'd tumbled into the darkness, but then the taxi swerved into the street, taking the first turn, and with a snap of taillights she was gone.

PART TWO

One Month Before

TROUBLE

The day I left for New York City, the summer heat was already clammy, the sky bright white. I stood on the side of the road with an old suitcase and a fresh black eye. I wasn't speaking to my mother. Still, she was all I thought about as I lifted my thumb into the wind—the last things she said to me, the worst things she thought about me, what she'd do when she found me gone.

My mother was the one who taught me how to hitchhike. The curving shoulder in the rippling shade of the willow tree was our spot, the city our intended destination. She also taught me how to cover up a bruise, carefully and in layers, how to light a fire in the woods without a book of matches, and how to hold a grudge.

Just one day ago, she had asked me to leave, and I couldn't understand what she thought she was teaching me. She hovered in the doorway to my room, not setting foot inside. She stood right there and said I needed to go away for a while, that she'd found me a place to stay. She had her old suitcase with the bad wheel ready for me, front flap gaping. She wouldn't meet my eyes. I sat on my bed against the wall, a cascade of dirty laundry like a pelt of wet moss between us. She didn't come any closer, as if she didn't want to ruin her shoes.

"You have to understand, Bina. He thinks you girls need some time apart. They're his daughters. This is his house. What do you want me to do?"

She was talking about her husband. I should have gotten used to calling him by his name—it had been eight years— but I enjoyed never doing it to his face, or where he might overhear. His daughters were two girls—one in my grade, one a year older—who wanted me dead.

What my mother should have done was found some loyalty. She should have chosen her own flesh and blood over the family she married into. Instead she was kicking me out. The suitcase was ready. The extra room could be used for scrapbooking or storage or cardio.

"It's just for a month or so." She looked at the wall. It was vintage basement cinder block, because my room was in the basement, painted sickly ripe honeydew before I ever moved in. "No longer than a month, I promise. You'll be back here by August. Aren't you going to say anything?"

"Say what? Say I didn't do it?"

"If that's what you want to say . . ."

I nodded. I'd made my pillow a tourniquet-style twist.

"So you're innocent," she said. "You're really telling me the girls made up a whole new story to spite you. Again."

And shame me. And break me in all ways they thought they could.

I couldn't keep straight what I was supposed to have done now, this summer, and it was only the last day of June. I considered the stories I could put up in my defense, the inventions I could mold with my mouth to make the girls sound more terrible, or at least a shade more terrible than me. It wasn't that I'd trashed Charlotte's room again, but that they forced me to do it, gun to the head, so they could get their dad to buy them new stuff. It wasn't that I'd stolen the laptop Daniella carelessly left out and sold it for drugs, like they insinuated, but that I was protecting it, and them, and almost got chloroformed and stuffed in the trunk of a car over it, and everyone in this house should be grateful and checking to see if I had signs of PTSD. My mind shuffled through stories, possible alibis, excuses, all of them powdery-thin, edging on desperate. I wouldn't know what might come out of my mouth until I opened it.

The problem was, my mother was long used to my lies. She remembered, surely, how I tried to convince her that her new husband was unfaithful, leaving lipstick smudges on his collared shirt in the hamper for effect. When I *did* trash both girls' rooms, spilling paint from the garage on their matching pink carpets and then acting innocent. It wasn't always directed at them, either. Sometimes I aimed at myself. When I said I swallowed all those pills, it was the hospital that had to break it to her that there was barely anything in my stomach to pump. She knew what I was, as a good mother would. She recognized it because she'd grown it herself, over these past seventeen years.

Besides, I was tired. Couldn't she read my face to see when I was telling the real and actual truth?

"I swear," I said.

My mother closed her eyes to take a moment.

Gazing back at her was like seeing what I'd turn into in twenty years. We even had the same laugh—people said so all the time. The same pale eyes, when they were open, eyes that shifted colors depending on the tone of the sky that day, or the shirt we were wearing, or the color of the paint on the walls in the room we were in. Same pinkish skin that turned pinker at the slightest infraction. Same curly hair on the both of us, unruly and pulled back by an elastic band. She'd stopped dyeing her hair different colors once she gave up acting, and ever since it had been brown, like mine. Same brown hair. Same hands. Same big hips. Same big lips. And when they parted, same smile.

At that moment, she wasn't smiling. I couldn't see for sure, but when she opened her eyes, I bet the mood in the room turned her irises an infected green. "The thing is, I talked to your sisters. They told me everything."

She'd called the girls my *sisters*. "Told you what?"

"What you did to get yourself in trouble. What you did with that boy. At school, in front of everybody. It's a wonder you didn't get suspended before summer break. And Daniella's boyfriend, of all people. How could you?"

The punch to the gut was hard. I stared at her.

The pieces weren't there to put together. They were vague enough to cause smoke, make fumes, and my mother was breathing it all in until she couldn't even see her own daughter. That was me. I was in the room right in front of her, and she couldn't see me.

"Sabina," she said, "I'm tired. Every time there's a problem, it's about you. Every time we hear something terrible, you're the center of it. And I'm not even talking about what you did to my car. How do you think this makes me look with *him*?"

Her husband again. The moment had come, almost as if I were watching her draw a chalk line dividing us on the basement floor. She'd called me by my whole name, the name on my school ID and on my working papers, not Bina, which is what she tended to call me instead, not Bean, the silly name she'd tagged me with as a kid and used only in private. She'd drawn the line. She was on the other side. She was with them.

"Think of this as a break," she said. "Stay away from the girls for a while. Don't go to that party tonight. Give them space. You'll be fine at Alicia and Andrea's. You know them—you met them at church that time you went, don't you remember? They're good, generous people to take you in. They'll pick you up tomorrow morning, before your sisters even wake up. Did you hear what I said about the party?"

The church was her husband's thing, not hers. The people she mentioned were blank faces. She knew I wouldn't remember. The suitcase was mine now, even though I didn't understand why this was the last straw among all the things I may or may not have done. She wouldn't believe me no matter what I said. It made me want to roll around in the clothes on the floor. To clear a place and feel the basement's very bottom, the coolest spot in the house, against my bare cheek. Tile, and under it a pool of cement. Maybe I wouldn't move for a month.

But I had a party to crash in the woods. I had my name to clear.

After she left the basement, the plan formed. It had twists and turns. It had legs. I pictured myself finding my stepsisters and their friends out in the trees where they always went to party, finding them . . . and then what? I imagined a rush of insults, brutal confrontations, choked-up truths. Them admitting it in front of everyone and driving through town in disgrace to go tell my mother. *We are such liars. We are made of lies. We lied.* I couldn't wait for her to hear it from their mouths.

But it wouldn't be enough. She needed to regret what she'd done. I pictured myself going home to pack. I saw my hands, slick and careful, gathering what cash I could. The girls' purses and underwear drawers would provide the bulk of it, but I'd also confiscate what I could from her husband's wallet, wedged in the back pocket of his work slacks and hung on the arm of the bedroom chair. They would finance my trip, even if they didn't know it. My mother would be stunned, and I'd be heading down the road before she had the chance to send me somewhere else. Knowing when to leave was another thing she'd taught me, since she was so lousy at it.

My mother liked to say that your worst mistake can lead to the best thing to ever happen in your life, that sometimes you'll look up and see you found happiness from something that almost wrecked you to pieces.

I assumed she meant me, and the circumstances surrounding how she had me. She wouldn't say that I came crashing through her window like a hurled brick. She wouldn't say that she could have been someone else entirely—better, happier, and more fulfilled—had I not been born or had she left my father sooner. All I knew was that she was going to be an actress until she had me and, practically minutes after, married him. She'd hoped to become one of those dazzling faces on movie screens, the ones with the artificial glow about them, silvery and soft, with pearly white teeth.

She moved down to the city after high school to chase that dream—to get famous, to be someone. She used to tell me how close she got, how tangled in the dream she was when she had to pull away. This was my bedtime story, the city its backdrop, and it led to the most dazzling fantasies. Part of that story, a glittering piece at its center, was the summer she left her boyfriend and moved into the boardinghouse where she was able to rent a room of her own in the city. The summer she almost made it happen, her face pressed up close to the glass, peering in. Then the news of me, and there she was, terrified and not even twenty.

The story ends like this: She is at her window on the fourth floor of the young women's residence where she has a room, which looks out onto the street, letting the lights of near a million windows warm her insides. Her feet ache, ball to heel, from dancing. Her hair is dyed burgundy that week. It's loose, the elastic tie lost, the curls set free. The shooting of the indie film she starred in had ended, and this is the night of the wrap party, they were celebrating, they'd saved money in the shoestring budget for this. "Don't go! Don't go!" they said. "You're still our star! Stay." But she had to go, she said. Curfew. The line producer called her a cab. Now she's at her window, feeling every feeling, remembering every moment, a burn through her toes.

That's when she hears him.

He's found her. He's down in the street. He's banging on the gate, shouting her real name, not the one soon to be in the film's credits, but the one on her school records, in the Hudson Valley, upstate, hours and lives away. If she had stayed at the wrap party, she would have missed him. But here she is, at her window, and there he is, my father before he knew it, at the gate.

The story broke off there. Simply hearing the sound of her real name in the darkened city street must have punctured everything and faded the picture to black. She would never tell more beyond it, as if all time stopped when she left the house to go back to him that July night almost two decades ago. The winter after, she had me.

Now, my own story was on the edge of beginning. All I knew was that I had to leave the basement, I had to go where I wasn't wanted, if I expected anything to change.

The bedroom my mother shared with her second husband was on the ground floor and had a straight, unblocked view of the driveway, not even a tree in the way. And my mother had heightened hearing in the dark, like a bat. I waited until she was preoccupied streaming a movie before carefully carrying the packed suitcase up the basement steps, not letting the bad wheel bang. I turned off the motion sensor that controlled the outdoor lights and slipped out of the house through the back door, tall and made of glass, where I could see in but no one could see me in the shroud of surrounding black. The backyard faced a bank of trees, and it was through that fringe, following a worn path illuminated by a well-aimed flashlight swiped from the hall closet, that I was able to bypass the driveway and make it to the curve in the road. There, I left my suitcase, camouflaged by a bramble bush under the willow tree. I'd come for it later. My mother taught me to never run away with only the clothes on your back.

I remembered. The first time I ran, I was nine—and she was with me.

The two of us stood on the side of the road, my ragged, frenzied mother and me, unbathed and anxious we'd get run over. We had a sign, careful calligraphy done with a rainbow of markers on a torn flap of cardboard: *Take us to the city. Good company. Cute kid. Mom can sing.* This last bit was an exaggeration. We had a suitcase and a milk crate of our most beloved things—everything we'd been able to rescue from the house before the hairy sociopath would emerge from his art studio (the garage) and find us gone. That was something we called my father to avoid using his given name. Saying his name aloud gave him power, and he had no power over us anymore.

We couldn't salvage everything we wanted from the house, and though my mother took me digging out behind the cherry tomatoes—we had rows and rows of them in the back garden—she didn't find what she was searching for. Time ran out. He was coming out any minute. He'd be done painting soon, and he'd know we were leaving him.

We gathered our things and walked a long way to the two-lane road, far out of view of the driveway. We found a bend where it was safe. The willow tree there gave us refuge. I mimicked the way my mom stuck out her thumb and the compelling come-hither face she put on for drivers, pulling them toward her as if she were a magnet. I wanted to help, and she said I was a natural.

We had a plan to head straight for the Thruway. We were aiming for the lanes going south, New York City–bound. Any moving vehicle would do, so long as it got us closer to the city, which was where our destiny foretold we should go. My mother would renew her career and go on auditions again—start small, student plays, short films, then maybe she'd get a vocal coach and try for off-off-Broadway. Her dream had been reanimated. As for me, I didn't have a dream yet, but my plan was to find one and wear it around in front of her so she'd recognize the same fire in me.

She said I'd go to school with the city kids. I'd have to force myself to not be so shy. Maybe she'd enroll me in tae kwon do or kung fu, so I could defend myself, because urban streets were different from the walking trails I knew in the woods, and a bear whistle wouldn't be enough down there. We'd find a place to stay.

What about the house you used to live in? I'd asked. *Why not there?* I knew the house was on the island of Manhattan. In her stories, the house grew tall into the night, taller than trees. It was red-bricked and eyed with many windows, gated and safe from fathers and ogres and other intruders, unless you opened the gate to let them in, and I would not open the gate, I would not be fooled. Any girl who needed a place to run to was welcome there—this she told me. This place was called Catherine House, which felt right to me, a whole house named after one girl. I imagined it nestled deep on the island somewhere, waiting for us with a light on and a cracked-open door.

But no, she said. No. We could not go there. Not today. And certainly not together. That house was not the place for her anymore, and it was not the place for me.

25

She wouldn't give it another word.

Instead we'd couch-surf, she told me, we'd camp out on floors if we had to, she had some friends from the old days, she had some numbers she could try. Never again would I have to call the neighbors from the speed dial she kept programmed for me when he was raging, like the time he got ahold of the fireplace poker and threatened to destroy his own art in the garage, then her, then me, all things he owned in order of importance. My mother and I were done with him. We lifted our thumbs high.

The car that stopped changed everything, but not in the way I wanted. It was a minivan with a silver fish on the bumper, and that was the first sign. My mother had warned me about these fish. She said they meant the people may not like us or trust us—they were Jesus people—but if they asked if we were Jewish we should not be afraid and hide what we were. We should look them in the eye and say yes. It didn't matter that we didn't know when the high holidays came on the calendar and we mixed all our plates and bowls and spoons. We were Jewish enough to most people, even when we weren't Jewish enough for some other Jews.

I didn't see the driver. I saw the two girls' faces first, smashed up against the back window, suction-lipped, bug-eyed. These were the sisters: Charlotte (older, meaner); Daniella (younger, same age as me, the smaller clone). It would turn true that they didn't like me, though it had nothing to do with religion. Their father told my mother he couldn't head out to the Thruway right then because he had a sack full of groceries and his precious girls were peckish for supper, but if we wanted a place to stay the night, well, they lived just around the bend, on Blue Mountain Road, and had a serviceable pullout couch. Somehow or another, he worked in that his wife was dead.

Within twenty-four hours, my mother had moved from the pullout couch to his bed. Within a week, the sleeping arrangements were permanent and I was taking the bus to school with the sisters. At dinnertime they said a thing called grace before we were even allowed to start eating, and my mother made eyes at me until I closed mine and took their squirmy hands. By December, my mother was saying we weren't going to be Jews at Christmas anymore, so we could help decorate the gaudy fiberglass tree. My father hadn't been Jewish, either, but even he didn't ask us to do this. We all wore white to the wedding at their church, all four girls, and my mother didn't know that underneath my scratchy white dress the sisters had written all over my stomach with my own markers that I had nasty hair and was dirty and homeless and smelled like poop.

She didn't know a lot of things, as the years went by. She didn't know that when I peered ahead at my future, I didn't see anything sparkling, the way she used to when she was my age. I saw a dark tunnel, and at the end more darkness. My mother didn't know that when the orange bottle full of pills popped open in my hands and spilled into my palms (the label said hydrocodone, three years expired, from when she broke her ankle on the driveway ice) I was only looking at them, seeing how they were shaped, how big they were, how many. I was thinking of what it would be like to disappear, that was all.

Most of all, she didn't know that I'd never given up on our plan to move to the city. I'd held it close while I slept, I kept it fed, over all these years. I remembered the name of the house where she said she lived and the street it was on. It was a place where a girl could go when she was in trouble. I remembered she said the whole room she rented there was as small as her walk-in closet now, but it was hers. There was only one window in the room, but it was her window. Late at night, she would sit out on the fire escape and dangle her legs into the dusky air and watch the lights of the city do their dancing. She'd think how, from far away, if anyone were gazing in her direction at the patch of city she was in, she'd be a part of the dancing lights for someone else.

It was a few days after we moved in with the man who picked us up on the side of the road that I got my mother alone to ask her. I was confused over why we weren't already on our way to New York City, which she called "the" city, to show the only one that mattered. This conversation took place in the master bedroom. Her favorite lotion was on the dresser. Her big yin-yang earrings were on the nightstand. She'd taken as many pairs of shoes as we could fit in the milk crate and the suitcase, and there was a small spill of them by the front door out in the foyer, but she had her special favorites stowed here in a jumble beside the dresser. Her lace-up boots. Her boots with the buckles. Her chunky heels worn only for significant occasions, peep-toe and purple. All her most personal things were already stored in the way back of the topmost dresser drawer.

I tried not to trip over the boots and climbed up to cuddle the pillows with her. I asked questions like: Why were we still here? When would we go? Could we go tomorrow? Could we go the day after that? Could we be down in the city surfing on couches by the weekend?

This was what she said to me:

"Soon. But, Bean, don't you remember? Weren't we so hungry?"

She patted my stomach, reminding me how empty it was because he'd stopped letting us have extra money for the grocery store. Here on Blue Mountain Road, there was always a full fridge.

"And weren't we scared?"

She squeezed my hand, to remind me how I'd flattened myself to hide under furniture when I heard him yelling. The new guy never yelled.

"Sometimes you do desperate things," she explained. "Like leave with barely anything. Like how we had to go without the car because he threw the battery in the pond, remember?"

I nodded. We did have to do that. I'd abandoned almost every toy I had and most of my book collection, because we didn't have the car to carry it all in. She even left her most precious piece of jewelry, as she'd taken the opal off her finger for the last time. (She would wear it on her hand only behind closed doors; she once let me slip it on, but the band spun a loose orbit, even around my thumb.) That ring was what we'd buried behind the cherry tomatoes—so he wouldn't sell it, she said. But when we went to retrieve it, we couldn't find it, even with all the holes we made.

There were so many other things we'd left on the walls, in cupboards and in cabinets, on shelves, under beds, and it would take years to catalogue all we lost, because we could never go there and ask him for any of it. Even after he abandoned the house in the Hudson Valley and moved down to the city to be an artist, he must have burned our stuff in a fire pit, or dropped it at the dump, because when we drove by to see what remained, we found a whole other family living there. When we snuck onto the property, we discovered a brick patio in the spot where the garden had been. Paved over, sealed shut to our search. The plants must have been ripped out by the root. We'd left by choice, but it felt like a sinkhole had swallowed everything we had.

My mother continued. "And sometimes you have to do something you don't want, so you can have a roof over your head."

I nodded again.

"Not everyone in the world gets their dreams to come true," she said, quietly while holding my hand. "Now how would that be fair? Understand?"

I did understand.

Time passed, years lost living in that house.

When we did make it to the city when I was thirteen, it was only for a visit, and one ruined by the fact that we weren't allowed to go alone. Her husband and the girls tagged along. They overtook our itinerary with the most obvious places, like Times Square and Macy's and the Empire State Building. They didn't even want to see the Village. They bought matching I ❤ NY T-shirts and FDNY hats—they didn't care about trying to find the block my mother said contained store after store only for shoes. They didn't want to get lunch at a cozy French bistro, or have falafel or Indian curry or dumplings in Chinatown. They insisted on eating Italian food at the Olive Garden. My mother and I got away once, saying we were meeting an old friend, and on the way downtown my mother told me all the things we would have done, if only it had been us two: Make friends with an alley cat. Get ourselves lost in the maze of the West Village. Read our fortunes in happenstance splashes of street graffiti. See a movie while the rumble of the subway traveled under our seats. For a meal, we'd buy knishes from a street cart to munch on, deep-fried pockets full of spiced potatoes, which were only a dollar when she lived there so she practically survived on them all summer. Next time, she promised. She pinky-swore. Next time.

Instead of seeing the old friend, we went to see my father. It didn't go well. After, my mother didn't want to plan another trip down to the city, just the two of us. She didn't want to pose for pictures in dark alleys or people-watch on a park bench or buy greasy food to eat right there in the street. She didn't even want to try on a dozen pairs of boots on Eighth Street. Months passed. I couldn't remember her ever speaking of us visiting the city again.

———

It came back later, waiting like a glowing gem dug up from deepest dirt and now sitting in open air, in the palm of my hand. The city.

This was the first thing that came to me when I dragged myself out of the trees after they ran me out of the party. When my knee gave out and it got to be too much to keep walking, I sank down on the asphalt, there on the dotted line. The dark behind my eyelids matched the dark on the road. I heard a rush in my ears. I pressed the heels of my hands into my eye sockets until I saw stars.

A van was rattling toward me, boxy and taller than an ordinary car.

I heard and felt it before I saw it—the growling hum, the rumbling under my body. I stood, my arms up, trying to catch the driver's attention, but the van didn't slow. It sped by so quickly it almost clipped me. So quickly I could have blinked and been back where I was, waiting for someone to drive by and save me.

When I opened my eyes again, the wooded road was empty. All that remained were the stars in my eyes, bright spots burned into my retinas, as if I'd looked where I wasn't supposed to. A single, pointed thought remained in my head.

The city. It was only two and a half hours away.

I could see it from a distance, like in one of those post-cards of the skyline at night taken from somewhere across the river. All shine and sparkle, dazzle and promise. I narrowed the focus in my mind on the skyline. It became smaller and smaller until it was just a window. A fire escape. A single light dancing.

My mother always said I had a vivid imagination.

I started limping along the shoulder of the road, leaning my weight every so often on a passing tree, but I stopped feeling the pain. It was almost like I was there already, swaying on new legs in the glittering night that used to know my mother, and now might know me.

———

I found myself at my suitcase under the willow when the sun was lifting up. It was officially the next morning, and I was channeling my mother, or at least who she used to be, positioning myself on a good, visible bend of Blue Mountain Road, in view of those faint and far-off blue mountains, with the bugs swarming my ears and the sun bearing down. Suitcase parked between my legs. Makeup slathered over my aching black eye. Thumb up and out. One good eye trained on the road that would lead to the city. No going back now. No fear.

Part of me wished she would drive by and see me standing in the gravel, melting in this heat, that she'd get out of the car and hug me to her and say she believed me, she'd never not believed me. She forgave me for all the ways I'd messed up, she would always forgive me. I could come back to the house. I could unpack the suitcase. I could stay.

Another part of me willed myself cold. That part wouldn't let me drop my arm or stop trying to flag down passing cars. That part stood firm.

I was ready, dripping with sweat and thirsty, if only a car would stop. I stared down Blue Mountain Road with purpose. The sun was directly in my path, and I aimed myself right for it, willing a ride to come, even though it hurt.

No cars would stop. They kept going, whizzing past, as if I were invisible or an obvious threat. This was taking longer than I'd expected, longer than I'd planned.

People rarely hitchhiked around here anymore, so maybe the drivers didn't know what to do when some lone teenage girl used the road as her personal bus stop. Hitchhiking was the pastime of murder movies, lost to the 1970s, and probably illegal now in the state of New York. But I had no one to ask for a ride, and I didn't have a car, or my license anymore—that got taken away almost as soon as it got issued, after I wrecked my mother's Toyota. All my cash was rolled up in my pocket. All my hopes were aimed at the next willing driver. It was this, or walk.

What came at me next couldn't be recognized as a car. It was a moving blur, veering onto the shoulder where I was standing, and I couldn't focus my eyes on any part of it. Then the distinct green of the approaching hood registered, and I saw the pinched face of the girl behind the wheel as she concentrated her aim. Charlotte drove a green car. Didn't she see me? She was speeding up, and she would do that for sure if she saw me, especially after last night. I stumbled back into the weeds, into the shade of the willow. The car kept going—our house was a half mile away—and two heads were visible through the rolled-down windows on the passenger side, one in the front seat and one in the back. Daniella and a friend. I saw their gaping mouths as they laughed, probably at me, showing their fangs, and something cold and wet washed over me as one of the girls threw the dregs of a soda out the window. Soon as it happened, it was over. The car took the bend and didn't turn back. No one looked at the retreating road to see me there with my suitcase. No one cared. I was out in the middle of the road, giving the green car the finger, when another car finally did stop, a gray hatchback with a strange man at the wheel. He slowed, seeming unsure, until he pulled over a few yards ahead and waited for me to catch up.

His window descended, and I felt the blast of cool air that let me know he had air-conditioning. But when he turned, he seemed to cringe at the sight of me. His knuckles tensed as he gripped the wheel. There was the state of my clothes: I was soaked from the backwashed soda and ice. But it was my face he seemed stuck on—he spent an intense moment taking in my face without saying a word. I checked my reflection in the side mirror. The marks, such an unnatural color, pooled under my left eye. The scab on my lip was crusted. There was something going on with my ear.

"You need a ride to the hospital?" he said, after a sizable pause.

"I'm okay." He didn't seem to believe me, so I added, "I saw a doctor, I'm fine, really. It looks worse than it is. Do you think you could take me to the train station? Metro-North?"

He still seemed so unsettled. I almost expected him to speed off in a squeal of tires, or tell me to settle for the bus. What he didn't know was that my mother had taken the train eighteen summers ago, so I would too, even if it was nearly an hour's drive. That was how her story started: window seat, river side, hopeful ticket: one-way.

"I'm meeting my mom at the station."

These were the magic words. I didn't give a backward glance at our driveway in the distance, or even the willow tree that had once been our spot, as I shoved my suitcase in his back seat and climbed into the front. I waited for him to ask where I was going so I could tell him New York City, but he didn't. He never asked. I worried my cheap drugstore cover-up wasn't covering enough, so I dug around for the sunglasses I'd swiped from my mother's dresser weeks ago (she thought she lost them at yoga) and popped them on. At this, he turned away from me, as if I'd blocked out all questions along with direct sunlight. That was a move of my mother's, and I'd done it perfectly.

I was a known liar, I was a thief, but I was also my mother's daughter. She'd know where to find me, if she chose to look.

VACANCY

"Wake up." A voice close to my ear. A streak of white light.

The train intercom crackled to life. "Next and final stop, Grand Central Terminal. New York City."

I bolted up in my seat. Strangers shuffled around me, and I wasn't sure who among them made sure I knew we'd arrived. I must have drifted off against the window—there was a hot spot on my cheek. My head pulsed with a painful ache. My mother's sunglasses, which I'd kept on the whole trip to camouflage my swollen, purpling eye, were perched crooked on my nose. I'd like to imagine she arrived at Catherine House wearing these same sunglasses—deep-tinted, a subtle touch of armor to hide her own bruises—but she got this particular pair years afterward.

The suitcase I'd stowed on the rack above me was still there, undisturbed. I had the cash in my pocket, the directions on my phone. I could feel my heart beating a little too fast, its echo in my ears, and as we coasted through the still-dark passages of Grand Central, it took over all else.

I was here.

The train rolled ever so slowly through a series of tunnels, seeming like it would never reach the station, that maybe there was no station, that the city was only a story my mother told me, or one I told myself. The overhead lights flickered off and on, and shadows hugged up against the scratched windows, wanting in. Passengers crowded the aisles, clogging the exits at either end of the train car, so I was left in the middle, still in my seat, practically alone. I lingered at the window.

A dim-lit platform drifted past, deep in the bowels of the station. Not a soul was on it. Murky sections of tunnel rolled by, unused and blocked off. The view was industrial and surprisingly fragile at the same time, like the bones of the city could be broken with a swift kick and no one was supposed to know. For a moment, I thought I saw a burst of nature in the grimy machinery, a wild tree growing out from the third rail, alien and budding the green of my mother's long-lost garden. But it was a splash of graffiti claiming the hidden space. It wasn't alive. The train sped up and blurred it to black.

At last we stopped. The lights came up and stayed up, and an underground station was visible. The doors opened, and people rushed out. I grabbed my suitcase, my hopes, my coiled nerves, my unformed dreams, and I stepped out onto the platform.

———

I might never have known how to find Catherine House if my mother hadn't kept the phone number all these years on the bulletin board in the bedroom she shared with him. Their room on the first floor had a door to the patio that they never kept locked, which meant someone could sneak around outside the house and get in that way, without needing the more visible hallway and door. She used the space over her dresser not for jewelry or a mirror, but to gaze back into her past, to have a reminder of who she was in front of her face every morning when she searched for clean socks.

Tacked to the board were photographs from when she was young, the kind printed on curling, glossy paper, her hair burgundy, or crayon yellow, or blue-black. Ticket stubs from movies and plays and ska shows. Keepsakes, like a withering four-leaf clover kept preserved in a plastic baggie, art postcards of starry nights or ponds with water lilies floating on top, beheaded birthday cards, a single clipping from the *Village Voice* about a festival screening of short films with her name in small type, circled, starred. Pinned at the base of the bulletin board were the emergency numbers any mother should keep on hand: poison control, local hospital, dentist's office. And there beneath all that, sparkling with pin holes, crusted with age, a card, CATHERINE HOUSE OF NEW YORK CITY, as if she might one day have a dire need to rent a room and escape us all.

I didn't have time to go through her drawers before I heard her coming, but I confiscated the card, and later, after a few echoing rings, someone did answer the phone when I called. There was a vacancy, the voice on the other end told me, eager, almost as if expecting this call. The room was mine, but I should get there, fast, and bring cash.

The thing was, it turned out Catherine House wasn't so easy to find in a physical sense. From Grand Central, I made it downtown, to the West Village. I was close, or should have been. Yet showing on my phone screen was a gray area, unmarked and untethered by cross streets. I wasn't sure where to find the address in the nest of gray, and it didn't help that on the corner of the actual street there were two signs with the same name. WAVERLY PL said one sign. WAVERLY PL said the other, as if the street split into two sides of itself. Here I stood, waving my phone in the air, when I stumbled into her.

She was on the sidewalk, near a blue van with dried mud crusted on its tires, though every street I'd seen here so far was smooth asphalt glistening in the high heat. The van was parked before a sign that said NO PARKING, and she was shaded by its shadow. Maybe that was why I walked right into her.

The impact sent me reeling into the sign, which was sharp-edged where she hadn't been and crooked in the con- crete. The suitcase toppled to its side, skidding off the curb.

The van was more decrepit the closer I got to it, with a clutter of mangled tickets on the windshield and a boot on its grimy tire—it might have split apart if taken out on a road. The girl had long eyelashes, and short hair that showed off her neck. Her skin was faint brown, her eyes were deep brown, with golden flecks, almost amber. At least I thought they were, as I'd only been close enough to see for a single moment. She'd materialized from out of nowhere onto this patch of sidewalk. Or one of us had.

"Go ahead," she said as she helped me with my suitcase. "Say it."

Not counting whatever anonymous stranger had woken me on the train, she was the first person on the island of Manhattan to speak to me.

"I'm sorry . . . What should I say?"

"Yes, that's good. Go on. Say you're sorry. For trampling me."

I couldn't tell if she was serious. She had my suitcase still, hugged in close to her, and I wasn't sure if she'd decided to keep it.

"I *am* sorry," I started. "I think I'm lost, and—"

She held up a hand to make me stop talking. "You're not lost." Then she turned, distracted. "You hear that, don't you?"

I wasn't sure if she was listening to something inside the van or beyond it. The city swelled with noise. It banged and clanged around in my ears and filled my head with a persistent, growing thrum, brimming in the back of my skull. My head was still hurting, and my eye was pulsing from last night. Maybe I *should* have seen a doctor.

"I don't hear anything," I said.

"Exactly," she said. "It's so quiet. Too quiet. When it gets quiet like this, you know something's off."

I gazed around at the block, unsettled. It wasn't that quiet. She was shooting a stare past the booted blue van, into the distance. I followed her gaze, but all I could see was a tree-lined block and another much like it beyond, a man on the sidewalk, then no longer on the sidewalk because he slipped into a doorway, a yellow taxicab speeding past, not stopping. Apart from that, we were alone.

"There's nothing going on," I said. "Not that I can see."

"You're positive?" I wasn't sure if she was playing with me or if she knew the city so well she could sense a foreboding tremor when I couldn't. If she knew to run when I didn't. All I could think was, if she did start running, I'd probably follow.

I shrugged.

"You should watch where you're walking, by the way. You could get run over." She pushed the suitcase at me, but one of the wheels was jammed, and it didn't go. I pulled it back toward me.

"Thanks." I didn't know what else to say, so I headed off, dragging the suitcase behind me, until I remembered I didn't know where I was going. She hadn't moved from beside the dilapidated van, but the sun had, creating a glaring silhouette that made the expression on her face impossible to decipher.

There was a cowlick in her hair, a swirl sticking up that caught my eye and wouldn't let go. I couldn't know for sure if she was smiling as she leaned her weight against the van.

I walked back in her direction. "Do you know where I can find this address?" I held out my phone, and that was as close as I got. "I think it's broken."

She took a step toward me. "Hmm," she said.

I had a thought. "Do you know this place? Catherine House?" I recited the street address. My mother may have stood on this very corner trying to find her way that summer long ago. I could sense her shadow, the faintest trace. "Do you know how to get there?"

"I might."

I waited for more, but there was no more. Instead she was staring at me, openly. She was taking in the state of my face. The sun was blazing, and every gouge and scratch and purple stain must have stood out. It cut through the makeup, making the mask I'd tried to wear all the more obvious.

"Is it that way?" I asked, pointing.

She tapped her foot.

"Is it that way?" I pointed in another direction.

She itched her nose, keeping her face neutral. "If you're supposed to be somewhere, you'll find it. If you're not, you'll walk right by and miss it."

What did she mean? There was something taunting about the way she'd said it, also playful, as if this were a grand and possibly cruel game.

I didn't want to play a game. I wanted to find the house and make sure I had a room. I wanted to plant myself somewhere and stay firm. I wanted my mother to come calling—and then what? I didn't have that answer. My feet hurt, the suitcase had tipped over and lay flat on the sidewalk, and there wasn't a single missed call from an 845 number on my phone.

I also wanted this girl to know where I was headed, to be going there, too. It was wishful thinking, but when I gazed down the block again, I knew. I knew the way my mother had known the perfect day we should leave my father, the way I now knew I shouldn't have gone to that party, the way I knew, marrow-deep, that I was meant to be right here.

Catherine House was down that way, and she'd been well aware all along. I crossed the narrow street, and then I heard her call out.

"Wait." She paused. "You have to tell me . . . Who did that to your face?"

My hand went up reflexively to touch it, the tender spots, the scratches. The memory of the night before seemed so far away, a world apart from this one, dense and dark and surrounded by the brittle branches of trees.

"Nobody," I said.

"Nobody smashed your face in?"

"Maybe I did it to myself."

Her eyes lit up at this answer, and not the way people crane their necks out windows to catch the mangled bits of a car crash so they can have something awful to talk about. Her eyes lit up with recognition, understanding.

"You're holding your cards close," she said. "Smart. Keep doing that. It's over there, by the way. Down that block and to the left on the next block. You'll find it. I'm sure you will."

I set the suitcase on its wheels, though it wobbled, and headed off.

"Good luck, and don't get hit by a bus," she called after me.

I sensed her gaze as I dragged the unsteady bag behind me, a prickling awareness on my bare shoulders. When I glanced back, just to be sure, she was still watching, staring until I turned away again.

Soon, sooner than I wanted to admit, I reached the block. Catherine House, same as my mother had described in all her stories, made of red bricks and rising five floors into the bright afternoon light. I felt it in my fingers, I felt it in the soles of my feet. Stars prickled awake and gathered, with a slight burning sensation, in the middle of my chest. This was certainty. This was the culminating click of self-determination and fate.

A black wrought-iron gate separated the building from the sidewalk, the glossy fence poles tall and ending in savagely pointed spikes. A plaque on the gate said simply: CATHERINE HOUSE—A REFUGE. Behind the gate was a short walkway that led to a steep set of wide steps. It seemed very far away, though in fact it was close. At the top of the steps was a giant front door, sleek and windowless. Curtains, dark and completely opaque, covered the first floor of tall windows. The only thing

45

that gave a hint of movement was the small stained-glass window beside the door, but I couldn't make out anything more than that.

I tried the latch on the gate. Locked. There was a buzzer and a small intercom nested in the gate—no name to claim it. I pressed the button and stepped back. Silence. I checked the windows again, and again tried the latch. That was when the giant door at the top of the stoop burst open.

A woman emerged, followed by two girls who were younger versions of her. A mother and her daughters. The girls looked stricken, the younger one sniffling back tears, but the woman appeared irritated, her face pinched. They carried crates and a box jammed full of clothing down the steep stairs and pushed through the gate, ignoring me. They went to an SUV parked at the curb and dropped the boxes near the back, to pile them inside. The gate was open, but I wasn't sure if I should walk in. It was only when the mother returned that she met my eyes and held them steady for a single moment that pierced me through. Something had happened. Something had happened inside this house.

"Do you live here?" she said to me.

I wanted to tell her I was about to, but I hadn't signed any papers yet, or paid any money yet, and I didn't have a room yet or, well, a key, but she didn't need me to say it. She'd noticed the suitcase.

"You're moving in," she said, her voice grim. "Don't. If I were your mother, I'd tell you to go home. Right now."

The urgency in her expression alarmed me, and I stepped back, the iron bars pressing cold against my spine.

"I should've dragged Lacey out of here before—" She cut herself short. Her daughters at the car had turned to listen, as if aching for information.

"Who?" I said faintly. "What happened?"

She didn't explain. I was useless. She pushed through the gate and climbed the stairs. No one had answered the buzzer, so before the gate swung closed and locked again I slipped in and followed, dragging the suitcase up behind me.

The other girls—Lacey's sisters, I assumed; I'd by now pieced together a whole family—had finished with the boxes and came running up the stairs, their cheeks tear-streaked, their long legs flying with grisly determination. They beat me easily, and once I made it to the top, the stoop was empty.

The front door was wide-open, and I slipped inside.

―――――――

"Hello?"

The door smacked closed behind me. The sense of being watched tickled at my shoulders, but I couldn't find the source. The woman and the girls were nowhere to be found in the low light.

It took a solid moment for my eyes to adjust. Once they did, my first view of the interior of Catherine House was this grand entry room grayed by shadows. A dimness filled the space, unsettling after the white-hot daylight outside. A crystal chandelier high on the ceiling danced shards of light all over the walls. A sweeping staircase curved upward, disappearing into the darkness of the upper floors. That must have been where the mother and sisters went. A decorative vase so large I could have fit myself inside stood sentry at the door. It probably cost more than a car. I had a sudden flash-fantasy of wielding a baseball bat and smashing the vase, destroying something worth more than I was. I'd done it before. A fizz of anger went through me and was gone as fast as it had come, leaving me alone on the gold-woven antique carpet. I would be different here.

I felt a strange familiarity as I stood on that golden rug—because I remembered it. The rug was what my mother had described—like walking on a tiger's head, though almost two decades had passed since she'd planted her feet on it. The rug was here, covering the floor, as it had been then.

To my left was a closed door, and across the way a darkened hallway, and there was a large open parlor to my right, with a grand piano and velvet furniture, also in gold. Perched all over the shelves were delicate figurines as well as pearlescent seashells and other tchotchkes, as if this were a forgotten museum. It wasn't as if time had stopped—otherwise the air wouldn't be so thick with pooled heat, the carpet threadbare in spots—it was as if no one wanted to admit that time had marched on outside this house, decade after decade.

"Don't touch," a voice said.

I'd drifted near a display table and had been letting my hand wander along the surface, fingering an ornamental box made of painted china and, beside it, a decorative elephant tusk I'd assumed was manufactured. I pulled my hand away, but I could still feel it: The tusk wasn't fake. It wasn't cold and long-dead, like a fossil. It was slick but warm, like living skin.

I whipped around to discover a girl curled up in a gold velvet armchair before the dark fireplace. There'd been a moment when my hand had almost snatched and kept one of the items, and if she hadn't spoken up I might have tucked it away in my bag already.

The arms and back of the chair were tall, a semicircle surrounding her. She had a book spread in front of her face, blocking my view. I noticed that the cover had no visible title, not on the front and not on the spine. The surface was soft, made of gold fabric a shade darker than the furniture.

"We're not supposed to touch the souvenirs," she said from behind the book.

"I didn't know, sorry. Hey, do you know who I'm supposed to talk to about the room?"

At this, she lowered the book, careful to conceal its contents. She had a pale face and a set of long, low-hanging bangs that made a severe slash over her eyes, swallowing her eyebrows. When she unfurled herself from the chair, she was much bigger than she'd first appeared. She rose to her full height, imposing and enviably strong. My head barely reached her neck.

"Who are you?" She dropped the book on the chair in a muffled thump, letting loose a cloud of dust.

I noticed she was keeping careful track of my hands, as if she were on to me. There were so many tiny, innocuous things in this room—so many. I couldn't imagine they would notice one missing.

"I'm Sabina," I said, awkwardly offering her one of my hands. It was empty. "But you can call me Bina. Everyone does."

She didn't take my hand. "And you like that?"

I blinked. "Are you who I talked to on the phone?"

"I'm Gretchen," she said. "And no. I *live* here. I don't answer the phone." She stared openly at all my deficiencies, and I expected her to ask about the black eye and the scratches on my face, which might have made me look desperate or sinister. All she said was, "You're here for the last room, aren't you?"

"I guess so?" I'd called only a day ago, before I snuck out to the party, but maybe the news had traveled to the other tenants. I wondered where the rest of them were, and if they would welcome me in, become my lifelong friends, if soon we'd be dangling our legs off the fire escape together. Hers would dangle so far.

"How'd you find us?" she asked. "How'd you hear about the room?"

"Craigslist," I said, not even sure why I said it.

But this made her laugh. "Good one." Her mouth softened. "I can see why you came." She tapped a black fingernail to the corner of her eye. "Not a moment too soon, am I right?"

I wasn't sure what she was insinuating.

"There's a girl on the third floor who got thrown down a set of stairs," she said flatly, maybe to show I didn't have it so bad.

"What about you?"

"Oh, no one's ever touched me," she said. I believed it. "It's just they kept putting me away. My mom has the twins now, you know, and I guess I was scaring the children. They kept putting me away, and now I'm here."

That only gave me more questions. I started to ask, but she shook her head.

"Let's stop," she said. "Not with *him* here."

She pointed into the front room, and there, as if she'd conjured him, was a man sitting on a bench, head in his hands. I about jumped. All along there'd been someone hidden in the curve of the rising staircase, and I hadn't realized.

"Should I talk to him about the room?" I asked.

"*God*, no. He shouldn't even be inside. We told him Lacey's not here."

There was that name again—Lacey. I was putting the pieces of some kind of tragedy together, imagining the bleakest things, the very worst. First a distraught mother and sisters, and now this man, clearly distressed and looking for his daughter.

"The rest of them are upstairs, getting her things," Gretchen said. "They wouldn't take no for an answer."

I was watching him, waiting for him to lift his head, yet also afraid he might and then I'd have to find something suitable to say.

"Don't be a vulture," Gretchen said.

I leaned in. She smelled musty, like the pages of the ancient book. "What happened to Lacey, anyway? Did she . . . die or something?"

Gretchen's expression held a beat too long, not a twitch or a muscle moving. "I told you to stop it," she said. She plucked her book from the golden chair and left the room, avoiding the man on the bench and climbing the stairs to the rooms above.

She'd left me alone with him, but what could I say? I didn't know his daughter. I didn't know what happened, if it was something terrible that occurred, maybe even inside this house.

Someone should be down to help me with my room any minute, I decided. I made a halfhearted circle around the parlor and then planted myself in the gold velvet chair Gretchen had abandoned. All I had to entertain myself with were the souvenirs that filled the surfaces of the room. There were some close by, arranged on a yellowing circle of crocheted lace. I grabbed for the closest item, small and eerily pale, like a mushroom.

My hands were cupped around the miniature ceramic bell, curious to know what sound it might make, when a prickling came at the back of my neck, cold though the room was stuffy. I had the immediate urge to put down the bell.

I craned around. Above the fireplace was a single black-and-white photograph in a gilt frame. A dark-haired young woman in a high-necked black dress sat in a high-backed chair, her hands folded and perched above her knees. It was the kind of pose someone would have made in order to sit for an oil painting centuries ago. Something about it wasn't entirely convincing.

She had a long face, a meager mouth. At first her expression seemed dull, and slightly sad. Then I checked again. I must have caught the image from another angle, because her waxy gray face had shifted. Now the set of her small mouth was locked. Her eyes formed two daggers. They were intensely black, without any warm flecks or pupils, and they met mine through the glass right as the voice came from the other room.

"Were you here this week?" the man called. "Do you know anything about where she could have gone?"

I flinched. I glanced once more at the picture before turning around. The young woman's mouth had relaxed, and her eyes were downcast. I thought I must have imagined the expression before.

"I just got here," I told the man. He was standing now in the center of the outer room, under the chandelier.

"Did she seem out of the ordinary to you? Did it seem like she would take off, no phone call, no email?"

"I just got here," I repeated, edging closer. "I don't know her." But now I was starting to collect questions.

"Of course," he said, as if he might not believe me. He turned to the tall stairs. "They told me to stay down here. Men aren't allowed upstairs."

I kind of nodded. "Are you her dad?"

"I am. My wife's up there. With the girls, Lacey's sisters. Getting all her things."

"I know, I heard." Curiosity drove me forward. The prickling was at the back of my neck again, the tickle of a dagger point pressing me on.

"They said she's not coming back here. They said she's gone."

I came closer. "What do you mean, *gone?*"

He didn't answer that. Instead he said, "This seemed to be a safe place."

A safe place. My mother had told me she felt safe in Catherine House. She felt protected. Once she opened that gate and left, the real world crushed in.

Bad stories my mother had told me of the city came at me then. Dark street corners, vacant subway platforms, sketchy men. My mother used to wander the streets at night before curfew, boots to her knees, wind in her hair, getting to know all the surrounding neighborhoods, open to whatever might happen. One time a gang of guys followed her all through Tompkins Square Park and she hid out in a twenty-four-hour bodega until they got bored and left. Another time a distressed woman almost pushed her in front of the 6 train. *You could have gotten murdered*, I used to say to her when she told me her stories, but I didn't say it with worry or judgment. I said it with awe.

But she was safe, she assured me. She had this house to go back to—and her stories always ended here, secured behind the gate, which was kept locked until morning. That was why the house called to me so, how high she'd built its castle walls in my head.

"We don't know what happened," Lacey's father said. "Being here was supposed to help."

He looked so broken. He was acting—and this was mystifying to me, from my own experience at having a father—as if the idea of not having his daughter in his life destroyed him.

I had one clear memory of my father from my early childhood. He was talking with another adult, and I was grabbing ahold of his pants leg to get his attention. He peered down on me from a great height, and I lifted my arms to him, thinking he was about to bridge the distance and pick me up. Maybe I thought he'd hold me aloft on his shoulders, the way I'd seen fathers do with small daughters, because I was small and I was his daughter. I could imagine the intoxicating feeling of being high in the air balanced on his two stout and sturdy shoulders. How I wanted him to lift me. How my arms reached. But my father stayed where he was, in the distant stratosphere of the room, his head near the ceiling fan, and mine far below, by his knees, too low for him to hear me call for him. He kept talking to whoever it was he was talking to, his beard hiding his mouth. I dropped my arms. He didn't lower his distant head.

"She was doing so well," Lacey's father said. He had a tight grip on my arm as he spoke. "I don't understand what happened."

I had no possible idea. He was holding me harder than he should have, pressing his fingers in until he must have felt the solid stop of bone.

"I don't know, either." I wrenched my arm away and glanced up at the stairs. The bend at the top wobbled with shadows. Wasn't someone expecting me? Wouldn't anyone who worked here come out and welcome me and help me get settled into a room?

"She was fine," he said once more. His teeth were showing.

I put something between us—a display table with three bulky wooden legs.

"Maybe she wasn't," I found myself saying.

"What did you say?"

"Only . . . I guess . . . maybe she wasn't. Doing fine. And maybe no one could see it."

His head tilted.

I'd said a bad thing—I knew it as soon as the words were out of my mouth. It was the start of a story, but his reaction made me stuff it back in. Maybe I should have apologized, but there was a remote observer inside me that wanted to see what he'd say back to me, what he'd do. He was her father. When everything went so wrong at home, after I'd crashed my mother's car and lied about it, after I'd skipped school for near a week and concealed it, once my mother reached the end of her rope—those were the words she'd used, about what I'd done to her, words that made me cringe—I'd brought up my father. *Maybe I should go live with* him, I'd said. *Live with that man?*

she'd said. *You?* Hell *no*. When I said I could call the gallery—
I'd looked it up online, there was a number and an address in
the city, the whole storefront could be seen in a blurred snap
on Google Maps—she said I shouldn't do that. He took all
the money he got when his father died and opened that place.
He never gave us a cent. Or called. Or sent a card. Does that
sound like someone who wanted me?

Lacey's father bowed his head. I wasn't sure what he would
do: shout at me, or push me away, or grab me harder this time.

I backtracked. "I didn't know her, I told you. I only got
here today."

There was noise on the stairs, and he stepped away and
crossed the room. Lacey's mother and sisters came down with
a suitcase and a few boxes. "That's the last of it," her mother
said. Her face was cool and composed, but her eyes held something heavier and tangled.

"Let me at least help with these," the man said.

"We've got it. Didn't I say stay in the car?" With that, they
all left through the front exit. I watched the door seal shut.
The room relaxed without them in it.

"That took long enough," a sharp voice called from the
stairs. A tiny, bony woman descended to the bottom. "They're
always so emotional. It's exhausting." A smile crept onto her
face. "Please forgive me for keeping you waiting. You can come
in now."

She lifted her arm to indicate the door beside the stairs.
I'd noticed it was closed before, but here it was, open. Who'd

opened it? "Aren't you here about the room?" she said. "That is what you came for, isn't it?"

I nodded.

"Call me Ms. Ballantine, I prefer it."

I hadn't called her anything at all.

She was small yet commanding, standing with marked intensity on the golden carpet. It was a wonder how much space she took up in the room though she was shorter even than me. Tight skirt, shiny. Blouse with ruffles, satiny. Jewelry of all shapes and metals and protrusions, around her neck and wrists and fingers, on her earlobes and pinned to her shirt, all gleaming. Her hair—an artificial golden yellow that mimicked the rug—was pulled back into a severe bun at the base of her skull. She could have been forty or one hundred years old. She was, I'd soon understand, the landlady and manager of the house, though not the owner. Catherine House was controlled by a trust, because its human owner was long dead.

"I'm Sabina," I said. "Bina, I mean. You can just call me Bina. My mother, she rented a room here a long time ago, and I know it's weird, but I thought . . ."

She was assessing me without any movement. Not a breath escaped her mouth. Even her eyes were still, unblinking. It was unsettling. Finally she shifted, sliding her fingers together, making the rings knock.

I started talking again. I didn't know what else to do. "I'm, uh . . . You said bring cash?"

"Don't be daft," she said, and most unsettling of all was how wide she was now smiling. "I know who you are, Miss Tremper, not that I've told the others yet. You still have to sign the paperwork. This here is my office. Come in."

It was only as I was walking inside, ushered in ahead of her, that the thought came to me: When we'd spoken on the phone, she'd assured me there was a vacancy. She'd said bring cash. Then she'd ended the call before ever asking my name.

THE VOW

I'D ALREADY EXPLAINED THAT I WANTED MY MOTHER'S room, Room 10, and after that I couldn't seem to stop talking. "Do you remember my mother?" I asked Ms. Ballantine. "She was going by Dawn Tremper then? It was before she got married?" I hated that my mother had changed her name, matching herself to the man she was with—it meant she no longer matched with me. "Were you here then, when she was?"

The details didn't help. Many girls had stayed here over the decades. Many wanted to act in movies or have their eager selves circled in a bright-hot spotlight on a red-curtained stage. More than a few went back to bad boyfriends and former abusers, or came to rent a room with welts on their arms, flinching when touched, saying they needed someplace to stay. A hundred girls might fit that description. If Ms. Ballantine remembered, wouldn't she tell me?

Instead she leaned forward and said, "Are we going to stop this charade now?"

"Stop what?"

"I was hoping you would call sooner, but I told her we had to be patient, that the day would come. And here you are."

A ripple of surprise ran through me.

"My mother called?" She must have known for a while that she'd send me away—since the Toyota in the tree, or longer? Since I turned fifteen, the first worst year of my life, followed by the next two? I thought she'd wanted me to stay with those friends from his church, but all along she'd known I'd end up here, as she had. My heart warmed for a second.

But if that was true, how did she know I'd take the card and make the phone call myself?

"Oh no," Ms. Ballantine said, correcting me. "No, no. Your mother hasn't contacted us in years. We do like our former tenants to keep in touch. If they're able."

"So she didn't call."

"No," she said, "you did."

Something inside me sank. I didn't admit that my mother had no idea I was here, that I'd swiped the number, along with some money from unguarded wallets. My mother surely hated me right now and was maybe investigating the legalities of getting a daughter disowned, and changing the locks, and pressing charges for grand larceny (how much did it have to be to turn "grand"?). I'd been talking about her as if we were close, two pinkies entwined and cycles synced, even today.

Still, Ms. Ballantine hadn't said she remembered. Decades of girls coming and going, room keys traded from hand to hand, a pile of names. I wanted my mother to be the most memorable, a shining face in the crowd, but nothing indicated she was.

I could even be mistaken about the name. My mother started going by Dawn the day she moved into this house. That was her middle name and her stage name, and now it was her ordinary name out in the world. I could see her in this room, her hair that rotated through a half dozen colors in a single summer, her unwieldy dreams, her overstuffed suitcase bursting with shoes. Now I'd get to see this place for myself, and I'd know her. I'd know her in a way I never did before.

Her last name then and mine all my life, Tremper, wasn't technically my mother's, either. She liked it better than our family name, which sounded too "ethnic" for her future in Hollywood, she said, where so many people recast themselves with smooth, bland new selves and pretended not to be what they were. Her invented name was borrowed from the place where she was from, Mount Tremper in Ulster County. She put it on her glossies. She answered to it at every cattle call. She changed it legally, at the courthouse. When I was born, she passed it along to me.

I was about to ask Ms. Ballantine again when we were interrupted. The door was partly open, and a girl's head peeked in. Dark hair in a halo of static. Wide, searching eyes that landed on me.

"Yes, we have a new tenant," Ms. Ballantine said. "You'll meet her later."

The girl stared. I felt naked in the chair, peeled open.

Ms. Ballantine waved her hand, a shooing gesture, and the head vanished.

"I apologize," she said. "But I have bad news." She explained I couldn't have Room 10; it was occupied. But this was such good news that all the rooms were occupied, didn't I think so? Even if I had to have Room 14?

I pictured the mysterious Lacey, all her belongings carted out and piled on the curb. Was I getting her room? What happened to her here? No matter. I said I'd take the room. It wasn't my mother's, but it was close enough.

Out of the corner of my eye, I saw another girl drift past the open doorway, slowing. Blond head this time, smoothed hair that flipped upward at the ends. Small pursed lips and not a word, either.

After her was a girl in purple, and another, a splash of red hair and red lipstick.

"Don't mind them," Ms. Ballantine said, so studiously unbothered it made me wonder if I should be concerned. My back was to the door, and anyone could have walked by.

I turned again. Across the way I had a view of the grand parlor, gold velvet on any object that could be encased in gold velvet, crowded with artifacts from places unknown, swimming with dust, and crowned with the portrait of the serious young woman in the gilt frame. The tenants weren't watching

63

me anymore—they'd scattered. The photograph on the wall—it was watching.

"Is there a problem?" Ms. Ballantine said.

The portrait. Were its lips moving, creating a faint blur beneath glass? Was the frame crooked on the wall now, as if it had skittered to the left? Did the glass in front of her face contain a strange, swirling mist?

"Could we, um—" I didn't want to put words to what I was seeing. "Could we close the door?"

Ms. Ballantine stood from behind her giant desk. She stalked across the room—it wasn't a large room and was crammed with filing cabinets, but I heard every clack and smack of her jewelry, and she wore a tremendous amount—and pulled the door shut. It wasn't until she was back behind the desk again, bulbous rings glistening, that she spoke the name.

"You're curious about our Catherine." When I didn't respond, she clarified. "Catherine de Barra. Our namesake and the owner of this townhome, before her tragic end. As I'm sure your mother told you. That portrait was taken when Catherine was a mere eighteen years old. The year she lost her father. He was her last living relative. After his death, she was all alone. Imagine."

Ms. Ballantine had called me curious, but *curious* was not the word I'd use. I'd say unsettled. Something caged inside that frame bothered me.

I found some empty words and said them. "It's a beautiful photograph."

Ms. Ballantine let silence sit between us, as if to call my bluff. The photograph was substandard, in fact—once you got close enough, the soft blur became clear. It seemed an optical illusion, with only the eyes and the mouth sharp. Everything else was clouded. I'd noticed that in the parlor.

"I mean, the girl in the picture—Catherine—she was beautiful."

Ms. Ballantine's eyes narrowed. Did I *see* the picture? Did I even *look*?

I did. I thought anger was very beautiful on a girl, so long as it wasn't directed at me.

"Catherine was not known for her beauty," Ms. Ballantine said. As she spoke, she went to a filing cabinet. "There are other ways for a woman to be remembered. I tell all our girls that—for their sakes."

She drew a stack of papers from one of the file drawers. "In Catherine's case, what beckoned all the suitors was her inheritance. Charles de Barra, her father, was quite protective before he died. Some say too protective. Some say . . . unhealthily attached." She shrugged, as if she wasn't one of those who would say that. "But after his death, word got out, as it does, and suitors crowded the rooms out front. They came bearing gifts. They came for weeks on end, but no one was chosen before the incident that took her life. It turned out she left the house to all of us. Somehow she knew we would need it."

The *incident*. I held on that word.

Us. As if I were already one of them.

Ms. Ballantine gazed with reverence at the dingy curtains and the low ceiling, cobwebs clinging to the corners. Then she turned and looked me straight in the face. Did she see an angry, unsteady mess of a girl? Did she recognize the true person I was?

No. She was only assessing my face. Only concerned with my outside parts and my surface. The bruises, the swollen spots, the banged-up lip, did make me appear desperate. That was what she seemed to be searching for—it was all she saw, all she needed to know.

"Catherine said you would come," she said. She'd raised her voice, as if she hoped someone just outside the room might hear.

I sat up very straight in my chair.

"Caring for this house all these years"—*how many years?* I wondered; something about the milky film over Ms. Ballantine's eyes made me suspect a great many—"being here for each and every young woman who finds her way to these doors, I often think of the tragedy of it all. I'm grateful to your mother for sending you, Miss Tremper. It's been almost twenty years since all our rooms were filled in the precise way we were hoping. When Catherine told me you'd called, I felt this little flicker. I couldn't think of the word to call it until this moment. Hope. She felt it as well, when you spoke."

She touched a ringed finger to a fat black phone on the desk. It had a wire plugged into the wall. One by one, in quick succession, these thoughts struck me:

She thinks my mother sent me here on purpose.

She thinks I talked to a dead woman on the phone.

Get up. Get out of the chair.

Walk to the door. Get your suitcase. Go.

But my body didn't move. Only my mouth did.

"I'm sorry?" I said. "Aren't you who I spoke to on the phone?"

She shook her head. She was saying what I thought she was saying. Behind the film covering her eyes—as if just on the other side of a thin white curtain—a light was shining. A bright, bobbing light.

There was a knock on the door, and another girl popped her head in. I tried to meet her eyes—but she avoided my gaze. "Excuse me . . ." She hesitated. "May I ask about the ice?"

"Yes?" Ms. Ballantine said.

"We wondered . . . might we need some?" She spoke so formally, her freckles darkening on her cheeks as she spoke, as if this were a bold question.

Ms. Ballantine leaned forward. "Yes, Miss Tedesco, thank you for checking first. We do. We absolutely do."

The girl's tense face relaxed.

"It looks like we'll be having the party," Ms. Ballantine said. She nodded. The girl nodded. The door closed. I'd not gotten out of my chair or made a run for it. I'd not moved a muscle. It was funny that they were talking about ice, because my fingers felt so cold as I gripped the arms of the chair. The mist I'd caught sight of in the portrait wasn't behind a layer of glass in the next room anymore. It was at my feet, creeping upward in a faint shroud over my legs. It felt like the lower half of my body was crouched in a tight freezer, but the upper half was still free.

Then gone. Any thought of mist or cold or the foreboding sense I should walk to the door and leave was over. All of it gone but the ordinary drifting dust inside the dim, cramped room. I could see my legs again. Ms. Ballantine was seated behind her desk as before.

I touched the tender spots on my face, my head.

That felt more real than any of this. But maybe I wasn't quite myself yet.

"Are you ready?" Ms. Ballantine said, a crinkle of concern on her brow.

"What do you mean? Ready for what?"

She touched the back of her head, base of the skull, left side, exactly where my own hand was. "You said your head was hurting and you needed a minute. Did the episode pass?"

My head was oddly clear. I nodded. The episode—whatever it had been—must have ended, and so swiftly I didn't remember it.

"Let's continue with the paperwork," Ms. Ballantine said.

Paperwork. That was what we were doing. I had a page in front of me on the desk.

There was the short-term rental agreement for me to review—I could afford only the month of July, but I knew I had a whole month to come up with a way to pay for August—then items for me to initial and sign. Ms. Ballantine offered a ball-point pen, encrusted in dust. She'd have to abbreviate the orientation tour, she explained, because she had to supervise setup for tonight.

"The party is tonight?" I prompted.

"Yes, that's what Miss Tedesco was asking about. She's tasked with running to the corner market for ice. With this heat, we'll certainly want it for the drinks."

I nodded again. I remembered some talk of ice, and my feet and legs and hands were warming again, feeling the summer humidity clogging the room.

"Did you bring anything you might wear?" she asked. "Cocktail attire is preferred."

"I'm invited?" I said.

She almost laughed. "Of course. Do you think you might have a suitable dress?"

That would depend on what was inside my suitcase. Before I'd even snuck out for the night, when I was in the shower, my mother had let herself into my room. She was the one who'd packed the suitcase and left it for me on the end of my bed, zipped and tagged with my name over hers, crossed out. She'd tried to fix the broken wheel with duct tape, but it didn't work. She probably thought she was being helpful to me, loving. She didn't realize she was being cruel.

My face was still stinging from the last party, not a day ago, which featured me drunk in the dirt, wishing I could dig down into the tree roots and bury myself in the warm black earth.

"Eight o'clock," Ms. Ballantine said. "Perhaps ask one of the other girls to lend you something."

We moved on once more. I turned over the cash for a single month's rent, more than I could afford. I tried not to think about how I had $94.59 after train ticket and subway fare, and no job and no prospects.

"One more thing before I retrieve the keys," Ms. Ballantine said, pushing a sheet toward me. "The vow."

She was serious. This sheet of paper began with a place for the date and the words "I do agree that I"—a wide gap where I was to write my name—"as a resident of Catherine House, a refuge for young women that has opened its doors to me as I promise to open myself to it, vow today the following . . ." It went on with a series of rules. Quiet hours were from ten to five. Breakfast was served between seven and eight thirty. A house refrigerator for our other food items could be found in the back hallway, but we were not allowed to use the oven or the stove. Curfew was ten o'clock on weeknights, midnight on weekends. Other rules included no smoking, no illicit substances of any kind, no high heels on the hardwood floors (this was because heels made scuffs; I made no comment about Ms. Ballantine's own heels), no pets, no hot plates in the rooms, no candles of any kind, no incense, nothing that burned or could start a fire.

Ms. Ballantine paused at a rule toward the end. It said that no males were allowed above the first floor, and she wanted to make sure I didn't miss it. No men or boys, none. No boyfriends, or boys who were just friends. No brothers or other relations, real or so-called. No dads or uncles. That staircase and every-thing above was a no-male zone at all times. She paused, even after I'd initialed the no-boy box, waiting to see what I'd say.

The rule was so completely ancient. It was binary and bor-ing and lifted from another time. Then again, I didn't want anyone in my room, no matter their gender. And if I asked someone in at this point, who would come?

"Okay," I said.

"Usually, here is where I get some back talk."

My mother must have felt safe in knowing that the person she'd escaped from was not allowed upstairs. Yet I was escap-ing something else. I saw a ring of girls' faces hovering over me, forest-fire flicker, the coming kick. Then I lost the image. It didn't matter—they couldn't have known I was here.

"No argument from me," I said.

The last item on the vow was bolded and underlined, so I couldn't miss it. Before she read it aloud, Ms. Ballantine took a moment to reveal what had caught my curiosity before. This boardinghouse was founded after Catherine lost her life trag-ically due to the incident that took her from the world too soon, not long after her father's death. That was how she'd described it, *incident*, a word with a skin of mystery around it. Catherine had gifted her home to other young women in her will, young women in trouble, young women who needed a safe place to shelter from the cruel, coarse world beyond the gate. So long as she was alive—Ms. Ballantine thumped her bony chest—she would make sure Catherine's wishes were followed. Catherine would have wanted her house to be a refuge in this dangerous, dirty city. And a refuge is a fortress. And a fortress is kept secured by secrets.

The last item of the vow was this:

29. I will not speak to reporters, authors, historians, or anyone else, excluding female blood relations in the first and second degree (mothers and daughters, grandmothers and granddaughters), about the goings-on inside the house, nor of the founder, though deceased, while in residence or afterward, effective up to 99 years.

The specificity of the ninety-nine years was off-putting, as by the time all those years passed, anyone who signed this vow would be dead.

But it was something else that caught in my throat. *Excluding* female blood relations, such as mothers and daughters. So a daughter could be told? Meaning my mother had signed this vow—she couldn't have rented Room 10 without signing—and must have known she was allowed to talk about the house's founder.

Yet she'd never told me about Catherine de Barra. Not once.

"Another problem?" Ms. Ballantine said. My pen was poised above the paper, but I hadn't moved. She may have thought I was having another episode.

"No problem," I said. I checked the last box.

Ms. Ballantine had me sign at the bottom of the sheet. "Thank you," she said, pressing my vow to her chest as if relieved. It seemed to carry more weight than all the cash I'd paid her. Though it was odd she was so worried about filling the last room—couldn't she have advertised it online and gotten a tenant in a snap?

"We were so happy when you called," Ms. Ballantine added. "It's rare when we have a legacy—and Dawn Tremper's daughter? I can't express what a surprise this was."

So she did remember my mother. A pain pulsed in my center.

"What's so surprising?" I asked. "I've known about this place my whole life."

"Of course you have. We didn't expect that Miss Tremper would"—she took a long moment to search for the word—"*want* her daughter here, after the way she left us."

I could almost see my father at the gate, ruining everything. If not for him (and me), my mother might have stayed a whole year, or longer.

Ms. Ballantine went to the wall and retrieved a ring of keys from the highest hook. "Shall we?" she said.

We returned to the foyer, which she pronounced *foy-yay*. Halfway up the first flight of stairs was a girl scrambling to the next floor, but Ms. Ballantine's shrill call made her stop.

"Miss Chaudhary, you have a moment, yes?"

The girl turned, and though it seemed as if she'd been in a rush, trying to sneak to the next landing before being spotted, she was all polite smiles when face-to-face. "Sure, Ms. B, what's up? Oh, hi." This part was directed down at me.

"This is Miss Tremper," Ms. Ballantine answered for me. I was to be called the same thing my mother had been called, almost two decades ago. "Room Fourteen. Why don't you show her up?"

"So it's true," the girl said. "We did get a new tenant." She was looking right at me. Had we met before? She was taller than me and noticeably thinner, a detail I reacted to subconsciously by sucking in my stomach. She was also exceptionally pretty, all cheekbones and light in her eyes, a puff of dark hair to her shoulders, brown skin, a warm smile.

"Room Fourteen," Ms. Ballantine repeated. The keys were still in her jeweled hand. She wouldn't let me have them. "There won't be an empty bed in the house tonight."

A shadow passed over the girl's face. "Sure, no problem." Then, to me, "I'm Anjali. I'm on the fifth floor, same as you." She bounded down the stairs for the keys (Ms. Ballantine gave them up).

"Nice to meet you," I said. I told her she could call me Bina.

"Miss Chaudhary, a moment first?"

Anjali leaned in.

"Did you happen to see Miss Mathis today?"

There were some low words I didn't catch, though I strained to, and then Anjali said, "I haven't seen Monet anywhere, all day." She was a bit colder as she said this, as if Monet weren't someone she particularly liked.

Ms. Ballantine glanced anxiously at the front door. "We need everyone here."

"I'm sure she'll be back tonight," Anjali said.

Ms. Ballantine said yes, surely she was right, and then she headed off, leaving me alone with Anjali at the bottom of the stairs.

Anjali's face was gray for a long moment. Then it cleared. "Want me to help with that?" she asked.

I gathered my suitcase and lifted it onto the step above me. "I'm good."

"Okay, if you're sure. There's no elevator, you know." She started up and then stopped, because I wasn't following. She'd caught me with my eyes on the photograph over the fireplace, trying to figure out why it had bothered me so much before. It was ordinary now. Subdued and barely even angry.

I didn't go any closer.

"Hey," she said. "I wouldn't stand there so long if I were you." She started bounding up the stairs, moving so fast I had to tear my eyes away to catch up.

We tromped up the multitude of steep stairs that twisted in a hard turn and had more twists the higher they climbed. I trailed Anjali, dragging the suitcase behind me.

Over her shoulder she asked, "So what brought you here? I ran away and couldn't ever go back—New Jersey, not so far, but it's not like I ever see anybody from home, so I'm safe here. You?" She said this so openly, stating it so plain, it stunned me.

"Upstate," I said. "And I'm just visiting. I'm here for the month."

She looked at me strangely, as if she didn't believe I would possibly want to leave so soon. I kept climbing the steps behind her and didn't offer more.

"So is that a black eye or what?" She slapped her hands over her mouth. "I can't believe I asked that, I'm so sorry. It's, like, sometimes I don't think before I say stuff . . ."

"It's fine." A lie came to me on a wing, so simple. All the traveling must have tired me out. I was having trouble with the details. "I was attacked. They jumped out of nowhere and . . . you know." Hold on. That lie was too close to the truth.

It was only the night before, but the whole way it had happened felt hazy and soft, the way things get when I'm drinking. Every so often, a precise image popped up. I could see a green sneaker with white laces in the air before my eyes, and then the sneaker blurred into an incoming missile, green and white, muddy and fast, connecting square with my face. That was only the beginning. I was cold again, like before. I saw tree branches, too many, cracking in a cascade as I slammed through. A part of the woods that was too dark, too thick, too remote from the road. Something going on with my ear, or inside it, this weird hum. My ankle giving out. Dry sandpaper covering my tongue. Pain in my ankle, and I sat down.

That was happening in real life. I was sitting on the stairs, and Anjali had stopped to survey me from a few steps above. Dust swirled in the air around the both of us.

"Are the stairs too much?" she asked.

"I need a second, that's all," I said.

"So you were mugged? That's what happened?"

Yes, that sounded better. "They took all my money and this piece of jewelry of my mother's. It was a black opal, very rare. I tried to fight, but . . ." Why had I mentioned the opal? Couldn't I have lied about at least that? I stood up, alarmed. My ankle still hurt, faintly, and there was this strange whistling sound way back in my ears, a small wind-storm caught in my head. I should have told her a roaring burn-down-the-forest lie instead of anything even connected to the truth.

"That sucks. Wait, what did they take again? An opal, you said?" She mentioned this pointedly, as if wanting me to say it again from my own mouth.

The black opal was no invention. It was the soft, dark, shining stone that my mother used to wear on her finger with the door closed, the one that barely even fit my thumb. She said she got it in the city, years and years ago, but she never said how she could afford such a thing, or from where. She wore it every once in a while, when we were alone, and kept it in the back of her top dresser drawer, wrapped in a plain blue cotton scarf that she once used to hold back her hair when she was cleaning the house. She'd joke around and call it her "schmatte," which, in Yiddish, means rag. It was so ordinary, so unappealing, that no one would expect it was guarding something so priceless. So grand.

Then one day she said she couldn't wear the opal anymore, it was too dangerous. Keeping it in the back of the dresser wrapped in the old rag wasn't enough. She had to move it. I last saw it the night we buried it, and I caught it only through the shield of the clear plastic baggie, which fogged up its shine. My mother placed it in the hole she had dug. She dropped the earth back in the hole between the rows of tomatoes and smoothed the surface, and we arranged some ragged weeds and leaves overtop to disguise it. He didn't help with the gardening. He'd never find it. My mother said we'd come back for it when we needed it, and this way we would always know where it was. The earth was warm and moist down in the depths of the hole. I felt it with my own hands.

"It was just something of my mom's," I told Anjali.

No robbers stole the opal from me. It was two and a half hours north of the city, where we left it. Buried deep in the ground.

A flicker crossed her face. "Never mind. So did they catch them?"

"Who?"

"The losers who mugged you and beat you up."

"It was dark. I mean, it could have been anybody."

"Too bad," she said politely, as if she'd lost interest.

I'd lost the ability to make anything I was telling sound good.

We continued climbing the stairs in silence, and as we did the pictures that lined the walls stole my attention. Tarnished frames showcased posed black-and-white portraits of young women, girls all grouped together in tight-packed rows (kneeling on the floor, seated in chairs, standing), as if these were class photos. I recognized the room they were in by the furniture, which was shrouded in thick, mottled skin. Downstairs in the parlor, the velvet had been warm gold, but in the photographs it was dismal gray. In every image, from one to the next, she sat stiffly in her frame, on the wall above the girls. The gathering had the appearance of a solemn sorority, with Catherine de Barra herself as patron saint and reluctant queen.

The first photographs were labeled with months and years from the 1920s, and the decades inched forward as we climbed.

Then there it was, the one particular photograph I was holding my breath to find. The dates matched.

I spotted my mother at once, top row, perfect center, closest to the fireplace mantel and the frame. My mother was dark-lipped, hair bobbed and curling toward her chin. The image was in black and white, so I didn't know what color her hair was that day. Catherine, hovering in the frame above her, was almost smiling. Almost. The picture was too small to make it out for sure.

I tried to look not at her and only at my mother, the one who mattered. There she was, immortalized with a knowing gaze, a sense of consciousness, as if I could lean my ear in close and she might speak. She was so unconditionally herself back then, and I wondered what that felt like. She was only nineteen there, two years older than I was now.

"Hey, c'mon already," Anjali called. She was far above me—I hadn't heard her climb.

I came around the bend to the topmost landing, where the stairs stopped.

"Okay, so this is it." She showed off a wide, windowless space filled with towering piles of shoes. "This mess!" she said, kicking at a stray fuzzy slipper. "I keep telling them and telling them. It's even worse on the fourth floor. Anyway, this is our common room, so you'll have to learn to live with it."

I walked the cleared pathway, trying to get my bearings. It was dark. It was hot. Floating flecks of dust gravitated to my mouth, and I had to spit some out.

The common room contained a few armchairs, an ironing board, a standing rack for drying clothes that was completely taken over by a war zone of underwire bras, and an open doorway leading to a shared bathroom. The bathroom was the only thing giving off much light, and when Anjali switched on an antique lamp, I had to blink at the sudden brightness. I sneezed.

"I know," she said. "If you have a dust allergy, you're cooked. At least in our rooms, we can open the windows." There were four numbered doors on the walls of this center room, 11 to 14. The room my mother had, Room 10, was on the floor below this one.

Anjali was gazing at the door to Room 14.

She paused, without putting the key in the lock. She hovered outside the door, didn't even touch it. "I guess this is your room now," she said.

She didn't have to say it: This was Lacey's room. Or had been and wasn't anymore.

Anjali slipped the key into the lock. But before she had the chance to turn it, the door opened by itself from the inside.

Anjali shrieked and grabbed me. I grabbed her back. The key ring flung itself onto the ground, clattering at our feet. Someone was in the open doorway.

I retreated and knocked over the bra tree until there was Anjali laughing and saying, "Oh, you scared us, Lacey. I didn't know you'd still be in there. Didn't you have to switch rooms?"

"Yeah, I'm on the second floor now. I forgot my plant," the girl said. She was holding a sagging little fern in a plastic pot.

The girl was . . . Lacey? In the flesh?

Flashbangs of random thoughts went through me. She was a ghost. She was a figment of my imagination. She was a hallucination. But it really was Lacey—looking a lot like her mother, and perfectly alive even though her family had been mourning her downstairs. Her hair was braided and pulled back off her neck. She had intense eyes that skirted away from meeting mine. There was a sadness on her face that caught

81

hold of me and reminded me of her father's grip on my arm, so urgent.

"What"—I could barely find the words—"*happened* to you?"

Anjali patted my shoulder as if trying to comfort me. "Nothing happened. Her parents tried to get her to come home before it was time," she said. "That's all."

"I guess I wasn't ready," Lacey said softly. She said it as if it had been out of her hands, some unspoken destiny she couldn't fight and wouldn't have dared to try.

Anjali said it differently. "Sometimes Ms. B helps us figure it out, and if she has to deal with our families or whatever, she deals with them." There was a serene expression on her face, as if her own family had been dealt with.

"I saw your mom," I told Lacey, "and your dad, and your sisters."

She nodded and pruned off a shriveled brown leaf from the plant she carried.

"Did they tell you she died or something?" Anjali asked.

"Missing," I said.

"I guess they didn't check too closely," Lacey said. "That was just old junk."

"Stuff some girls didn't want," Anjali echoed.

"Random sweaters and things girls from before left behind . . ."

"That got stained or shrunk in the wash."

"I think there was an old set of curtains in there."

Anjali nodded to confirm.

"They saw what they needed to see," Lacey said.

Anjali laughed. "You look like you saw a tarantula or something." She pinched Lacey and let me witness the pinch. "See? She's fine. She's right here."

"Who are you, anyway?" Lacey said to me. "Are you new?"

"You didn't hear?" Anjali answered for me. "This is Bina. She like literally just got here." She motioned to my crooked suitcase. "I guess she has your room now."

Lacey didn't acknowledge this or welcome me. She turned to Anjali. "That means there's someone in every room."

They met eyes for a long moment.

"Are there not enough seats at the dining room table or something?" I said, breaking the silence.

Anjali laughed, an uncomfortable too-loud snort. Lacey said only, "Or something."

Anjali leaned closer to Lacey and lowered her voice. "Ms. B was asking about Monet. Was she out again last night?"

Lacey confirmed this. "Pretty sure." Her plant quivered in her arms, even though her face was perfectly still.

"*Where* is she going?" Anjali whispered, a note of judgment in her voice. "I don't get it, she's such a—" She stopped talking because Lacey was eyeing me, as if to keep her in check. I was thinking of all the ways people had talked about me, at home, must have still been talking, lighting up phones, eviscerating me, setting me to ruins, saying this, saying that, and all the more after last night. It made me not want to ask, made me not want to know. A girl should be allowed a fresh take when you meet her for the first time, shouldn't she? She shouldn't have to step into a room with her shoulders already burdened by old mistakes and the names she was called before. If that was the case, no one would want me here.

Anjali leaned back and set her voice to a normal volume. "Anyway, see you later. What are you wearing, that white dress?"

Lacey said she was. She'd made sure it wasn't with the stuff her family took. She headed off down the stairs.

I would have asked more questions maybe, but I was so struck by the room. My room. My very own. I peered into the doorway at a plain, tightly bound bed that took up most of the space. Anjali and I both squeezed into the room, so small I could spread my arms and press a hand on each wall. Three walls were white. The fourth was red brick, coarse against my fingers. Everything in the room was clean, as if no one had lived here before, though Lacey had, as recently as that morning.

I wanted to close the door right then, I wanted to be alone between the tight four walls, unbearably hot because there wasn't an air conditioner or a fan, but Anjali lifted the window for some air and then perched on the end of the small bed.

"You'll need those," she said, pointing at the dropped keys on the floor.

I retrieved them and took a closer look. There was a room key and a second, smaller key, together on one ring, and that was all. Anjali explained that there was no key for the front

door. Past curfew it would be secured, and no banging or begging on the intercom would allow us in. We never needed a
key for it in daytime.

"What's this one for then?" I asked. It wasn't big enough
for a full-size door, and it was murky gold and grimy,
as if a hundred sets of hands had gotten their grease all
over it.

"The little baby key gets you into the private garden. It's
for our house only. No one else is allowed in."

This was my own set of keys, proof I lived somewhere, on
my own—and it was a whole house, gated and tall, with its
own garden. I closed my fist, and the keys were warm, and
weightier than expected.

"Yeah, so if you need anything, let me know," Anjali said.
"I'm across the way, the door that doesn't have all the shoes
piled up in front of it."

"Not the shoe monster," I said. "Got it."

"The party's at eight. You're going, right? Of course you're
going. You have to go. We can't have it without you."

"What am I supposed to do, just meet everyone?"

"Yeah," she said. Her eyes flickered. "Everyone. Be sure to
dress up. She likes it that way."

Ms. Ballantine did seem overly formal. I was standing,
and Anjali was still sitting, and she wouldn't leave. Maybe she
was trying to be my friend. I'd forgotten what that was like.

I cleared my throat, trying to make it obvious that I wanted
the room to myself, when I noticed it, on the wall behind her:

a random extra door carved into the wall, blocked by my bed, painted the same white as the wall.

"What's that?" I said.

"Huh?" she said, and turned.

The door was short—it came up to my neck, and I was only five feet tall. Even the knob was painted white, as if to blend in with the wall. In order to open the door, we would have had to move the entire bed, an impossible task with two people crowding the space on the floor.

"Hey! My room doesn't have one of those!" Anjali said. Before I knew it, she'd reached out to take the knob.

Something came over me. I lunged, grabbing her hands, grabbing them hard, holding her back by the wrists.

I had a frantic, furious need to do it. On the other side of that door was nothing I could let her or anyone see—I felt that in my bones. It was mine and mine only. This was my room and not hers, and that was my door.

I couldn't say why I kept her there, trapped, all so she wouldn't touch a doorknob, but there was nothing else I could have done. Her wrists were so thin, the veins and arteries and bloodwork palpable under her skin, and I was holding so tight. My nails dug in. I could have snapped her wrists like twigs, and it was something I thought about: how strong and capable you can feel one moment, how small and powerless the next.

I didn't know how long I held on, but when I finally came to, Anjali was backed up against the dresser, shielding her wrists. Red marks peeked out from where she tried to cover them.

"What's wrong with you?" she said.

"I don't know. I'm so sorry." And I was, but there was a tiny fizz of energy in the depths of my chest, and it bristled. Burned. If this was an episode like the one I'd had downstairs in Ms. Ballantine's office, I wasn't sure what to make of myself. But I couldn't let her know that. "Are you okay? I'm really, seriously so sorry."

"The door can't even open," she said. "The bed's like right in front of it."

"I know."

She inched away from the dresser, careful to avoid touching me. The last thing she said to me before she left the room was, "I hope you like it here."

Faintly, in the back of my ears, I heard a hum.

Now I was alone. I told myself it didn't matter if my neighbors hated me—that was nothing new. I told myself it didn't matter if they all talked about me before the party even started. This room was mine, and I needed to unpack and stake my claim. All that mattered was the fact that I was here, in this house, having this chance to be someone far away from who I was at heart. I might grow a new heart here. I might change into an entirely new person.

I zipped open the suitcase to see what my mother had packed inside. There were tightly rolled coils of shirts and jeans and socks and pajamas, her signature style of arranging her dresser drawers. There were toiletries in zipped pouches. My prescriptions. My vitamins. My toothbrush. My phone adapter.

She'd thought of everything . . . except something formal that I could pull off as a cocktail dress, because why would she think I'd need that?

I was about to close the suitcase when the note slipped out. She'd carefully folded it around my hairbrush and written it small, in her rounded block letters that were so much like mine I should make a conscious effort to change my handwriting.

Bean: This is temporary. Give the girls some
time to cool down. It's their house and you know
I always try to respect that. I'm not choosing
them over you. I'm giving you

I didn't read the rest.

At the head of the bed was the window. I shoved it open as wide as it would go. Immediately off the window ledge was the fire escape, a black iron cage that gave me a miniature balcony, if I wanted to use it. Down below were the streets of the city, filled with millions of strangers who I hadn't disappointed yet. I craned my head out the window, and I breathed in the air.

I reached out my arm—I didn't like heights and didn't want to risk the rest of me—and I opened my hand, and I let the note from my mother go.

The moment passed, and in the quiet of a summer city afternoon, reality set in. My mother didn't know where I was. This was a first in our relationship, unknown territory. If anyone could understand wanting to be in this city, wanting to claw through the sidewalk to set roots here, anyone on this Earth, it would have been her.

Yet she was no longer the same girl who'd dangled her legs off that fire escape, and she wasn't the same woman who'd grabbed everything she owned and flagged down strangers in their cars to rescue herself and her daughter. She wasn't brave, and she wasn't trying to be somebody, not anymore. This was worse than when she converted and bent in the pew to pretend to pray. I barely recognized her lately, and we had almost the same face.

Didn't she remember running? Didn't she remember all the things she said to me pre–Blue Mountain Road, pre-sisters, pre-grace, pre-Christmas, pre-settling, pre–giving in? Back then, the window we'd had to escape was so small, and it had closed tight. But not for me. I made it. I made it out, to New York City.

Here was a vow, and this one was for myself:

Like Lacey, I would find a way to stay.

THE WOLVES

I MUST HAVE LAIN IN BED FOR AN HOUR, CONSIDERING texting my mother and not going through with it, not even reaching for my phone to check again if she'd tried to contact me. My head pulsed, a faint knob of pain in the back from the night before, though I couldn't remember if a foot or something else had hit it. A beer bottle maybe. Green glass. I pressed the spot, trying to massage it, but that didn't help. My eyes closed, and I let them stay that way. I was curled up on my side, lying diagonally on the bed so I could catch the slight breeze from the window. I felt it rustle my hair the way a hand would. My mother used to do that to my hair when I was a little girl. In the background, five stories below, I heard the blare of a siren, cars honking in the street, some random weirdo shouting, maybe at nobody. City noises, gloriously alien in my ears—the way I'd always imagined them.

Lying there, stretched out on my bed, listening to what was outside and the growing sounds inside in the common area as my new housemates came back to their rooms and started to get dressed for the party, I noticed a smell. So faint at first, a tickle in my throat. Then a rising wave, much stronger. A distinct, sweet, cloying stink.

That wasn't cigarette smoke. I breathed it in, and it calmed me. Definitely weed. I started sniffing, seeking out its origin. It seemed to be coming from the floor, seeping up through the cracks between the floorboards, from the room directly below mine.

I pressed my body to the floor, not minding the smell so much, not minding at all. I heard humming. The girl below me. She started by humming a melody, but I couldn't catch the song. I tried to make the sound clearer by suctioning one ear to the floorboards and plugging the other, straining to catch it.

The vow made it clear that there was to be no smoking. Smoking weed would surely get the girl kicked out—if anyone told.

I kept my ear to the ground, and the smell teased my nostrils. I sneezed. Right up against the floorboards.

She stopped the song midnote.

I held very still, sensing movement beneath me, some rustling, a scraping sound, then a careful silence. It felt as if someone had an ear pressed opposite mine, to the ceiling. How could anyone have climbed up there—on the dresser, with the desk chair balanced on top? I had no idea, except I sensed the proximity. A sensation of warmth spread from the floorboard through the pressed side of my face until it was so hot I had to pull my cheek away.

Whoever my downstairs neighbor was, she was flouting the rules. She was doing what she wanted and only what she wanted, and I wondered what kind of life that might be like to walk around in, how dazzling were those shoes.

That was when I heard it.

It sounded distinctly like knuckles knocking on wood, and it was coming from the small white-painted door behind my mattress.

I crawled close and put my ear to it. I was sure I'd heard three sharp raps against the wood, coming from the other side, but now there was silence.

I leaned forward and put my eye to the keyhole. Only darkness. I listened, concentrating with all my might, and . . . nothing.

When I was backing my eye away from the keyhole, assuming I had imagined it all, I heard a sound that could only be human coming from the other side, in the dark pocket inside the wall.

A sneeze. Someone was in there.

I jumped up and grabbed the whole top mattress and flipped it sideways. Same with the box spring, which had a frilly skirt that flopped over my head like a white sheet as if I were playing ghost. I dove for the knob and turned it. The door creaked outward, and I didn't have the space to open it the whole way, but I had room enough to see if anyone was standing there.

There was no one and nothing. Only shadows.

The sound must have been the house settling. The air ducts breathing. A hollow trick from inside the walls.

But wait. What had this door revealed? A closet? An unnecessary and very, very dark closet? I tried to wedge it open wider, but the box spring was in the way, so I pushed myself through, into the darkness.

———

It was dark behind that short white door until I found the string dangling above me. I pulled it and, *click*, a lightbulb blazed to life, allowing me to see the walls—plain red brick—and the width of the area, which was narrow, only space enough for maybe two people to stand shoulder to shoulder, as long as their shoulders touched. Then I noticed the stairs.

This was a stairwell, not a storage closet.

I gazed up into the black, where the steps got erased. If I'd discovered a hidden staircase at home, and the stairs led into complete and total darkness, and there was nothing that forced me inside, I would do the sensible thing and hustle out of there, close the door, seal it shut, never open it again. Yet only the first day of my new life, and already I felt a different sensibility taking up residence in me, this unfamiliar electricity, this growing, humming charge.

The stairs lifted only as far as the ceiling of my room, and then stopped in a blind corner. I'd have to go up there to see.

One step at a time, the string connected to the bare lightbulb ticking as it swung, the wooden stairs cool beneath my bare feet, I reached the crook at the top, where they turned. The landing was narrow, and the next flight twisted again. It had to lead to an attic. I didn't know why I kept going, why it mattered so much that I made sure.

I kept my hands on the wall, one on either side, both sides brick. It was like climbing the inside of a chimney.

At the top of the second flight, I expected to find a door—otherwise why a hidden set of stairs at all?—and there was a doorframe, the tall outline of it clearly visible in the wall. A doorframe, but where a door should have been was a bricked-up section of wall, blocking off any way of getting to the other side. The bricks were sloppy, as if they'd been hastily stacked, with fear and with force. Mortar sealed every crack.

I pressed my ear against a cool patch of wall, but bricks were solid, dense—they didn't carry sound.

I pressed my hands to the bricks, seeking a hollow in the mortar somewhere, a crevice or breakaway where I might be able to peer in. Down on my knees, I found a hole, black and gaping, and I lifted my eye to it. Inside was more black, soft and somehow inviting.

I slipped my finger inside to see if it was indeed a hole, and my finger went in all the way to the knuckle—the hole was deeper than I could reach.

I snatched my hand back.

When I put my eye to it one more time, I swore there was movement, a shifting of the shadows, from darker to darkest. Then it came into focus. I saw a girl in that darkness, but far away, farther than possible, as if I were peering through a telescope trained on a distant spot. Her back was to me as she walked down a dense, wooded road. Something tugged at me, something familiar, and I was tumbling forward.

———————

Time behind my eyelids has ricocheted backward, to the night before.

I am walking down the road, around the bend from the willow—the old highway that has no streetlights or real shoulder. I'm on foot, because I don't have a driver's license anymore, or a car to borrow. My mother told me not to go, but here I am, seeking it out—the party.

The air smells so clean. I'm wearing the same clothes, gripping the same small flashlight from a keychain without any keys. I'm vibrating with purpose. The anger is fresh, not yet sour and puckered. I picture two figures on a target in the distance, and that steers me on.

In summer, parties here are always outdoors, the night sky open to shouting, the ground of dirt and moss gone damp with spills of cheap liquor and beer. That means there are no visible walls or edges, no door to keep someone out.

I know where to find the party, concealed in the woods and away from the road so prying adults won't be alerted and shut it down. When I stand on the outskirts, watching the group gathered too close to the campfire, I feel the pull at my ankle, as if something from deep down in the soil wants to hold me back. But it's only the snarl of a tree root, and I tug my foot free and head into the noise, nearer to the flames.

I don't belong, though it's dark enough that I'm able to blend in, fish out a beer from the cooler, take a perch on a rock at a distance from the fire. I'm searching for them. Light flickers over faces, creating sinister eyebrows and beaked noses, mouths shadow-shaped into leering sneers. The bottle in my hand is as green as the tree canopy in daylight. I'm holding it to my lips, tipping it back. Next I know, the bottle is empty and I'm getting another. The plan is wobbling. Or I am. I came to confront the sisters, but I've lost the bottle and I'm too far from the cooler to grab one more. I hear my name. Some guy from school is calling. I hear a group of girls at the fire, talking loud, though not at me, never at me, and beneath that, the far-off howl of some kind of animal. I think of being mauled by a wolf and living in its skin all through winter, which would mean I'd never make it out of here, not ever.

But listen—some guy is calling my name.

"Who's there?"

My body goes looking. Away from the fire, from the cooler of beer and the people not welcoming me in.

Something's not right. I've been lured into a dark clearing, but no boy is here.

What happens next is swift. The alcohol may confuse things, and maybe words were exchanged, maybe there were warnings and threats, but the first thing I understand is a low kick from a green sneaker with clean white laces that seem to glow in the dark like teeth. Then other kinds, all kinds of shoes in all colors, multiple feet.

I hear myself cry out and stand to take it, but I'm not sure what I'm supposed to do. The girls have grown countless arms in the dark. The trees themselves have joined in. I can't fight them off, can't keep them away. Among the girls are two I've grown up with since I moved into their house when I was nine. My older stepsister—a year older, a head taller—is wiry and strong, with solid radar in the night. My other stepsister uses fingernails. Their friends are along for the ride. A sparse stand of birch trees sways above and behind them. The attack lasts a few minutes. It lasts all night. The world goes dark for a second, but I blink and come to.

Go home. We don't want you here, someone says from above me. Someone else pours warm beer over me and then drops the bottle, not caring where it lands. Beer has leaked into my ear and pooled in my head, making my thoughts float.

When I next lift my eyes, the girls hold sticks aloft, grabbed from the ground and torn from trees, to show what's in store if I don't leave. My arms are up, and I'm scrambling away. As soon as there's room enough to bolt, I run.

I feel them behind me, giving chase. Fuzzy patches of movement in the darkness, gray. Howls carrying through the air, coming after me.

By the time I reach the break in the woods and see a glimpse of paved road, I haven't heard anyone behind me for a while.

I wait, bracing myself. I'm wielding my own stick now. I'm waving it in the air, not sure where to aim.

Nobody's there.

Nobody's even close. The trees swish in response, but I'm alone now. Sounds of the party filter through the brush— oblivious and going on without me, as it should have all along. It's far away in the distance, separate from me.

I can't catch my breath, and every part of my body feels hot, the pain rushing through me from one place to the next, swallowing me in waves. I can't see clearly through my eyes. One is a pinhole of low light, not usable at all. The other side is blurry. My ankle gives out, and I sit down within view of the road.

"I'm right here," I yell into the woods, as if someone might still be coming for me. "Where'd you go? I'm right here."

Wake up. Those two words again at my ear like the lightest touch of a hand. I bolted up with a sting, as if someone had pulled my hair.

I'd forgotten where I was so completely that it took many blinks of my eyes before I recognized the four solid walls around me (three white, one exposed brick), the window, the desk and chair, the mirror, the dresser, the suitcase my mother packed for me, the closed and locked door.

The door behind my bed was sealed shut, the mattress and box spring in front of it as before. I was not on a set of stairs in the dark. I was on my back, in my tiny room. My eyes were cloudy, as if my ability to see were brand-new.

I waited for my heartbeat to return to normal. I waited for my thoughts to clear. I breathed.

As I was lying there coming to realize I couldn't possibly go downstairs tonight and I would have to skip the party—it wasn't like I had a single thing to wear—I heard a voice coming from the window over my bed.

The voice of a girl.

"I heard you moved in. I have something for you." Followed by a whisper of movement.

"Hello?" I said, but she didn't answer, she didn't say who she was.

When I rolled over, I found the dress dangling off the windowsill, half hanging onto the fire escape, half draped on my pillow. It shifted in a gust of wind, shimmering slightly. A black dress with iridescent accents of deep blue. Cocktail-style—I was sure of it, though I'd never before thought about what that might mean. The note folded up around one of the straps didn't have my name, but in an awkward burst of bad handwriting it said this:

Black and blue. Made me think of you. Borrow
this and see you at the party?
—Monet

PART THREE

THE WELCOME PARTY

THAT EVENING I TRIED TO FORGET WHAT CAME BEFORE AND only think about what might come now, tonight. I dropped the black-and-blue dress over my head and let it fall down my body. It was cool to the touch, its outside slick with shine, the inside velvet-soft. The zipper rippled against my hip, a faint scritch-scratch on skin.

There was a mirror on the wall of my room, perched high enough for a face. If I were taller, it would have shown my neck and shoulders, but at my height, it sliced off my chin. The reflection showed a sweaty nest of frizzed-out hair, a purple eye, a scabbed lip, two tomato-flushed cheeks. When I stood on the desk chair to get a view of the dress, the mirror lost my head and stopped at my knees. I became a body only. I could have been anyone, even Monet, my mysterious downstairs neighbor the others were whispering about, the one so generous with the contents of her closet.

The dress slithered around my legs, pooling over my feet. I stepped off the chair. The dress may have been too long, made for a tall person, but if I kept track of the hem when I was walking and didn't trip, maybe I'd blend in downstairs.

In minutes my hair was up, my face cleaned and recovered with makeup, and I headed down. As I descended, I could hear the chatter coming from below. It lifted through the stairwell, a scatter of conversation and laughter. Every girl in the house must have been there.

I paused on the second-floor landing, hidden by the angle of the wall. The last time I'd crashed a party was a nightmare, a mistake. I pictured all the tenants of Catherine House turning on me, their frenzied faces forming a circle around me. When I ran, their arms waving sticks through the corridors, chasing me down all the stairs and out the front door, shoving me through the gate onto the street, howling like they were no longer human. Even the air smelled like it was happening again, sour with beer and sweat, warm and earthy, like a mouthful of dirt.

I couldn't escape. I'd brought it here with me. If I closed my eyes, I would see it, as if it had never stopped and the night didn't end.

I turned to go back. All I wanted was to close myself behind the door of my little room.

I took a step up, but something caught my attention.

The Catherine House girls in the closest posed portrait, center in a series from the 1920s, seemed familiar for a moment. Only, I hadn't studied the portraits from this decade. I'd started paying more attention only as I climbed and as they became more recent and might be a group containing my mother.

Now, certain faces stood out. A couple of them were ones I swore I'd seen before. One of them had dark, distinct freckles, as if someone had taken ink to her face. I leaned in for a better look.

At the same time, a girl rushed up the stairs around the corner and almost slammed into me. Dark-clothed, dark-haired, pale-faced beneath the swift slash of her bangs. I knew who she was. Gretchen, the very first girl I'd met here.

She cast an indignant snarl at me. Her chest was heaving, and clasped to it, again, was the gold-bound book. "You're late," she snapped. "You almost made me climb all the way up there to get you."

"Why were you coming to get me?"

"Anjali didn't want to. Ms. B made me volunteer. What's taking you so long, anyway? It's almost nine." Then she noticed the dress I had on, its shoulder strap slipping fast, and her expression sharpened.

"I was getting dressed," I said. In truth, I'd slept away most of the afternoon and into the evening. I hadn't eaten—I couldn't remember the last time I'd had solid food. Then there was the door in the wall. The stairs. The bricked-up passage—to where, and what? Sliding on the dress had distracted me from everything, and Gretchen had distracted me from the portraits on the stairwell wall.

"C'mon already," Gretchen said. She had my arm and was pulling me down the stairs. "This party wouldn't be happening if it wasn't for you. You're the guest of honor."

"I am?" I said, uneasy. She'd muttered those last words out of the corner of her mouth, as if she didn't want to say them.

"Don't pretend you don't like it."

"Why are you bringing a book to a party?" I asked. She was even more antisocial than me if she planned to sit in a corner and read.

"I've read it eleven times already. I practically know every word." She said this defensively, as if well aware I wouldn't get it, and as soon as we hit the bottom of the stairs, she let go of my arm and headed for the chaise lounge. To anyone who would listen she announced, "I found her. She didn't jump out a window or anything. She just takes forever to get dressed."

No one really responded.

There was a chatter of voices, faint music coming from somewhere I didn't see. I entered the parlor and felt a sinking sensation under my toes as I stepped onto the carpet. The gathering was quieter than I expected, but still intimidating, with a room full of a dozen or so young women. They all showed an awareness that I'd entered, and a few girls smiled at me, though they went back to their conversations. No one approached. Ms. Ballantine didn't swoop in. I stood in a pool of my awkwardness, soaking in it. Minutes passed. I didn't understand how I was the guest of honor for anything.

Scanning the room, I found Anjali. She was smiling and talking with her hands, deep in conversation with a few other girls, so graceful in a pale-yellow dress that dipped down her back. There was a faint discoloration visible on her wrists— the red marks I'd made had darkened—and I only hoped no one noticed. I found Lacey, wearing off-white with a high neck and no sleeves, the toned muscles in her arms showing, but she didn't meet my eyes. Even she was smiling, but I was too far away to see any expression beyond that on her face.

I would have gone over to compliment their dresses, I would have joined the conversation, I would have, but I stayed put.

The entire front parlor was furnished in that collection of gold-velvet claw-footed pieces from another century, same as in the photos on the stairwell and matching the chair I'd sat in when I arrived. A faint scent rose from the furniture, from its golden, lumpy skin. Fabric freshener, cloying with gardenias, and beneath that, mildew. The gold-velvet couch, low and deep like a boat, fit four girls, and four girls exactly. They nodded at me but did not get up. I found a space by the wall and fiddled with the dress straps that kept falling from my shoulders. The shadow there was cooler, out of the way. There was no central air in the room, and a trickle of sweat ran down my back. A ceiling fan whipped in vicious circles, raining down gusts of warm wind.

Ms. Ballantine saw me and offered a tight smile, but she didn't make a move to cross the room. If this party was meant to welcome me into the house, wouldn't Ms. Ballantine have clinked a glass and called out my name? Or something? She only kept an eye on me. A number of the girls did, subtly, sideways. I adjusted my shoulder strap again.

Around a grand piano, lid up and keys quiet, a few more girls gathered, whispering, their backs to where I stood. Then the knot of girls opened—whispers ceasing—and a head lifted from the rest.

I knew that girl.

How she'd fooled me.

She had known I was trying to find this house, and she could have easily pointed me in its direction from the start, but instead she played games. She lived here, at Catherine House, all along. Now the girl from Waverly and Waverly was dressed for the party, with lips dark and eyes black-lashed, daggered at the edges. The shirt she wore was black, the neckline low, with pants instead of a skirt. All of that made sense. But her hair . . .

It had been short when we spoke on the sidewalk, I was sure of it. Now it was lavender-tinged, shoulder-coasting, noticeably transformed. *Was* it her?

She didn't acknowledge me at first. What she did was play with a piece of hair by her ear, pulling it back so the shiny lavender locks revealed underneath, tucked away, that her hair was shorter and dark as before. She tugged it free, let me notice, then tucked it back in. Something inside me swiveled and swerved. Something shook loose.

It *was* the same girl. Only now she was wearing a wig, and for some reason she wanted me to know it. No one had to tell me her name was Monet.

She made a show of looking me up and down, taking in my dress, so I had to acknowledge, had to let her know I knew.

Thank you, I mouthed. *For the dress.* I didn't have a way to ask how she could have possibly known I'd needed one. Did Ms. Ballantine tell her? Did she guess?

She shrugged, as if to say it was nothing.

All this happened from across the large room, amid chatter, glasses clinking. Girls and furniture and the body of the piano stood between us, but it felt like she was huddled up next to me at the wall, my mouth to her ear.

I tore my eyes away and edged, from my spot against the wall, closer to one of the short display tables. Each dark, oiled wood table was hip-high. Displayed on lace doilies were so many random objects. Souvenirs. Artifacts. I let my fingers dance over a vanity set made of silver, showing a silver-plated brush, mirror, and two fan-shaped barrettes, and a small silver comb. The comb had the tiniest teeth, sharper than expected. I was poking one into my index finger when I was interrupted.

A blond girl pushed her face into my view. The first thing I noticed after her overwhitened smile was her bright hair, which seemed to be everywhere. She was holding a small glass plate of sweating grapes and cubed cheese, and pushing it in my face. Apparently the food was meant for me.

"Take it before I drop it," she said. "Monet said I should give this to you as an apology for this afternoon, but for *what*? What did she do?"

I balanced the plate in my hand but didn't try anything. The grapes were dripping with condensation; a puddle pooled under them. I couldn't bear to put one in my mouth.

I remembered what Monet had said to me on the street, only hours before: that I held my cards close, and that I should keep doing it.

"I can't say," I said. "It's something between her and me." I liked the way that sounded, coming out of my mouth, about her. A blooming secret I'd created this moment.

The blond girl blinked a few times. I'd rattled her.

"I'm Bina, by the way," I said. "I moved in today."

"Yeah, like we don't know. I'm Harper, third floor."

"Fifth," I said, wondering if it meant something in the house, the floor your pocket-size room was on, if that would determine a thing out of my control.

"Yeah, we *know*," Harper said.

So they knew my name and my room, but they didn't know anything else about me. My makeup was fresh, though the heat made me worry I'd sweat it off. I could say anything at all happened to me: accident by car or skateboard, mugging like I'd told Anjali, even a simple clumsiness, like I'd walked into a door.

But Harper didn't mention it. Maybe she was being polite.

"How long have you been staying here?" I asked her.

"A while," she said vaguely. She averted her eyes to a gold tasseled cushion on the couch.

I wanted to ask what brought her here—had she gotten in trouble, and what kind? Was she hiding from something, and if so what, or who? But she didn't seem particularly bothered and told me without prompting.

"It was my stepdad," she said, gazing almost blankly back at me. "He tried to murder me, so I tried to murder him. It was a whole thing."

"What?" I said, startled.

She popped a grape into her mouth, chewed, swallowed, popped another. "You were wondering why I came to Catherine House, right? Sob story, blah-blah-blah, he-said-she-said and all that. Who knows what happened anymore? It was such a long time ago."

She seemed about my age, but she was acting like this was something that had happened years ago.

"But I'm safe here. We all are." She paused, and a flare of awareness shot through her eyes. "Even you."

Now I was the one to wonder what she knew about me. This room must have been clogged with secrets, but I could focus only on my own.

Ms. Ballantine drifted by, and Harper's face went studiously blank again, flat as an unmarked board. "Love the dress," Harper said loudly. "So shiny. Where'd you get it?"

My body did the betraying. Before a conscious thought entered my mind, my head was turned toward the piano, to seek her out. She was talking to one of the other girls, her back to us, the line of her long neck making me so curious. The wig seemed like another game she was playing, maybe even for my benefit. What were her secrets? What was her story?

"Hello," Harper said. "Your dress? Where'd you get it?"

"I bought it," I said. "At a store?"

"Right," Harper said. "I've heard of those things. *Stores.*" It was plain who the dress belonged to, I realized, it was recognized and known, and she had been testing me. I'd failed without even trying.

I'd noticed Lacey crossing the room near us. "Hey," I called to her. "Wait."

She kept going on her way to the finger foods, but I reached out to touch her arm. It was so cool.

"I'm in Room Fourteen," I said, once she stopped moving.

"I *know*," she said. "I saw you upstairs, remember?"

"Did you ever," I started. Harper was listening intently, watching my mouth. I leaned closer to Lacey for a crumb of privacy. "What's up with that door?" I finally asked, unsure how to put it all to words, what I'd felt when I reached the top of those stairs, my hands against brick, my eye to the dark and impassable crevice. Had it even happened at all?

"What door?" She spoke far louder than my liking.

"The door in the wall. The one behind the bed?"

Not that many hours had passed, but the sadness in Lacey's eyes had faded—though a shadow was still there, something unspeakable. Harper had a similar shifting shadow in her eyes. Gretchen had one. Even Anjali did. Did all the girls carry an unspoken heavy thing they wouldn't let out, even when they were smiling?

"Oh that," Lacey said. "That's just a storage closet. I found an old vacuum cleaner in there and a bunch of hangers." She said this with a straight face. She didn't *seem* like a liar. And yet.

"You know what, Bina?" Harper said, cutting in. "We were all wondering how you found out about Catherine House anyways. Like, it's not advertised. You have to really go poking around, or know someone who knows. But you showed up out of nowhere. What's that about?"

"I do. Know someone who knows. My mom. She stayed here a long time ago, like eighteen years ago. She had Room Ten. I wanted that room, same as hers, but Ms. Ballantine said—"

Nerves got me talking, but I cut myself off, because they both seemed so surprised. I'd been warned to hold things close, and here I was talking about my mother.

"Eighteen years?" Harper said. "That's so . . . specific."

I shrugged. That was how long it had been.

Harper shot a look at Lacey. "*Eighteen years*," she repeated, with emphasis.

"Interesting," Lacey said. That small admission made her pay true attention to me for the first time. She noticed my black eye blotted down to lavender, my broken lip painted over in an attempt to hide the cut, the cuticles I bit to shreds

113

on my fingers, the chipped nail polish from weeks ago, the sandals that didn't match my dress with the hem too long that I'd stepped on again. She noticed.

Did it bother them that my mother had been a tenant? Other girls were peeking over. The girl with the dotting of freckles all across her face—Ms. Ballantine had called her Miss Tedesco—was watching me openly. For a moment, I thought she was the same girl from the 1920s photograph on the stairwell. But she wasn't. She was the girl who asked about ice. That's who she was.

Monet was the only one in the room not in the least concerned with what I was doing. She was standing before the fireplace, gazing up at the framed photograph of Catherine de Barra, the house's grim namesake.

All those eyes on me created a desperate need to scratch at my hip bone. The fancy silver antique comb I'd swiped from the display table and slipped in through the side zipper of my dress was tickling my skin, its teeth nipping where it was tucked into my underwear, right at the waistband. One of the teeth was especially digging in. And now it was all I could feel, it was all I could think about, and I had to do it. It couldn't wait. I had to.

With slow movements, trying to be casual, I gave in and scratched. Harper and Lacey didn't seem to notice, and the girl with the freckles didn't seem to notice, but across the room someone had turned, someone had stopped studying the portrait on the wall, someone saw me scratch, and this someone smirked.

To cause a distraction, I reached out to the closest item on the closest display table as if to admire it. I didn't care what my hand found. It happened to be a paper fan, purple-flowered, delicately painted, the surface oily and slick.

As soon as my hand was on it, Gretchen was beside me. She snatched the fan from my fingers and set it back on its bed, made from a yellowing lace doily. "I know it's a hundred degrees in here, but I told you not to play with them," she said. "All of these were Catherine's. These were gifts from her boyfriends, and souvenirs from her dad, when he traveled the globe. They were here when she died, they're here still, and we're not supposed to mess with them." She stood guard between me and the table.

"Sorry," I said. "I forgot." The itch had stopped. The comb in my waistband was tingly against my skin now, a delicious sensation.

Gretchen smoothed the doily and was about to step away when I asked her: "How do you know all that? Who told you?"

"Catherine," she said. I immediately thought of Ms. Ballantine and the phone call.

But Gretchen didn't mean anything weird. She lifted the book—she had it even now, concealed behind her back. Its gold cover was satiny, sewn together. Many corners of its pages had been turned down.

"Catherine wrote down every gift anyone ever gave her," she said.

"Really?" I said. "In that book?"

She nodded, fever spots spreading on her cheeks.

"Catherine de Barra did," I repeated, sensing the photograph looming behind me. "That was hers? Where'd you get it? Can I see?"

"Not on your life," Gretchen said. "This is her *private* diary. But if you're wondering where that fan came from, imperial Japan. Her dad brought it back after he was away for four months. He came home with it in December of 1917." She closed her eyes as if rummaging around her memory for the exact date, as if I cared to hear it. "The thirteenth. A Thursday. She thought he'd left her to die in this house all alone. She would wait at that window, watching the gate, to see if he showed." She pointed into the foyer, at the stained-glass sliver of a window beside the front door, just narrow enough for a girl to stand, her eyes peeking through a shard of blue glass, or a shard of green, of gold, of warm red, depending on how tall she was.

"What do you know about how she died?" The question was out before I knew I was about to ask it.

"Catherine?" Harper said, butting in, her mouth twitching.

"Ms. Ballantine said something about an 'incident.'"

Gretchen shook her head. She knew, and she wasn't telling.

"We can talk about that, can't we?" I asked. "Do you know what happened?"

Harper's eyes went wide. A girl on the couch bolted upright.

"Don't *you* know?" Harper said. She paused. "You know about the roof, right? Your mom . . . I mean, she *must* have told you."

Lacey nodded. "If her mom was really here eighteen years ago, she would know."

A crawling feeling. My head nodding. *She told me. I did know. I was only checking, asking like that. Of course I knew.*

I looked to the portrait, I couldn't help it. Monet had gotten much closer. She was tall, much taller than me, so when she reached the lip of the fireplace mantel, she was a whole head and shoulders above it and level with Catherine's posed feet.

Monet was close enough now to touch the glass with her finger. I wanted to ask her if the picture of Catherine had changed at all since she'd started watching it. If right then, before her very eyes, the mouth had shifted into a sinister smile. Just to see if I was alone in what I saw before, all alone.

Monet didn't appear to be the least bit surprised or frightened. I knew it then. She couldn't see the picture moving at all. That was only for me.

All along I'd been trying to avoid it, but now I had to see.

Catherine had a stern set to her mouth, her lips tight and flat like a ruler. There was no smile. Maybe there never had been a smile. Her hands were still clasped on her lap, in a knot above her knees. I knew I should leave her be.

Yet I found myself moving. My feet barely had to do the walking—I was pulled by a string. I was wheeled on a dolly. I was there before I knew it, at the mantel, pushing past Monet to take the space front and center, my neck lifting, my eyes gazing up. Catherine wasn't scowling anymore. Her eyes were deep black pools, perfectly serene. Her mouth was loose and coming open, a hint of teeth showing. There was no mist or fog—it was all so clear. On her faint gray face was a new and undeniable grin, a hard beam of light that landed straight on me.

My ears stopped taking in sound.

I saw Catherine de Barra herself, there inside her frame facing the foyer, I saw a ripple come over the image, a faint blur as she shifted in her chair. She was closer to the front of the frame, closer to the glass. She'd adjusted the way she was sitting so I could see it better. See what was on her hand.

There, protruding from her finger, was a dark object, glimmering so brilliantly that I almost thought I could reach through glass and time and remove it.

In the photograph, she was wearing the black opal, the very one. That was how my mother had found it, eighteen years ago—it hadn't come from the city outside; it had come from this house.

Black opals are beautiful, but some myths say they can also be terrible, even cursed. They are as shiny and lovely as they are said to be angry and foul of mood. I'd read all about them, and I didn't believe a thing about their bad hearts. People were ignorant, afraid. I'd touched one, held it, tried it on the once, and I knew it to be good. I've read that they are also as distinct as a handprint, no two the same. Before we buried it, my mother would remove it from the back of her dresser drawer, where it was camouflaged by her ugliest underwear. She would unwind it from the plain blue schmatte and let me watch as she slipped it on her ring finger, where a wedding band would go, and she would say she was alive today because of it, and let's never forget that.

I never did. I committed it to memory. I dreamed of it, sometimes, even after we moved away.

And so, I would have known it anywhere. I lifted my finger to the glass, and Catherine de Barra's finger, on the other side of the glass, reached out to touch mine. Her eyes sparked and seemed to contain a thousand different colors at once. The black of her irises was only a trick—inside was everything.

A hand landed on my shoulder. I broke my stare at the portrait and turned, an insistent ringing in my ears.

Ms. Ballantine had come up behind me. Her face had changed, softening, the apples of her cheeks glowing.

Everyone was looking—more at Catherine than at me. I'd awoken something inside the picture, and now everyone in the room noticed. Maybe they saw the colors swirling in the blacks of her eyes and felt their hearts beating in a way that was urgent and right.

"We were hoping, weren't we, girls? We were all hoping," Ms. Ballantine said. She squeezed my shoulder and would not let go. "Welcome." A true smile broke open on her face, as if she'd been holding it in for such an excruciatingly long time, yellow teeth exposed and not even caring I could see them.

I'd proven myself. I'd shown I was meant to be in this house, as my mother had been almost two decades ago. Ms. Ballantine saw me in a new light. Everyone did.

"We have everyone we need now," Ms. Ballantine announced to the others as they gathered closer, wrapping around me in a tight ring. "She's the one we were waiting for. She's here."

Time turned sticky. Time spilled slowly forward. Molasses. There was champagne, and there was wine, though most of us were underage. Ms. Ballantine looked the other way. There was loud laughter, dancing, spilling champagne and wine and crushed cubes from an endless supply of ice. I met the other girls, each one, even if there were too many names to remember and I couldn't recall who I'd met already, and heard the reasons that brought them here to rent rooms. Some had run away, and others had been kicked out. Some were hiding from mistakes that felt too heavy to confront. No one could tell me exactly how many weeks they'd been here, how many months, only that it had been a long time. The faces and hair colors and moving mouths blended together after a while. Some of the girls seemed dressed for another time, as if this were a costume party and we didn't all get the memo. Others wore tattered dresses, as if they owned only a single one. I noticed these things, but none of it mattered, really. They all wanted me here. No one was running me out of the house for crashing their celebration—no one.

There was a moment when it seemed like more than four-teen of us had come to claim the remaining empty chairs and openings on the furniture, that when there was nowhere left to sit, young women pressed in around the piano, they lined the standing shelf where the cold drinks were served, they occupied any gap they could. I even thought I spotted a young version of my mother, at the back of the crowd, so short she was squeezed between two shoulders, but it was only the gold-framed mirror mounted on the wall, a quick flash of my own reflection. I appeared so giddy when I saw myself, so alive.

Maybe I should have understood what was wanted of me—why everyone would welcome me in so enthusiastically, what kind of circle I was closing by being the last girl. It was assumed I knew, because my mother must have told me.

I acted like I did know. I figured it would become clear to me sooner or later.

When the candles were brought out, and the party moved out to the garden, I followed at the tail end of the crowd, not sure what was happening but swept away and willing to swal-low my questions. Ms. Ballantine led the procession out the front door and down the stoop, through the tall iron gate and onto the sidewalk, and then through another gate beside the house, where it was dark and smelled, strangely, a lot like home. This was the private garden space, locked to our neighbors and tourists alike. Here, she said, we would pay our respects under open air.

It seemed more choreographed than an impromptu visit could be, and when we had walked in a line through the gated space to form a circle in the darkness, I began to have an inkling.

I was the only one who hadn't known we'd end up here. My candle flickered. The faces of the girls shown in that flicker were solemn, full of concentration, but never confused, never uncertain.

I got distracted keeping the flame out of my hair, which had come loose, so the flyaways were everywhere. It was too dark to see our city garden, how big it was, what was planted, if it had trees and how tall. I could smell the plants and sensed myself surrounded by their not-unpleasant muggy heat. There was soft, yielding dirt under my sandals instead of flat concrete. There were small spots of light from our candles, wobbling and fluttering in the night air like fireflies.

Ms. Ballantine clapped her hands, and we quieted. The glow of her candle made the jewelry on her fingers shriek with light. "Now we are all here," she said—and I sensed her nodding in my direction, though I could barely see the shadowed movement—"and now that she's awake and listening, we will try to reach Catherine, to see what she wants of us, to see how we can help her, and if she'll let those of us leave who want to go."

This set off some faint murmurs near me, a flurry of attention, girl to girl.

Ms. Ballantine clapped again, and the girls stopped whispering, chastised. "First, the offerings."

I kept myself back as one by one the girls approached a dark space at the center of our ring. They seemed to be leaving items on a raised ledge of some kind, a tall stone, and, as they did, whispering a message, saying a thank-you. I couldn't follow the words exactly. In the glow of the candles, I thought I caught a shiny coin, a souvenir yellow taxicab, a candy necklace, a bottle-opener keychain.

Soon it was my turn, but no one had warned me or prepared me to take part.

"What am I supposed to do?" I whispered to the girl next to me. It was Gretchen, who only shoved me forward, and then after her, Harper, who gave me a gentler nudge. Ms. Ballantine waved an arm to usher me to the center, and so I stood there, the others all around me. I found the monument and put my hand on it, touching the offerings.

Leaning in close, I found what appeared to be a dark hole in the ground right beside the monument. I couldn't sense or see a bottom. The light of my candle didn't reach that far.

I had no pockets, no bag or purse. All I had was the comb I'd stolen from the parlor—and maybe it was sloppy of me to pull it out, maybe I would regret it in daylight, but it was all I had to give.

"I'm sorry I took it," I whispered to the dark, unknowable space at my feet, as if Catherine were listening and might understand.

There was a hush, and then a few mutters I couldn't make out, but no one called me on it. I stepped back into the ring of candlelight, where I'd been before, the comb no longer tickling my waistline. I felt empty.

"Now let's listen," Ms. Ballantine said. She closed her eyes, and the fire danced on her eyelids. It danced over everyone's eyelids but my own, because the whole time my eyes were open. Then across the way, I noticed another pair of eyes that did not close—Monet's.

The others listened. The tenants and Ms. Ballantine listened, and Monet and I fake-listened, but there was nothing to decipher, nothing to translate, nothing whatsoever to hear. Quiet blanketed the garden, as if a whole city weren't on the other side of that gate.

After a time, Ms. Ballantine sighed, which indicated the listening time was over. Her shadow in the night seemed deflated, thinner and more bent than before. Had she expected her ghost to talk out loud, in front of everybody? Perform for us?

"I do apologize," she said. Disappointment tinged her voice. Now her candle flame stayed away from me—as if avoiding even touching where I stood.

Murmurs. Rumblings. A few hushed complaints. Then a hand—I wasn't sure whose—squeezing my own as if I needed comfort.

"Thank you," Ms. Ballantine said to us all. "Thank you for trying. It's been eighteen years exactly, to the month, and with Miss Tremper now here, I must have thought . . . But I was mistaken." She stopped, fumbled, and was quieter when she next spoke. "She'll show herself to us another time."

She blew out her candle. The girl with the freckles—at my elbow, I hadn't noticed her before—did, too, with a hard hiss of breath.

Eighteen years, Ms. Ballantine had said. That was the summer my mother lived here and may have stood in this very circle holding her candle flame and listening for the dead. Another thing she'd never thought to share with me.

The circle disbanded. Whatever magic had electrified the parlor and set us off drinking and dancing had fallen flat outside. I wasn't so special anymore, was I? I glimpsed Ms. Ballantine heading for the gate. Girls followed, until only a handful of us remained. What was supposed to have happened? Why did I feel like I'd let everyone down?

"Should we head in?" one of the girls asked. "It's almost midnight."

"That's it? It's over?" someone else said. "Ms. B?"

"She left," I said, speaking up for the first time.

The garden was set between buildings, and directly above it was the night sky. For a moment, the rooflines overhead turned jagged, like mountains, and that was familiar to me, that was something I knew. I could have closed my eyes and transported my mind back to where I started, but I didn't want that. I refused.

"What's the point of you, anyway?" a girl shot out from the

darkness. "I thought you'd come for a reason. I thought, with you here, something would change. But nothing changed."

She was a vaguely familiar face, but I couldn't recall her name. "What do you mean?" I asked. "If you don't like it here, why don't you go live somewhere else?"

"What did you just say to me?" She got up in my face. She seemed furious, buoyed by it as if whatever had happened with the candles had been her last straw.

Monet intervened with her body. All of a sudden, she was there in front of me, as if shadowing me all along. "She doesn't have what we need, obviously. She can't help us. Leave her alone."

The other girl put up her hands in surrender, and then both of them—Monet and whoever among the tenants had been so upset at me—were gone.

A couple more girls filtered away until I had a small pocket of space of my own deep in the garden. I was near the offerings, near the black spot at my feet that felt like it went down and down until nothing could be made out below. Monet didn't come back. I could hear the last few girls whispering, but no one stepped over. The drinks I'd had (how many? my mind scrubbed details) made me want to catch my balance, and I reached out a hand. It landed on the hard-edged stone of the monument.

My hand began to close. A growing warmth inside my fist. I'd left the comb—everyone had seen me leave it, even if they hadn't recognized where it had come from—but that wasn't what found itself captured in my grasp. I didn't even know what it was at first, only that there was weight in my palm now. I'd taken something else, and it was the taking that calmed me.

It felt like a small oblong stone. Ordinary and cold at first. The band cut a groove into my flesh as I kept my fist shut. The longer I held it, the more the stone warmed. It sparked and hissed. Something inside it rumbled and spun. When I parted my fingers and peeked in, I understood immediately and at the same time didn't think it possible. I kept my fist closed to conceal it. I was trying to make sense of it. The black opal ring had been buried in the ground upstate—deep in dirt; I'd seen it myself eight years ago. I'd witnessed my mother do the digging. Then how that patch among the rows of tomato plants had been paved over and covered in bricks to make a patio. How it was gone. Gone forever. We'd never rescued it.

Yet here it was. In my hand.

As soon as I squeezed it in recognition, there was a shout.

Harper was crying out, and she was pointing up into the sky.

"Look up," I heard Gretchen say. "I can't believe it, look up."

I emerged from the dense section of the garden and went for where I could see beyond the tree covering. I craned my neck to the sky above, shifting grays on gray. Light caught my eye, and I followed it to the place everyone else was pointing. And there it was. There *she* was.

Five stories over the garden was a thing none of us would name. I saw it, and I couldn't blame it on the champagne, or the wine, or the still-pounding spot in the back of my head making me dizzy, needing to lean on the closest girl.

I'm not sure how I imagined a spirit would manifest itself. This wasn't the photograph reanimated, not a replica of the young woman who'd posed for the camera in the tall-backed chair. It wasn't so much a girl as a light. The glow was almost blue. The shape of her—the sense she had a shape—was three-dimensional, but the backdrop of city lights could be made out through her.

She was at the edge of the rooftop. She wavered there for a long, heart-stopping moment. We all saw her up there—the few of us who stayed.

Then she disappeared entirely, blotted from the city sky as if a light had been switched off.

I felt a part of something, then. The small group of us together, barely allowing ourselves to move. Simply waiting. The stretch of rooftop—ours and all the other buildings around it—was empty, but we held still until we were sure it was over, and then we allowed ourselves to move again, to blink our eyes, to breathe.

"Did you see?" Harper asked. Her hand was in Gretchen's. The others who remained were huddled close together, chins lifted.

I nodded. I had seen.

"That's where she jumped from," someone said. "It's exactly like in the stories."

"She didn't jump." Lacey spoke from out of nowhere. "She fell. It was an accident."

"She knows we're here," Gretchen said. "She woke up. Something we did . . . something that happened tonight . . . it woke her." She was staring with intensity and longing up at the roof. But I knew it was over.

I was afraid to slip the ring on my finger, so I kept my fist closed. Still, I felt it. The opal in my hand had gone calm, and cold.

Lacey was near me now, her breath on my bare shoulder and her off-white dress practically aglow. "You did it, didn't you?" she said, finding my eyes in the dark as best she could.

I didn't even open my mouth.

I found myself staring up at the empty edge. Only my first night, and this would be a thing I would not tell a living soul. No one outside this space would believe me; we would all keep this secret through our lifetimes plus ninety-nine years, unless we shared it with our daughters, or—maybe, not that they deserved it—our mothers.

I caught sight of Monet at the fringe of the remaining group. She'd removed the wig, and her ordinary hair stuck out, the silhouette of the cowlick giving her away.

"It's almost midnight!" someone called, and a sense of urgency leaked from the others. Quickly, they blew out the last few candles. In a rush they headed out of the garden for the house's gate and, beyond it, the towering stoop. "C'mon," someone said to me, and I followed. "Somebody lock the garden," I heard someone else say. I didn't see who stayed behind to lock it up, but I lingered at the gate for a moment, gazing out. I almost wanted to follow the sidewalk and see where it took me, head to the west side or the east side, downtown or uptown, let myself be led by shifting signs parsed from the moving crowd or the slack summer wind. My mother used to do that in her stories.

But I couldn't. It was near midnight. I had to go in.

It was when I was back in the house that it came over me, sudden and strong. Dizziness rushing in like a wave. Through it, faintly, I heard the grandfather clock toll twelve times. I felt funny, slippery, and it wasn't the slinky dress. My stomach was a roller coaster riding up into my head. I needed a glass of water.

Should I have stayed upstate, where I was safe in the trees, safer than I realized, because it was what I knew?

I wasn't sure how I ended up in my room. I must have been helped up all those stairs, as I had a faint memory of leaning my weight on someone else, being dragged up the last flight, almost carried. At one point, I was puking into a cold porcelain toilet and someone—it might have been Anjali—was carefully holding back my hair, giving me a sip of warm water from a plastic cup and wiping it when it dribbled down my chin. I didn't even remember getting that drunk, but I must have. I was cold. Then warm, and covered by something soft. I think I asked for my mother, but she was so far away. The pattern on the backs of my eyelids bloomed like a black stone full of uncountable, incomprehensible stars.

The opal had been in my hand, I swore it, deeply burrowed into my fist. It was only when I was in bed, at some point during the night, that I realized I didn't have it anymore.

LIARS AND THIEVES

I WOKE TO A RATTLING AT MY OPEN WINDOW. I WAS STILL IN BED. It felt like days had passed, but it was only the next morning. The sun was creeping its way up, burning orange at the edges. My head was buzzing and the light was confusing, but most confusing of all was the noise at my window. It was a person. Before I knew it, that person was crawling off the fire escape and into my room.

She jostled into me. "Move." There wasn't room for the both of us in the bed, so I found myself sprawled on the small patch of floor, gazing up at where she'd planted herself by my pillow.

"Where are you— What are you—" My words were chopped up in my mouth. They kept getting stuck or lost altogether.

My mind struck a match inside me, then sucked it dark fast. For a moment, I couldn't remember much of anything.

132

Then her name came to me. It was Monet, the girl who lived downstairs, in the room directly below my room. I was in Catherine House; I wasn't home. I remembered everything.

She was wearing her dark clothes from the night before, but the shirt was wrinkled and smeared, and her pants were rolled to the knees. Her feet were dirty, her legs streaked in dried mud. Her hair was her regular short-chopped style, no sign of a wig. In a trick of the light, she'd become so unreal she turned practically translucent.

But she was genuinely here.

I was trying to tell her she had the wrong room, but it wasn't working. She was curling into my sheets and balling up her body to go to sleep. She had my pillow crunched into her face.

"Monet," I said, nudging at her. "You can't stay here."

My own head was pounding. I very much needed to close my eyes and lie down.

"Hey," I said.

I pulled on her arm, her leg, her other leg. Her limbs were heavy. She'd closed her eyes, and mascara streaks made delicate butterfly lines all down her cheeks. Her smudged mouth opened, and a small drop of drool slipped out onto my pillowcase, glistening.

"I think you're confused." I kept trying. "You're in the wrong room."

No response. When I nudged her one more time, she simply sighed.

It was almost officially morning—the sun rising and blazing between buildings told me—and a strange girl had taken over my bed. Surely no one else was awake in the house to help me deal with this.

I sat for a while in the small space, considered compacting my body into one of the dusty, puffy chairs in the common area, or admitting I was awake and getting into the shower before anyone else did.

I went to the bathroom, took my time, splashed water on my face, brushed my teeth, and came back, but she was still there.

Then I noticed how she was curled up so carefully at the head of the bed, her knees tucked in, leaving the whole lower half of the mattress empty, almost on purpose.

I took the bottom end, that small area of space between her body and the wall, and I said aloud, "Okay . . . I'm going back to sleep now," as if that might rouse her, but it didn't. She wasn't budging.

She'd stretched out her leg a few inches, and now one of her bare toes was touching my bare arm. I peeled open an eye to see if she was still there, and she was. She'd opened an eye to check to see if I was there, too.

Caught, we both snapped our eyes closed at the same time.

―――――――――

When I woke for the second time that morning, the sun was in my face and the bed was empty except for me.

Still, I sensed I wasn't alone in the room and rolled over. She was standing beside the bed. I covered myself as best I could in case she was looking. She was.

"Hey," she said from above. "Morning."

She eyed my exposed legs, and then her eyes traveled upward, to the rest of me, and I remembered what I was wearing. I'd never taken the dress off before falling asleep, and now it was rumpled and wrecked, one of the shoulder straps knotted, the hem torn in the front. I was starting to say I was sorry, but she caught me and spoke first.

"Looked good on you. Maybe a tad too long, but the colors were perfect. Anyway, I don't need it back. What am I going to do with it now? You keep it."

"Thanks," I said. "But what are you doing in here? And couldn't you use a door?" I pointed to the ordinary door that led to the common area, not the one I didn't want to think about, right there behind the bed.

"I was passing by and thought I'd stop in," she said, indicating the wide-open window with the black-barred fire escape attached. I assumed she was joking, but I didn't ask. She said it as if I didn't understand the simplest of things—that the Earth wasn't flat, that rocks weren't for eating—and she couldn't bear having to explain. She turned and resumed whatever she'd been doing while I was unconscious, which I guess was poking through the few things I'd put out on my desk. My phone (blank as a brick, without a single notification). My key ring with the two keys. My wallet (cash and useless ATM card only, no credit cards—I watched her confirm).

"Um," I said tentatively. I didn't have the words. I sat up. I couldn't really stand, because the room was so small and she was in the way. "Are you leaving?"

"I didn't think this is how our first real conversation would go, Bina," she said. "I thought we'd be past this by now."

That quieted me. We didn't exchange a spoken word at the party, but we did have a connection. I couldn't deny that.

She was still going through my things. Checking my desk drawer. My pants pocket. Inside the toes of my shoes. She hovered over me, her dirty feet all over my floor, her hands slipping into the drawers of my dresser, where I'd dumped the balled items of clothing my mother had chosen. She felt around beneath them, then, satisfied, closed the last drawer. All that was left was my suitcase.

Her back was to me when she spoke. "I wasn't named for the painter, you know. The man."

"You weren't?"

"I was named for my great-aunt, twice removed. Want to know something about her? She was a revolutionary. She gave up all creature comforts to fight for the voiceless, the suffering, the powerless. Last my family heard, she studied up on her Spanish and joined an armed leftist group in the jungle, fighting for the people. She had many lovers in the forest and would send us back locks of their hair in envelopes with dried leaves and flower petals. Never signed her name, but of course we knew they were from her. She died in a great battle, and they carried her body through the trees to the river, and then they let it float back to civilization covered in flowers so someone would find her and fly her home." She said all this and stopped, waiting for my reaction.

"She did what?" I said, trying to piece it together. I couldn't help but be impressed. I knew how to recognize a great liar, could even taste that tanginess in my own mouth. I suspected she liked to put a thing out into the air only to see if it would sound true or flutter down to the ground and die. I admired her talent, because I couldn't tell, not entirely.

"Where are you from?" I asked.

"Are you asking me what I am?"

I didn't think I was, but I flushed that she'd called me on it. I knew I looked Jewish—I'd always known, from the way people would say certain things in front of me, then add as an afterthought, *Oh, that's just a joke, you know we don't mean you, right?* But it was a rude thing to wonder about a person. She was right. When it came to her, I'd turned rude and curious about all the things.

"Some parts of my family are from Iran, some from France, Italy, Cuba, you name it. Plus, I have three Australian cousins. But to answer your question, Colorado. Where I'm from, the mountains are taller than you could even imagine and we have gangs of wild horses roaming around in our backyards. The air's so thin up there not everyone can breathe it. But that's just an address. Really, I'm from everywhere. I'm a part of the whole world. I'm the future, really, because one day everyone's going to look like me." The cowlick in her hair was quivering as she spoke, and her eyes were bright and her arms were gesticulating and bare. I couldn't tear my eyes away—at least I didn't want to.

I was beginning to suspect she'd invented absolutely all of it. How glorious.

"How about you?" she said. "Where are you from?"

I hesitated and got ready for what might come. But when I opened my mouth, nothing near worthy spilled out. "The Hudson Valley," I said, so simply. "A town up there. You wouldn't know it."

"Why would you tell me that?" she snapped. Disappointment in her voice, even disdain. "Anyway, that's how I got my name. How'd you get yours?"

The problem was, I couldn't meet her eyes and lie. "My mom. She found it—Sabina—in a baby name book. She liked the way it sounded. That's all."

She sighed, deeply, as if she knew what I was capable of and that now, here, in the face of a master, I'd choked. "You really need to come up with some better stories," she said.

She'd poked around in my suitcase—it was empty, every pocket and flap. She was now at the closet, noting the few items, the collection of empty hangers. I had no interesting or revealing secrets, at least not where she could find them.

"Did you come in with the rest of us last night?" I asked.

"Didn't you see me behind you?"

"No."

"Didn't you see me slip in right after you did and close the gate?"

I tried to think. "I mean, I don't remember. I wasn't feeling too good last night. So you stayed out? All night? Where'd you go?"

"You didn't hear me say that," she said.

She stood there with the most unreadable face I could imagine, and I hadn't been able to read her this whole time. It seemed like a mask on a stick, one made with cardboard and two pinholes for eyes poked out, held over her real face.

"You don't have to tell me." I could piece it together on my own. The dirt on her feet gave her away—she must have spent the night in the garden. Was she teasing about being right behind me and missing curfew?

I noticed that she was leaning her weight against the wall, as if spying all through my things had worn her out and she needed to rest now, to take a moment. Her breathing was kind of labored, too, though the air in the room was perfectly okay. Maybe this was why she wouldn't leave.

"It's your first morning, so I'll tell you something," she said. "You'll miss the good breakfast if you sleep too long. All that'll be left is the cereal and the bread. They take away the toaster, and they stop serving eggs. But sure, take your time if all you want is cornflakes and dry toast." She made no move for the door herself.

I swung my legs over the side of the bed, and she had to move away, closer to the door. Yet she didn't make any effort to open it. Was there something she wanted from me? And would I have minded so much if she stayed?

"You still have an hour," she said. "I'm only telling you for tomorrow."

"Oh."

"Then again, who knows if you'll be here tomorrow."

"What do you mean? I just got here. I rented the room for the whole month."

"So you're staying?"

"I'm staying."

"Even though you're the one who woke Catherine up? And you don't know what she wants from you?" She was trying to scare me away. Ever since she ran into me on the street and toppled my suitcase, she'd been trying to get rid of me.

"What does she want from me?" I asked. Everything that happened after I stepped up to the portrait and put my finger to the glass the evening before had a different kind of light to it. I could hardly face it in my memory.

My mouth went dry, even drier than it was. In the back of my throat, there was a taste that was gritty, like a faint coating of dirt.

"I'm messing with you, Bina. I know you're not leaving. I was only wondering if *you* knew." I was noticing how drained she appeared, her light-brown skin more tepid than

I remembered, as if she'd spent the whole night sipping drain cleaner and was mildly poisoned by sunup. Hungover like I was, that's all.

"I signed the lease," I said stupidly.

"And the vow," she added sadly. "We all put our names to that." She said it, but it wasn't like she followed the rules. I already knew of a couple she'd broken.

She leaned forward, changing the subject. "I have something for you . . . Do you want it?"

"Sure," I said, confused.

"That's why I came up here. To give it to you. It's yours. Now where did I leave it? Oh, right. Out there."

I peeked out at the fire escape. I didn't believe that this was the reason she'd climbed into my window at three or four in the morning, or whatever time it had been, but now I was curious.

"What, you're not afraid to climb out there, are you?" she asked.

Even back home, where the cliffs met the night and my friends—before I lost them—liked to touch their toes to the vacant air at the mouth of the ravine, I stayed back, on solid ground. Even then, I kept myself apart from them, so apart that when I needed someone to have my back, no one was left. "I'm not so much a fan of heights."

"Good to know. Don't worry, I won't make you climb the ladder. You'll find what I brought you on the windowsill. Outside. You'll just have to reach out there to get it."

I slipped my hand out and patted around on the ledge. All the while, my eyes were locked on hers as if she could keep me from falling.

When I found it and pulled it in, even she seemed surprised. "There was a good chance it could have dropped in the wind and gotten lost forever," she said. "I don't think Catherine would have liked that, do you?"

I couldn't be sure if she was joking.

In the palm of my hand was the silver comb from the display table downstairs. The same comb I'd left as an offering in the garden. She'd known somehow that I hadn't wanted to give it up.

It had felt delicious to take it, that sense of sneaking something that didn't belong to me and making it mine. I'd had it snug and cold at my waistline until it warmed to the temperature of my skin. But I'd thought I'd lost it forever. Like the opal.

I stiffened. The comb wasn't really what I wanted anymore.

"What's wrong?" she said. "I thought you'd like it back. Even if you shouldn't have it in the first place."

"Thank you." It was in my hands, and the sharp teeth and the smooth, shiny surface reminded me why I took it, but it wasn't enough.

"Remember the vow?"

"You know I remember the vow. You just said we all signed it."

"Then you'll remember what's squeezed in there between curfews and hot plates. No theft. Theft is cause for eviction.

Now, I think it means stealing from other girls, because who here wants one of those grimy old teacups downstairs? But still. You should watch yourself." She knew, as much as I knew, that there would be a next time. That this was habit and I'd only just begun.

"It's not like you follow the rules yourself." I pantomimed a swift inhale of a tightly rolled joint and then waved the smoke away.

"Touché."

She heaved herself up off the wall. For someone who'd scaled the fire escape to get up here, it seemed to take a lot of effort. She went for the door.

"Wait. Don't go yet. I want to ask you ..."

"Ask me what? All the questions you couldn't ask last night?"

I nodded.

"All the questions you don't even know you should be asking?"

A chill crept along my arms, though the morning heat was already rising.

"Sometimes a person can't tell you what you already know," she said. "Sometimes you have to see it for yourself. Then you'll believe."

She must have meant the figure on the rooftop, that outline created out of blue light. A single flash that disappeared. I should have been scared to think of it, wanting to run from this place. But I was more curious than afraid.

"Why did Ms. Ballantine want Catherine de Barra to wake up?"

She laughed. I liked her laugh. "If you were sleeping for over a hundred years, wouldn't you want somebody to wake you up already? I'd figure you'd be so hungry." She said this so matter-of-fact.

I shrugged. It was a silly answer to the wrong question.

"How did she die? I heard some of the stories . . ."

"If you're so interested in all of that, you should ask Gretchen. She sleeps with that diary she found. I'm shocked she hasn't eaten the pages out of it yet so no one else can read it. But do you want to know what I heard?"

I nodded.

"You want to know what people said back then? What was in the newspapers?"

The creeping sensation was now up my back. Behind me was the door in the wall—I was abruptly aware of it, and then it was all I could think about, the fact that I was right up against the extra, unwanted door.

"It all starts with a terrible boyfriend . . ."

"It does?"

"Obviously," she said, as if the story couldn't begin any other way. In fact, that was how my mother's story had started, which made me want to listen all the more. "He wanted to keep her, and he wanted everything she had all to himself. So he thought he'd come here and curse her. That way, she'd do whatever he said. Right? He knew she liked presents, that she collected things from all over the world that her father brought her. She had her collections in every room, on every shelf and table, some even showing from the windows, so he had to bring her something *really* different. Special, even."

Though her complexion was still pallid, her eyes shone. Maybe she was making this all up. Maybe. I didn't care.

"A black opal," she said. I kept myself so still. "Very rare. But he was such a dumb dolt of a thing and believed what people told him, that it was evil, cursed after a countess in Prague died while wearing it and someone stole it off the gnarled finger of her cold corpse. What he didn't know was that this opal was really *good* luck. It saved that countess, helped her escape and run away to whole new lands, safe and apart from him forever. She lived a long, happy life because of it. So when he gave it to Catherine meaning to trap her? Didn't work. She didn't want him, she couldn't be bought. She left him downstairs and told him not to dare follow her, but he did. He started chasing. So she ran up all five flights to the roof, and—" She whistled as if to create a gust of wind. Her hand formed the shape of a bird, and it flew.

"That's impossible," I said. "There's no way to reach the roof from in here, is there?"

"No." Monet cocked her head at me. "There isn't. But I haven't even gotten to the weird part."

"You haven't?"

She smiled. "So she fell, or she jumped, or maybe he pushed her—nobody knows for sure, and it was this giant question mark for a long time. But the biggest question mark of all was what happened to her body."

She waited for me to react, or to guess.

"They never found it. The story goes, she went over the edge of the roof—and disappeared into thin air."

I scoffed. It was a quick reaction, like nervous laughter, but Monet didn't blink.

"So she never landed?" I asked.

A single shake of her head.

"So no one knows what happened to her," I said. "If she died, or escaped?"

It was only a story. A story that ended right where she'd left it. In the air. In the night. The way she was staring at me made me feel like I was in a police lineup, and she was on the other side of the one-way glass, trying to determine if I'd done the crime.

"I'm deciding if I should trust you," she said. "Should I?"

"You can trust me."

"Can I? I barely know you."

"You can," I insisted.

"Tell me why you're here then, out of the blue. Tell me the truth."

I didn't know why I longed for her trust so badly. This whole time, I'd been wanting her to get off my bed, give me back my pillow, leave my room, and whenever she was about to take off, I wanted her to stay a few more minutes, I wanted in.

"The real reason?" I said. "The real truth?"

She waited.

"There was a fight." Even speaking of it trampled me over inside. "With my mom."

"She didn't beat you, did she?" She traced a circle around her eye. "Because we should call child services."

"I'm not a child, I'm practically almost eighteen."

She heard that and smirked. The boardinghouse didn't rent rooms to anyone underage, not technically.

"I mean, I *am* eighteen now."

"Right, of course you are," she said. "Go on."

"The fight happened after. I was going to leave before that, anyway, when my mom kicked me out. She heard a rumor about me, and she didn't even ask me if it was the truth."

"Like she kicked you out on the street?"

"No, she wanted me to stay with some friends of hers. For a month." Saying it aloud turned it flimsy. My whole reason for being here could be swept out the fifth-floor window, and me with it, down into the gutter.

"So did you tell her the truth?" she asked.

I shook my head. I'd wanted her to know it, innately, the way a mother should know.

Monet was leaning against the bare brick wall. She could have said so many things, and yet she didn't, and I was grateful.

"You know how it is," I said. I shrugged and glanced at my blank, dark phone. I wondered if I should call my mother.

"The thing is, I don't. Know what you mean. I don't even have a mom."

"Oh god, I'm so sorry." Had she hinted at a tragedy, and had I missed it? Didn't she mention a mother and father and great-aunt and cousins, a whole family?

She stretched, getting a kink out of her neck as if she'd slept funny. She did look so tired. "She took off. The last time I saw her I was maybe eight or nine? She got this urgent overseas call in the middle of the night and hopped a helicopter. I was at the window, and she waved. Then she flew off into the clouds. She was heading west, for the Pacific. I haven't seen her since."

I didn't know how to respond.

"I figure she's CIA. She could be watching me from the window across the way as we speak."

The lie had flown from her lips like the helicopter, and as a kindness to her, I accepted it without a word.

"Man, you'll believe anything I say. Maybe she lives in Ohio or Idaho somewhere and drives a Toyota, works in real estate, does yoga on Wednesdays."

"Does she?" I said quietly. My mother drove a Toyota. She worked in a real-estate office, as the office manager. She did yoga on Mondays and Thursdays, and sometimes Sundays, in the afternoons, if she was up for it.

Monet shook her head.

I changed the subject, as swiftly as if I'd run the light in my mom's borrowed Toyota when I'd been drinking and swerved to take a turn so fast that I hit a tremendous oak, centuries old, impassable. The oak had no give, but the Toyota crumpled. That wasn't a story I was going to tell Monet.

"Thanks for the comb. And thanks for not telling anyone I took it."

"I would never," she said. "And I decided. Right now. I'm going to trust you. I'll keep your secret, if you do something for me."

She trusted me. My eyes lifted to meet hers. "Of course," I said, probably too fast. But I meant it.

"Let me see it."

"Let you see what?"

"You have it. I can almost smell it in the room, but I can't find it anywhere. All I want is to see it, to be sure. Where'd you hide Catherine's ring?"

I blinked, and so did she, and an awareness shot back and forth between us. I didn't think of it that way—as belonging to Catherine—or even as something to be worn on a hand, because I hadn't let myself do it yet.

Also, she was wrong. I'd had it in my fist the night before, and then my hand was empty. I'd lost it, the way I may have lost my mother.

"It's like that, is it?" She turned toward the common room. "Don't forget, breakfast starts soon. Get there early. I need to sleep this off." She said this without a glance back, and slipped out for good this time, through the door.

Catherine House served one meal a day to its residents. Down a series of hallways, short and swiftly turning, dead-ended and short-stopped, the floors covered in peeling linoleum, there was the dining room. I followed the instructions from the day before: Walk through the kitchen antechamber and write your request for eggs or omelets, if you wanted any, on the sheet of butcher paper on the counter by the door. No one was there to see what I wrote, but I left my name, *Bina*, and my preference, *scrambled*, and the number, 2.

I waited, to say good morning or thanks for personally making me some scrambled eggs, but the view into the kitchen showed only a cast-iron pan on a cold burner, empty, and a carton of eggs, half-full, on the cutting board. "Hello?" I called.

No one came out, so I pushed through the swinging door to enter the adjoining dining room.

The linoleum stopped here, and creaky hardwood floors took over. My first step inside the room announced me with a high-pitched shriek. I'd hit an extra-creaky spot. At this, four heads lifted. Gretchen and Harper and two other girls were at the very end of the long dining room table, as far from me as they could get, and my entrance had interrupted their conversation. The surface of the table between me and them was practically oceanic. I turned, awkward, making the floor groan again, and searched for something to drink. They went back to talking as if I weren't even there.

It wasn't what I expected, after the night we went through and what we'd witnessed. I thought I remembered Harper's arm slung over my shoulder, Gretchen whispering in my ear, some girls whose names I didn't catch—bonded moments that made me so sure we'd be friends in the light of morning. Now I was stung by their lack of greeting. Ashamed.

Set up on two smaller tables by the door were the cold food items to choose from: yogurt, cereal, fruit, a few pastries. Next to a stack of bread was a toaster, and a stick for retrieving toast when it got stuck. Pitchers of juice and water sweated on the sideboard, goblets arranged in rows beside them.

I set my bread to toast and filled a bright-green goblet with orange juice. I took a seat in the chair at the end of the table, as far as possible from the others.

Their voices were hushed, but the ceiling in this room was high and some of the sounds carried. "What did she look like? Are you sure it was her?" I heard one of the girls whose name I couldn't recall say. I heard an attempt at describing the blue light on the roof, and I heard Gretchen say she knew, positively and without a doubt, that it was the founder of this house herself, if not in the flesh then in some other form, trying to communicate with us.

A cold breeze at my back made me jump in my chair and I almost knocked over my goblet. A shadowy arm swiftly slipped a plate before me. It gleamed with fluffy yellow eggs, a bloom of a flower for garnish, and a delicate sculpture made of an artistically carved orange slice, the most elegantly prepared breakfast I'd ever seen.

I must have stared at the plate a moment too long, because when I turned around to say thank you, whoever had served me was gone. They must have been fast. The door to the kitchen wasn't even swinging.

I scooped up some eggs and lifted my fork, and it was near an inch from my mouth when a quiver of movement made me lean in closer.

The eggs were squirming on the fork.

The entire pile on my plate moved and crawled over itself. The yellow was alarming and leaking ooze. Whatever had come from the kitchen was horribly still alive, not meant to be eaten, as if someone were trying to trick me, or feed me poison.

I dropped the fork and shoved the plate away into the middle of the grand table. The plate knocked over a salt-shaker—heavy, bronze—and the booming sound as it toppled and spilled made the other girls glance over at me, curious.

I waited for a scream of reaction when one of them caught what was writhing on the plate, but nothing. None of them seemed to see what I did.

"Aren't you going to eat that?" Harper said.

"Breakfast is *the* most important meal of the day," another girl said, smiling, as if reciting something she'd heard from a regressive TV commercial from the '50s. Her hair was sculpted into a blond helmet with the ends flipped up. She must have spent an hour under a hair dryer getting it to perform.

Their eyes bored into me, much like the rows of black-and-white eyes on the stairwell walls. In fact, it was hard to tell the difference. The back of my head began to pulse.

"You can have it if you want," I told Harper. "Anyone who wants it can have it."

I was feeling so hot. I remembered my toast and went to get it from the toaster. It was cold and hard, but inanimate, like Styrofoam. I dropped it on my plate; no butter or jelly could save it.

When I glanced at the eggs again, nothing was wrong. Nothing was moving, and the cheerful flower embellishment was bright purple. Harper smiled at me, and so did the girl with the hair flip. Gretchen was stone-faced. The fourth girl scrunched her face in concern.

"Is she okay? She's not eating."

"Maybe she's hungover."

"She should really eat her breakfast."

"Whoa, check her out, she's turned green."

"What did you say?" I heard. All four were watching me. Gretchen was the one who'd spoken. She was pointing at me with a lifted fork.

"I didn't," I said. "I didn't say anything."

"You're Becca, right?" one of the girls said.

"No, no, her name's Bina," Gretchen said. "Remember?"

"It never happened until she got here," another said, plain as fact.

"That's true," Harper said, cocking her head to the side. "None of us saw Catherine before, until you got here."

I couldn't read their expressions. I sensed they blamed me, thought I orchestrated it somehow, whatever had gone on in the perplexing dark, high over our heads and in our hearts, our stomachs, our minds. At least in mine. I couldn't sense if this was a terrible thing worthy of punishment, or if they liked it and welcomed me all the more.

"You need to come out with us tonight," Harper said. "We're going to see if Catherine comes back and—"

Gretchen slapped her arm. "Not yet," she said. "Not here."

Harper blushed and lowered her eyes.

But I'd lost the opal, if I'd even had it at all. My memory, when I tried to turn to it, puckered into a small black hole. The opal wasn't anywhere in my room when I'd searched for it after Monet left. Nowhere. And whatever I believed about what happened in the dark the night before, whatever I thought I saw and made everyone else see—it was connected to that stone I knew I'd held in my hand as certainly as I knew it was buried, unreachable, under a patio more than a hundred miles away.

Gretchen had her arms folded across her chest in a gesture of menace. "Aren't you going to eat something?" she said.

Before I could answer or try to take a bite of toast, Anjali miraculously came rushing in, jumbling with noise, making the floorboards shriek all over again. "I overslept!" she announced. "I can't believe I missed my chance at eggs." She poured herself some cereal and turned to face the table. "Hi, Ana Sofía! Hi, Gretchen! Hi, Muriel! Hi, Harper!" The shift in mood was dizzying. Then she saw me. "Bina," she said, her voice more contained. "Hi."

Anjali could have taken a seat anywhere at that giant table, but when she'd finished assembling her breakfast, she sat catty-corner to me, our elbows practically touching. I was grateful, though not sure why she'd chosen that chair. "Hey, are you going to eat those?"

I shook my head as she pulled my plate of untouched food toward her.

"Perfect," she said. "So . . ." There was an awkward moment, grapefruit bit stabbed on the end of her fork. "How are you feeling? Any better?" Her cheery tone seemed forced, as if someone was watching us. In fact, they all were.

I kept my voice low. "Better, I guess." She must have been the person who took care of me last night. In fact, I was sure she was. She may have even put some fresh bacitracin on my lip.

"That's good. You must have had a lot to drink, huh?"

I couldn't remember, but it didn't sound unlike me.

"Anyway, glad to see you're okay." Something in her eyes—a flicker there—indicated she may have wanted to say something else, but she did not. Maybe she'd seen Monet slipping out my door when the sun was up, and that made her wary. Maybe she still held a grudge about when I'd stopped her from opening the small door. I saw the mark of my grip on her wrists. The bruises were purple now. Not pretty like the flower on each of our plates, more like my eye. I felt like a monster, which was a familiar feeling.

Anjali started eating as the others finished up.

I decided to say something. "I'm so sorry about yesterday, in my room . . . You know, after you left, I opened that door—"

"No, no, stop," she said, jabbing the words in. "Stop talking."

"What?"

She was eyeing the girls across the dining room as they gathered their dishes to leave.

Once we were alone, she lowered her hand. "I don't want to know anything about it," she said. "Please don't tell me. I didn't stay out in the garden, but I heard about last night. It's happening again, and I don't want to be a part of it."

"What did you hear? What's happening? They said nobody saw Catherine until last night."

"Why didn't you tell me who your mother was? It happened eighteen years ago, when she was here. That's what I heard."

Some girls pushed through the swinging door and entered—also late. I noticed that not one of them was Monet. She'd been so intent on me making it to breakfast, yet never showed for it herself. Instead she'd needed to sleep in, as if she'd spent the whole night out dancing in the chaos of the city I hadn't had a chance to witness yet.

While the others were busy at the sideboard, banging around as they poured themselves juice, Anjali leaned in.

"Listen," she hissed. "I took it from you for safekeeping, but I don't want it in my room. I don't even know how you got your hands on it, but you can't be dropping it on the stairs— anyone could have found it. Even Monet."

My face must have gone gray. It was in her eyes, plain as if she'd said it from her mouth. She was talking about the opal. It was real—not a dream.

"Your door was locked, but I left it there, outside your room."

I was so relieved I could hardly speak. "Thank you," I said. "I've got to go." I stood up and pushed back my chair, making a screech. I hadn't eaten anything, but I also wasn't the least bit hungry. I rushed through the swinging door into the empty antechamber that connected to the kitchen. My name and order for eggs was crossed out on the butcher paper, dirty dishes and green goblets stacked on top. The kitchen was still empty. The faucet in the industrial sink was running, but no one was there.

———

As Anjali had promised, something was waiting by my door. It was wrapped in a T-shirt, folded, refolded, burrowed inside. The opal ring was cool, its surface smooth, the band thin and silver. If I'd dropped it somehow while climbing all the stairs last night, the stone didn't chip, it didn't break. It was perfect, the way it had been on my mother's younger hand.

With it was a note in neat, curled handwriting, unsigned.

Get me out of here.

It made no sense. I'd thought Anjali was happy here. I'd thought every girl was. Had she even written it?

Something made me search the empty common room. The area was dim, dusty, and crawling with the gnarled shadows of the bra tree and the wobbly lampshades. A stack of shoes had spilled all along one wall, creating a dark lake. No one was up here with me, though a prickly whisper in the back of my head asked, was I sure?

I carefully shredded the note and disposed of it down the toilet. Not everyone wanted to be here. Not everyone considered this a safe place. Anjali wanted to go, but I'd only just arrived. I wanted to stay. Still, when I went back to my room to get dressed for the day, I locked the door.

DIRT AND CONCRETE

THEY WANTED ME TO JOIN THEM IN THE GARDEN THAT NIGHT, but something kept me away. It might have been the pressure of expectation, all those eyes on me, but I told myself it was only a desire to see the city, to see what I might find in the growing orbit around the house.

I slipped out the gate in front of Catherine House and started to walk. I got lost in the maze of the West Village and then found my way east, where the city's grid of streets began to make sense. As the hours passed, I let myself stay out as late as I could stand it. There were no stars to be seen in the sky, but the building lights twinkled. And there was so much to pay attention to in the street I barely thought to look up.

I hovered outside the windows of restaurants, reluctant to spend my remaining money and sit at a table all alone. I tried on near a dozen pairs of shoes on Eighth Street. I was a six and a half, my mother's size, but I couldn't afford a single pair.

I found a used bookstore and a branch of the public library. Once, down a narrow alley, I thought I saw Monet poised at a splash of graffiti with a can of spray paint aimed high, but when I blinked it was only a blur of movement and a plain brick wall. Another time I thought I saw her ordering from a street cart. The girl who turned around had a different face and was eating only a pretzel.

My head was hurting in that familiar spot, and by the time deep night had fallen I had blisters on my heels, a burning in the balls of my feet. My weak ankle gave out when I stepped on a patch of crooked cobblestone, and as I sat rubbing it on the curb while a stream of black-clad legs swept past, I marveled that it hadn't crumpled hours earlier. No one bent to see if I was okay.

It was close to midnight. When I looked across the street, where cobblestone met pavement somewhere in what I thought was SoHo, I saw her again. She had brighter hair this time, burgundy in the shadows, bloodred under a streetlamp. She disappeared into a subway tunnel before I could get up and follow her to be sure.

I didn't know where she was headed, but curfew was coming. There was an urgent beating in my chest to tell me it was near, that I had only minutes to get back to Catherine House and many blocks to cover. A magnet was pulling me, and I couldn't resist.

If I didn't make it, would I have to rough it out in the street, like some of the people I saw setting up boxes under construction awnings? (One was a girl my age; she had nowhere to go, dark circles under her eyes, a busted suitcase. I left her a dollar in her paper cup, and she yelled after me that I'd ruined her coffee.)

I was close to a panic when I finally reached the block and the black iron gate containing Catherine House and its tiny concrete yard. Beside it, through a different gate on the street, was the garden, but there was no time to even peek inside. There wasn't a moment to spare before buzzing in and leaping up the stairs to the top of the stoop and getting myself through the sleek front door.

I had to catch my breath on the other side, safe in the foyer, holding the arm of the coat stand to get steady and make myself right again.

When I looked out at the street below, I saw that the chain was already on the front gate, though I hadn't seen anyone who worked in the house go out and take care of it. I saw Anjali on the stairs inside, but she acted like she'd never left me a note, and with it traveling the pipes of the septic system, I wondered if I'd invented the words, and her desire to go. What did she expect me to do? Couldn't she leave if she wanted?

The others tried to knock on my door to tell me about Catherine, but I ignored them. I avoided her photograph. When I put my ear to the floorboards upstairs, the room beneath mine was a tomb of silence. I'd made curfew—as far as I could tell, all the other tenants had but one. Monet had not.

When I next saw her, emerging from the fourth floor at two in the afternoon with wild hair and bleary eyes from sleeping in, she seemed sickly again. There was a point when she had a coughing fit and someone offered her a dusty lozenge found in the cushion of the gold-velvet couch.

"Where *were* you?" Harper hissed at her in the linoleum-covered winding hallway between parlor and kitchen.

Monet motioned that her lips were zipped, but she was zipping them all for herself. None of us knew where she spent the long, late hours of night, or why.

My first week in the house went by like this, day after day. I didn't have the money for movies or shopping, and I had to be careful about spending too much on things like a fan to cool my room. I lied on my résumé to say I'd graduated from high school, but none of the retail counters where I left it gave me a call. Riding the subway every day would have cleaned me out. What I could do was walk, and I did, from Tenth Street to 110th Street, from east to west, up the island and down.

In the nights, light-headed after another day of walking, my phone dark after another day of no calls, I let myself listen to the room below mine, my ear suctioned to the floor. I was drawn to do it. I knew I shouldn't be so nosy, but I had to know how close she was.

I could hear her climbing the fire escape long after curfew and settling in when everyone else was asleep. A few times, I caught sight of her bare, swinging legs as she rattled around out there, passing my window to whatever was above—the roof, I suspected. She didn't stop in on her way or leave a gift or a note on my windowsill. She'd defended me in the garden my first night, but she didn't acknowledge it in any way since. It was almost like she was waiting for me to do something to catch her notice again.

In her room, she stayed silent for long stretches and then talked to herself, whispers I couldn't quite catch. She listened to sad songs, ones that were vaguely familiar to me, like old hurts. She slept through breakfast, so I started to do the same. She must have dreamed, but I never heard her shouting in her sleep as I woke myself up doing. I wondered if anything scared her, even the dark, dusty rooms of this house and the young woman with the black, shifting eyes downstairs, who the other girls said hadn't shown herself since.

The small door in my wall, I kept blocked and sealed shut.

The garden, I avoided without asking myself why.

When I slept, my dreams were memories, and always the same running nightmare of home.

———

By the end of that first week, my mother hadn't called to ask where I was, and curiosity got the better of me. I'd been checking my phone, expecting a series of messages, a string of texts, wanting to make sure I'd made it to the church people's place okay, then when she didn't hear from me, turning worried, getting serious, skipping emojis, asking me where I was, what happened, why I didn't show. My phone had weak service inside my room, the brick walls so thick, but I would have seen her attempts at contact when I was outside. There wasn't a missed call for days.

First thing Saturday morning, before I could stop myself, I pulled up her name in my favorites and called. I heard a faint hiss of air on the line and then a high-pitched beep as I lost the signal. I tried again, right next to the window, practically leaning half my body outside, though the sight of ground through the slats in the fire escape gave me the spins. The call dropped.

I didn't get a good signal until I was out on the sidewalk. I stood across the street from the house so none of the girls would hear. It seemed so taboo to miss our mothers.

She answered straightaway. "Bina? Is that you? I'm driving. I can't hear you. Bina?"

She'd called me Bina, not Sabina—in fact, she kept repeating it as if she were surprised I'd called—a sign I chose to interpret as good. I softened, and it left me off guard, a door open.

"It's me," I said, and let those two words hang. Not that I was sure she could hear with the wind in her ears, a static roar into her mouthpiece. She must have been on the highway with the windows down. That was something she liked to do now. I imagined she appreciated the way the wind threatened to peel away all her layers of hair and skin and flesh and muscle until she was down to the bone, and free.

An exhilarating sense of power twisted its way through me. This was what it felt like to make your life your own, something I'd only witnessed my mother start to do. She'd failed. I wouldn't fail. I wanted to share this with her—wouldn't she want this for me? Wouldn't she be proud?

I surveyed the street—my new home. The block was made up of narrow apartment buildings and brownstones, some gated and none taller than five stories. They were in a series of hues from brown to tan to red to brick and back to brown. There were sidewalk trees, a corner store with a warm-green awning at one end of the street, a red-doored pub at the other, a bright-blue mailbox, a few random people out walking well-groomed dogs.

It was picturesque, like a movie set of the city, which happened to be the way my mother had described it to me when I was a child. It could have been plucked from her stories and made real. I wanted to tell her, but she could hardly hear anything I said.

All the while I kept saying, "Mom?" into the phone.

She was kind of screaming over the wind. "I'm in the car. I can't hear you. Did something happen? What happened? What did you do?" She had her hands-free headset on— she could easily roll up the windows and talk; she didn't want to.

"I'm not at your friends' house," I burst out. "I didn't go."

"You're not what? I can't hear you . . ."

It spilled. It spread clumsily all over my feet. Where I was, that I wasn't coming home for a month at least, that maybe she could send money? I was in the city, like we should have been for the past eight years, and I might not come back ever again, at all.

The power filled me now. Mine.

"I'm supposed to be meeting the girls, but I'm pulling over," she said. Her voice got so much clearer after she stopped the car, without wind shouting her down. "Please tell me you're not at your father's." She didn't use one of our sloppy monikers for him; she called him the low-down dirtiest thing she could, which was *father*, emphasis on *your*.

"You are," she said. "Aren't you?"

Her voice had shrunk so small that it squeezed my heart—more than squeezed, it flattened. There was so much I wanted to say, but then came the still-raw memory of the last day I saw her, when she brought me her old suitcase, one wheel so worn it traveled with a limp, and told me she was kicking me out. That was stronger. That was louder. I couldn't even remember why I'd wanted to talk to her.

"I can't hear you," I said, and ended the call.

I headed back across the street, for the stoop. There was a breeze, cooler than the temperature inside the house, and it touched my arms and skimmed through my hair, lifting it from the damp, hot back of my neck. The light wind brushed my face, where the bruises and scratches still felt tender and fresh. Maybe the air and the sun would help them heal so I would stop looking like a victim and wouldn't keep having people ask what was done to me. I closed my eyes for a second, to gather myself, when I heard it calling to me and I forgot all about my mother.

The loud creaking sound was insistent. Sharp. It skittered through my body, twingeing into my head. I had to make it stop.

The sound was coming from beside the house, from the lot sandwiched between the building and the town house next door. It was the private garden where we'd all gathered on my first night, the one I'd been avoiding all week and hadn't yet seen in daylight.

At its center was a gate with a shining gold lock, but I didn't need a key, because the gate was open, and that creaking was its unsteady swaying in the wind.

I grabbed it to make it stop, and then it happened.

Somehow I wasn't closing the gate, as I'd planned. I was stepping through it. I was going inside.

Once I did, something rippled over me. It rinsed through my body, a soothing calm. The gate swung closed behind me, and the sound ceased. I kept walking. The area had felt so much larger in the dark, but in truth it was only the width of a narrow building. It was cluttered and fragrant with living things growing from the ground, with gnats, with rustles of movement, a forest hush, but it was still small and walled-in.

I let my palm rest on the rough skin of a tree. It seemed

a kind of tree too old to be growing here, in the middle of a concrete city, caught between brick buildings. The trunk was tall and gnarled, knots bursting out, and the overhanging branches provided cool patches of shade. When I looked upward, all I saw were tree branches and the ceiling they made over the garden. No peek of sky was visible from this spot.

This place reminded me of home in a way that made me want to sit on the ground and touch the blades of grass. Home, before I'd ruined it.

As I was trying to figure out which way to walk, I almost tripped over a wooden signpost covered in an unruly swirl of ivy. At the top was the sign itself, an arrow pointing at the back of the garden, which was impossible to see from the entrance. The sign said:

GRAVESITE

The arrow led the way.

I felt no surprise. It hadn't been said outright, but it had been suggested. I should have figured that was why we'd all come outside my first night, to pay our respects.

The path through the green growth was trampled, and I followed it to the end, near a brick wall that must have been the back of another building. There, a short wrought-iron fence marked off a small section of earth. I knew even before I saw with my eyes that Catherine de Barra was the name engraved on the gray monument. All around were wild weeds, green and growing, horned and clawing, but the base of the headstone itself was clean and carefully tended. A circle of worn, cleared ground surrounded the area—enough space for a small throng of mourners, if they packed in tight around the gravesite, tight enough to touch.

On top of the monument was a collection of items, some weathered and rusted, oxidized into green, but some shiny-new and recent. Those had been left only a week ago. The candy necklace had been ravaged by squirrels and maybe (I couldn't bear to let the word form) rats, but the miniature yellow cab was intact. There was also a tarnished gold bracelet. A silver button. A moonstone. A tiny black ceramic cat. All offerings for Catherine, from the girls who lived in her house.

A stone bench, meant for a single visitor, was set beside the low fencing that surrounded the grave. I sat down and saw that at my feet a small tomato plant was growing. Tomatoes, in a city garden, right near a grave. Someone must have planted them here as another kind of offering.

I felt an odd pull to touch them. These were cherry tomatoes, fully ripe and perfectly red, small and plump and ready to be picked, the same kind my mother once grew. I remembered the exact taste of them. Tangy but also sweet.

I plucked one from the vine and held it in the center of my palm. I was about to lift it to my mouth and pop it open with my teeth when I heard a new sound.

Not a gate creaking this time, and not the wind through the low-hanging leaves. Something else.

I wasn't alone here.

The sound was tinny and artificial, not from nature. The electronic alert of a cell phone ringing, and not far away, from an overlooking window or the street. Close. It was coming from the other side of the gravestone, where the shadows hid a patch of tall grass.

I must have crushed the tomato when I'd heard it—I felt the pulp and seeds in my hand. I dropped it to the grass and circled the fencing, and there, lying in a patch of unshorn weeds, was something green—too green. It was plastic with a glassy, almost-neon reflection. I leaned in closer and caught the pattern on its skin, reptilian. A fake-crocodile purse.

The purse was stuck on the short fence that surrounded the gravestone, and I pulled until it came loose. Some muck and dirt had gotten on it. I shook it off. The crocodile skin—slick and cold to the touch, turning my stomach—was flapping open, revealing that the contents of the purse hadn't been pillaged. There was the wallet and a nondriver ID for a Lacey Rhonda Garnett. A depressing DMV portrait and her statistics: She was five foot seven. She was eighteen years old. She was from Connecticut.

My hand was in the purse again. Slithering in, separate from me, an insistent snake. Almost $200 in twenties was in the wallet. My fingers itched to slip the wad into my pocket, but I abstained, at least for the moment. I decided I'd bring it back into the house and leave it in Lacey's mail cubby. She'd find it there, eventually. The only question was if she needed to find it with all the money intact.

But the phone wouldn't stop ringing. The cell phone at the bottom of the purse was lit up with an incoming call. A blocked caller ID. It could have been Lacey herself, calling to see if her purse and all its contents had landed in friendly hands.

I hesitated, and then I answered.

"Hello?"

No words on the other end. Only labored breathing.

"Lacey, if that's you, I found your purse. It's Bina—you know, from the fifth floor? I found your purse, and I—"

"Stop," the voice said. I heard the faintest touch of wind, as if it weren't a road the caller was on but a high rooftop. No one told me that, but I saw it so clearly. A rush of vertigo in my knees.

The voice sounded gravelly and weak. This wasn't Lacey.

"Who is this?" Something told me I didn't want to hear the answer.

The person on the other end ignored this question. Maybe she thought I knew already.

"Hello? I said, 'Who is this?'"

"You look so much like your mother."

I lifted my eyes. Up and up, following the long brick expanse of the side of the house until the perimeter of the rooftop was in sight. In daylight the colors were orange and yellow. They went white where the sun hit. White until I couldn't see anything out of either one of my eyes, the good one or the bad. White like what a dead body sees from under the sheet.

I flung the phone away from me.

As I did, I happened to lose my balance, and I happened to glance down and see it. The trail of hair on the ground behind the statue, long and deep brown. Braided.

My hand reached out to touch it. The braid of hair was heavy, because it was attached to something. A neck.

There was a body hidden in the shadow behind the gravestone. A girl with long braids, the same way Lacey wore her hair. This was her. This was her, on the ground, in the dirt, in the flesh. Her eyes were crusted closed. She lay on her back, arms limp at her sides. A prescription bottle was open beside her. Orange, white cap. The label was smeared with dirt, the name of the pills too blurred to make out.

I went for her, stumbling over the grating that surrounded the grave and almost dropping down, half on top of her and half on Catherine de Barra, buried underneath.

As I got ahold of her, Lacey's eyelids jittered, and her arms jolted, and I heard gurgling coming from her throat. She was alive, and I had to help her.

Everything moved fast after that.

At some point I removed myself from the garden. I must have. I'm not sure if I yelled out for help from some passersby or if I called 911 from the sidewalk because I couldn't get a working signal again and I couldn't find Lacey's phone that I threw. I was outside the garden as the ambulance pulled up, my arms up to flag it down, and she was inside, and I wasn't sure why I didn't stay beside her.

Two EMTs burst out. Lights were flashing. Someone pushed me away. Someone else pulled me aside.

"The garden," I said, pointing wildly. "There's a girl inside. I think she took some pills, but she's alive, she's alive."

The EMT asked me for her name, and I told her. I tried to offer the purse, which for some unknown reason I had on my arm, but she didn't want it. She asked where Lacey lived, and I pointed to Catherine House, and then I said I had her room, and then I said she moved rooms, and I didn't know what I was saying so I stopped talking. The EMT asked me if I was all right and what happened to me, and that part was confounding until I understood her mistake.

"Did someone hurt you?" she asked, indicating the bruises on my face. "Do you want to press charges?"

"No, no," I said. That? That was old, already taken care of, I already saw a doctor (I lied). It looked worse than it was. This wasn't about me. This was about the girl in the garden. This was about the girl.

She told me I seemed flushed and I should sit down and wait there.

She went in through the gate after her partner, calling out for Lacey as if she'd been buried in an avalanche and needed to know there was someone searching for her, she was not forgotten, she would not be alone, not ever again.

I was on the sidewalk, sitting on the curb. I felt something on my face and realized I'd started to cry. I couldn't bear the idea of Lacey's being out there all alone, under the tree with no one helping her or even trying to find her all that time.

Ms. Ballantine was on the curb above me, her thin shadow swaying. She'd come out of the house and now glared with intent at the garden gate, which was wide open. She wasn't even bothering to go in. No other staff members came out of the house to join her. I still hadn't seen anyone else who worked there. No one who cleaned or cooked or assisted Ms. Ballantine with what she did as landlady and manager of the estate.

A police cruiser arrived behind the ambulance, and now two officers were in the garden, one guarding the gate. Now it was clear we weren't allowed to follow.

"Who called the police?" Ms. Ballantine asked in a flat voice. The sun seemed to be bothering her eyes, and she put up a hand to shield it from her face. Instead it hit mine.

"I called nine-one-one," I said, taking claim. "She's still alive. I can't believe it, but I think she's still alive."

She looked down on me. I had to squint, and even then I couldn't see the expression on her face.

"Why are you sitting in the street like a beggar?" she said. "Get on your feet. Get up." She pulled me upright.

I was holding Lacey's purse—the green plastic cold in my fingers—and all I wanted was to get rid of it. When I tried to hand it off to Ms. Ballantine, she pushed it away with a flinch, as if I'd offered her a severed finger. I would leave it in Lacey's cubby after all. She could get it later—I hoped.

A hush emerged from the open gate, but it wasn't peaceful; it was jarring. I wanted to see in, but I also didn't want to watch Lacey die. I imagined the scene instead: her cheeks losing color, her eyes showing only white . . .

"How did this happen?" Ms. Ballantine said to me. "How could you?"

I didn't understand. I'd found Lacey before it was too late. I'd done a good thing. I could already picture her family—her mother and her father, her two sisters—pulling up to the curb and running out to take her in their arms. She would go home with them after all. She needed them. It was where she belonged.

What did I do to make Ms. Ballantine so angry?

"You shouldn't have called," she said in a low voice, uncomfortably close to my ear.

The police cruiser at the curb said all. It was sinking in that there was a reason Ms. Ballantine wanted to keep the authorities away. It could have been about the garden, where everyone gathered in the night. Maybe there was something in there the city was not supposed to find, because if they found it, they might take it away from us forever.

And I was the one who'd sounded the alarm and led the way.

A minute later, both emergency workers came out. Neither was holding a body. No one was escorting a girl.

I stepped up, even though the panic was flooding my chest. "What happened?"

"There's no one in there," one of the EMTs said to me.

"What do you mean?" I started for the garden gate, but they blocked my way.

"There's no girl." This repeated in my face. People passing slowed on the street—the ambulance called their attention—but they weren't trying to get a peek into the garden to see what happened; they were looking at me. Everyone was looking at me. I was the thing to look at.

I noticed the old woman across the street with a gray cat in her arms. The yowling animal struggled in her grasp, butting its head against her chin, but the woman held fast, on thick exposed legs with slippers, mouth slightly open, judging me.

There was talk of my wasting the emergency workers' time and calling in a phony report, and I wasn't sure if I was going to get into trouble. Then the police turned to Ms. Ballantine. There was something in the garden they needed to discuss with the property owner—could she come this way?

She walked in, head held high. Again, I wasn't allowed to follow.

"Miss," the EMT said to me, her face right up in mine so I couldn't see past her. "Are you hurt? Do you need medical attention?"

I shook my head. It was Lacey who needed help. She was the one who swallowed all the pills. They might have to pump her stomach, which was supposed to hurt horribly, I'd heard, and she'd probably want company at the hospital. Where was Lacey? I put my hand to the back of my head and held it, to calm the thumping.

"Did you fall? A concussion might be what's causing this confusion. Why don't you—"

When the EMT reached out her arm, as if she might touch me, I barely escaped. I moved away as quickly as I could, and it felt like they were on my heels again, the whole pack of them. At any moment, they would catch me and take me down. If I skidded and stumbled and hit the pavement with my bare face, would it feel so different from leaves and twigs and pine needles and tree roots and dirt that night in the forest?

I stood on a patch of random sidewalk a few blocks away. I stayed there a long time, loitering, nursing my ankle. When I circled the block again and saw that the ambulance and police car were both gone, that the crowd had dispersed and no one was across the street keeping tabs, I knew it was safe to come back. They'd forgotten all about me.

It was late afternoon by the time I climbed the stoop leading back into the house and felt something wet and warm flick down onto my shoulders, like a rainstorm had found me. A few more drips, this time on the top of my head.

Monet was there, her legs dangling off the fire escape.

She was holding a bottle and had been dribbling water down on my head. Our rooms were in the front of the house, and she'd descended a few flights to sit at the lowest level of the fire escape, a single story suspended over the stoop.

She seemed so unbothered. The word must have not gotten out about Lacey.

I wiped my hair and looked up to her bare legs. Today she was wearing a midnight-blue pageboy wig. I was beginning to suspect she'd visited a Halloween store and bought herself a collection on clearance.

She held up the water bottle again, and I ducked, shielding my head.

"I'm only messing with you," she said. "Don't be so serious."

I wasn't laughing. "Hey," I said. "You haven't seen Lacey today, have you?"

"Funny you should ask . . . I have."

"Is she okay? I thought I saw—I thought something happened to her. I guess I was confused."

"You weren't confused."

Wasn't I? I held up the green reptilian thing that had been hanging on my shoulder. In a way, it was evidence. "I have her purse."

"I see that. Listen, you weren't confused. Lacey's upstairs in her room, recovering. She shouldn't have tried to leave again. Ms. Ballantine's going to have a talk with her."

Recovering. Tried to leave. Upstairs in her room. How did she get back inside, avoiding the EMTs and the police and even me, right out on the sidewalk? There was only one way out of the garden, as far as I knew.

Monet put a finger to her lips so I wouldn't ask. "Don't you get it?" she said. "You shouldn't have called nine-one-one.

Not about something happening in here, with us. We have to take care of it ourselves."

"I need to go check on Lacey." I headed up the stairs.

"You sure?" Monet said. "Maybe the one you need to worry about is yourself." She seemed to know things about me she wasn't telling. I'd sensed that from her the very first time we met.

I kept climbing, but before I could open the door she called down once more. "How was your walk today? Did you wander around SoHo again?"

She knew my habits. She knew where I was.

She gazed down on me as if I should know what was coming right at me, as if she were shouting directions from a moving truck.

Then she climbed the ladder to the fourth floor and into her room beneath mine.

I didn't know which room was Lacey's now, but I went to the second floor and called her name. Finally one of the doors popped open and Lacey herself stuck out her head. Her face was puffy and pillow-creased from sleep. Her braids were loose, without any leaves or debris from the garden in them. She was alive, but she didn't seem too thrilled to see me.

"Hi," I said. I had my hand on the door, which she wouldn't open all the way.

"Hi, what?" It wasn't that she was being mean—more that she was being careful.

"I just needed to see if you were . . ." Dead? I couldn't say it.

"Can't you see I'm still here?"

I leaned in, hoping no one in any nearby room was listening. "Do you need me to call your parents?"

She leaned back, gaining distance. There wasn't a speck of trust in her eyes. "It won't matter."

It was a perplexing thing to be so content with something no one else seemed to want anymore. How many of these girls hoped to abandon their rooms in this house but felt tethered here, feet in cement and willed to stay?

Couldn't Lacey have gone home with her parents when they came for her stuff? I had questions, but the insistence in her eyes told me I should stop while I was ahead. All I ended up doing was holding up her purse so she could see. "I have this for you."

She pushed her hand through the crack and grabbed it. The door closed in my face. I hadn't taken anything she'd miss from her wallet—no money, nothing worth even a cent, though I could have.

On the stairwell heading back to the top floor, a familiar face came into view. Dark freckles like black ink spots; shifty eyes, gray. She slipped by me without stopping, a blur of motion swallowed by shadow.

"Hey," I called after her.

She was gone, though her feet didn't even make an audible patter down the stairs. When I looked at the closest portrait of the tenants—I was smack-dab in the middle of the 1970s, aimed right at 1975—I almost thought I saw the girl who'd avoided me on the stairwell. But hadn't I also spotted her doppelganger in a photo from the 1920s? Maybe I did have a concussion.

That night, in my own room, while I was hiding Lacey's library card, the one item I'd slipped out of her hideous purse, I let myself go over my slowly growing collection. Each day I had something new to put in the hollow space behind the radiator. I removed each thing so I could run my eyes over it and remember where it came from—the place and the moment. The comb was the first—how the silver caught the sunlight, how it gleamed. Also from the parlor downstairs, I had a tiny ivory elephant. Little carved ridges in the body made it feel like a crushable thing. A ceramic ashtray, a folded purple silk fan, a rook from a cobwebbed unfinished game of chess. From the open doorway of a room on the third floor, I had a delicate necklace, a string of tiny silver seeds. Other items from the house included a beautifully decorated spoon from the sugar bowl in the dining room and, from my own common area, one of my floormates' abundant shoes. I took only the left one.

All I collected were items they wouldn't notice: the beaded necklace among the other beads, the hair clip dropped beside the sink, the red-inked pen nestled among the black.

But at the far back of the hollowed-out area behind the radiator, burrowed in deep, I had something else, something special. I didn't have my mother's blue scarf to wrap it in, and I'd returned Anjali's shirt, so I used a sock.

I'd thought of selling it—I'd scoped out a pawnshop in a basement storefront in the East Village—and I'd stood, wavering, on the top step, not yet ready to go down and see about giving it up.

I wanted to ask my mother how she'd gotten hold of it— how it could have possibly appeared in a photograph from a hundred years ago that hung, framed, behind a pane of glass, over the mantel, and ended up in her possession, but I couldn't call to ask. If Monet was to be believed, which of course she wasn't but sometimes I pretended she was, it was from a countess in Prague who escaped to live a new life, and beyond that I didn't know who else had worn it or where else it had lived.

My mother once told me it was a gift—but from who, and for what occasion?

She also said it saved her life.

I removed the opal from its cave and let it loose from the sock. Within a moment, it was on my finger, and I was closing the lights and crawling into bed. I slept with it tucked under my pillow, my cheek on top. It was a hard knob digging into the mattress, oddly as cold as a cube of ice that never melted, but I was so comforted by the weight. I had to pull it out. To see.

For a moment, the smooth black stone captured the light and shimmered, showing it wasn't black after all but a swirl of many colors, uncountable colors, changing by the moment and shifting from every angle, the way opals do.

Some girls wanted to leave Catherine House, and I couldn't fathom why. With it on my hand, it felt like nothing bad could happen within these walls, beneath this roof, to me.

CITY OF STRANGERS

A COUPLE DAYS LATER, I SPOTTED THE BLUE VAN AGAIN.

It was parked at the end of the block, when before I swore it had been around the corner near Waverly Place. Someone had moved it, even though its tires were still locked by the city and its parking tickets still wriggled in the wind. Now it was much closer to Catherine House. I could see it from the front stoop.

I left the gate and crept closer. Wrinkled stickers, rust swirls, and dents made it seem urgently out of place, a desperate girl screaming into a stone-faced crowd with everyone looking the other way. The porthole windows were covered by curtains or, it occurred to me as I checked more closely, loose and soiled clothes pressed up against glass to keep curious eyes out. Murmuring came from inside, an argument of some kind. Heated and furious, then shushed, then contained. I rested my weight ever so gently against the side of the van, trying to get my ear closer. A hubcap was missing, and one of the tires was bald.

The van door could have slid open with a roar, and any monstrous thing could have happened, but I stayed put, listening.

Placing my ear against the side of the derelict vehicle, dirty and sticky with some unidentified city substance, was like cupping my ear to a seashell. Ordinary, earthly voices stopped, and something else made itself known. A rush of wind could be heard coming from the belly, the air whipping itself into a frenzy, battering against walls and breaking branches, as if a forest of trees crowded inside. Then it calmed, as if it knew I was there listening, and I recognized the sound. I knew the exact timbre, the swell and hold, the crunch of leaves underfoot, the rustle, the whisper. It was the sound of home.

I pushed off, went running. Not for the boardinghouse but beyond it—I didn't even know where. Uptown or downtown, east or west, closest avenue or any beyond. I was far away from the van in no time—and some passersby, probably tourists, saw me running and seemed alarmed, but others, surely locals and used to minding their own business, didn't bat an eye.

I slowed to a walk, and then I was walking for a while. A stretch of blocks came and went. At some point, I stopped. I'd come this way for a reason, and I didn't want to let myself know it yet, but things were taking shape. Something clicked.

I knew that lamppost. A yellow storefront on the corner pulsed with familiarity, and I found myself pulled toward it. I stood beneath the yellow for a long moment, under the protruding awning that kept me out of the sun, until I saw the flowers lining the block. I remembered.

The only time I'd visited the city, I'd come here, to this place. That lamppost, this awning, and my memory shrank my hand to child-size. I sensed the ghost of my mother's hand in mine.

It was the visit my mother's husband and his daughters ruined, when I was thirteen. Something else happened that visit, something that took us here.

We'd separated from them for an hour or two. She wouldn't tell me where we were going, but she'd led us to this corner and stopped. There was so much noise. Color. Activity. I wanted to memorize every inch, to drink in the outfits and accents, to carve my initials in fresh concrete so they would dry and stay forever, like some initials I'd seen. We stood in the glow of the yellow awning while she got herself together. Her fingers were trembling, which made me hold tighter, glancing up at her, trying to understand.

She breathed out. Then she led me down the next block, a street filled entirely with bright, blooming flowers and plants in pots. We traveled for what felt a long time through green shade, which sometimes reached over my head, and it confused me, this part of the city so much like upstate, as if we'd returned to our garden we'd had to give up. But she set me straight: She said this was only the flower district. It had made me think this city must be made up of different divisions, magical islands separated by crosswalks, and if someone wanted a daisy in the city of New York, they had to come to this street only and nowhere else.

Now I was back. Somehow I found myself here again.

A series of flower shops and gardening stores lined the street now as it had then. Not a thing had changed. I walked, buckets of bright blossoms and tall arching ferns on either side of me, basil and oregano and other herbs and spice plants giving the air a tangy scent, and the roses, every last color to be imagined, crowding the sidewalk. To walk this street felt different, now that I was taller and more sure. I could see up and out. I could see where it ended.

When the block was over, the city emerged again, gray and charming in a different way. A traffic sign glowed at me with a beckoning figure: WALK.

I came to a stop right in front of the same destination from that visit with my mother so long ago, when she'd forced herself to ask my father for money. This was where he worked.

My father still owned the same art gallery he'd opened after my mother left him—there was some kind of small inheritance he got after his own father died, and he used it all for this. We'd always known where it was, though we'd visited only the once. I remembered the wide pane of glass, the white insides. I remembered some pictures on the walls and an ugly, stumpy figure in the center of the floor—a sculpture of something I couldn't understand, maybe an animal of some kind, a creature. It was lumpy to the touch, colder than I expected. Something slimy had come away on my wandering hand, as if the sculpture were oozing and alive. My father had yelled at me for touching it.

As for my father, I'd forgotten what he looked like in specifics, but I'd recognize him if he were there. He was my father. He would know me, and I him.

I hadn't meant to seek him out. My feet had done it for me. They'd traveled through the corridor of flowers and carried me here, for this. I would tell him who I was, and I would ask him for money, and I would be able to eat lunches and dinners in restaurants and buy new shampoo, and wouldn't even have to think of pawning the opal then. He'd never sent a child support check in his life, and when we'd visited those years ago we'd left empty-handed. He owed me, and my mother, and I would tell him. I hadn't known it at first, but it was why I'd come.

Through the glass, I could see a series of large paintings hung on the walls—long legs and bare bellies, pinkish flesh and flushed faces—but the art barely registered. I sensed he was close, the tremble of my mother's hand again in my hand. She never wanted to ask him for anything. She would have torn me away from this place before she'd let me go in there and ask him for as much as ten dollars. My being here was the last thing she would have wanted. She would have shoved me down the sidewalk and into the green.

And yet I didn't move. He was in there on the other side of the glass, I felt it.

"I don't get art sometimes," I heard from behind me. "I mean, why's it always got to be naked girls? Are we so special they can't be satisfied painting a tree?"

Her low voice made me unsteady.

I turned.

Monet was resting the weight of one leg on a fire hydrant. She kicked off and came closer, running her fingers through her hair. It was blond today. Her bare arms gleamed in the sunlight, muscled and curved the way an artist might render them in permanent, glistening paint. I wondered what it would be like to be her.

I wanted to act outraged that she'd found me here—confront her, make *her* unsteady—because of course she'd followed me from the house. She had to have.

But the thought of it pleased me. She'd followed me.

She moved up close to the glass, and now we were both there, hip against hip and shoulder to shoulder, peering in.

"Which one's your favorite?" she asked.

They were all blurs to me. There were nipples and bellies and pointed toes. The girls in the paintings all had dark curly hair, sometimes a hand running through it. They could have been one girl.

Monet squinted. Her mouth fogged the window in the shape of a crescent moon plunged out of the sky and lying sideways.

"I like the giant one in the middle," she said. "In that one at least she doesn't look dead and murdered on that hideous plaid couch."

The mention of the couch caught my attention, and I found myself studying it instead of the painted girl. The hideous plaid couch—tan and brown, composed so it mimicked a hunched creature itself, moldy and furred—prickled my memory. The arms were tall, the cushions sunken. I recognized it from somewhere, maybe.

Monet seemed to think I was ignoring her question on purpose.

"Don't be so sensitive," she said. "People tell you that all the time, don't they?"

I nodded, because they did. I was gullible, I was sensitive, I was too unsure in my own skin. She didn't know me, but she knew that.

"Are you stalking me?" I tried to smile.

She shrugged. "You're the one who called the cops over. Maybe you thought you knew something you don't. Something you can't know yet. Because you're not supposed to."

The way she spoke made the sunny street dark for a moment. I heard the whistle of wind, as if I were back inside that gated garden, down on my knees in the dirt by the grave, where the city didn't seem to touch. I had dirt under my fingernails. I noticed it right then and tried to pick it out, but it was so deep in there.

"You're going to see some things while you're here, and

they're not going to make sense. And you're going to try to make sense of them, but your brain is too small to take it in. So stop fighting."

The dirt was embedded under my fingernails, and I imagined it, plush and dark, seeping into my blood and contaminating me.

"So why are we here?" Monet said, sweeping her hands over the view of the empty gallery. "Out purchasing some art to liven up your tiny room?"

I scoffed. "I have fifty-three dollars to my name."

I was about to say more, but I saw him then. I saw him.

He was standing near where I recalled the slimy sculpture had been when I'd visited. His shadow was wider but just as tall. He still had that beard. I remembered the beard, and I remembered something else. When I'd touched the sculpture and he'd yelled at me, he'd also pushed me away from it, a shove that landed me on the ground, which was concrete, hard and cold. This alarmed my mother, and a fight began, one that propelled us out of the gallery soon after, without any cash in hand and with him yelling after us that she was a greedy Jew whore for coming to ask him for money after refusing to take his calls for years. I plugged my ears until we were across the intersection and in the flowers again, back with the flowers, away from him, safe, but that wasn't what hit me as I saw him standing there.

It was that I didn't want a thing from him after all.

My mother had taught me that. How had I forgotten?

It was too late. He was looking out the wall of windows, straight at me.

Monet didn't notice my father, even though he was the one person inside the gallery and he was right there. She had eyes only for the paintings. "How much do you want to bet a dude painted those things?" she said. "I'll bet you twenty bucks it's a dude. If you win, you're up to seventy-three bucks. C'mon, let's go in. Let's see."

I should never have come here. That was what I was thinking. I should never have walked the street of flowers and ferns, knowing where it would take me. I should not have come. I should turn around right now. I should never see this man again. I should go. My mother would want that.

Monet was grabbing my arm. She was heading for the glass door. She was opening it and pushing me inside, before I could even protest.

The gallery space was a squished storefront. It seemed smaller now than it had all those years ago. Every wall was white. The ceiling was white. The floor was gray, and hard, as I remembered. The exposed pipes were painted white. The doors were white. There was no furniture apart from a desk and a single stool, and those, too, were white.

Monet was offering her smile to my father, and he wasn't looking at me at all anymore. He was looking only at her. It was hard not to. His eyes ran from her face down to what was below her face, and took their time there, did a few circles down there, until he came back up again and met her eyes.

If Monet minded some strange creep checking her out like this, it didn't show.

He had a dark, scruffy beard. He had big, ugly hands. He reeked of cigarette smoke. He had a fat, veiny nose. I wondered what my mother ever saw in him, and worse, how many of his genes I carried, how much my aging future would be like this.

"Don't be shy. Take a look around."

Monet had no idea who he was to me. "Why, hello," she said. "Hello, hello. We were wondering if you could tell us a bit about the artist? Like, what is *his* name?" She winked at me.

A phone rang behind the white desk, and my father held up a stubby finger. I was relieved to see I didn't have his hands. He'd be right back, he told us—well, he told Monet. He acted as if only one of us was there. He hustled for the desk and answered a white phone. He turned his back as he spoke, which allowed me to escort Monet to the far side of the gallery, where the girl in the painting—it had to be the same subject in all the paintings—lolled listlessly with limbs outstretched on the hideous plaid couch. Either the artist had limited skill in animating the human form, or she really was a corpse and it was a brilliant interpretation; I couldn't decide. That was art, I guessed.

I just let it out. "That's my father," I told Monet. "I don't think he recognizes me."

"Who? *That* guy?"

I nodded and indicated she should keep her voice down.

"That guy is your dad." She whispered it, flat. I couldn't tell if she was teasing me.

"This is his place," I said. "That's him."

"I don't see *any* resemblance," she said, and this soothed me. She made a box with her fingers, as if miming the frame for a photograph. She gazed at him through her finger-frame. "Maybe in the nose."

I cringed and covered my face.

"Kidding. Seriously. But are *you* being serious right now? Did I interrupt a family reunion?"

"He didn't know I was coming."

"So," she said. "When's the last time you saw him?"

"I was thirteen. Forever ago."

"And he doesn't recognize you?"

I shrugged.

She grinned. "And you came here to—what? Claim your fortune? Go into the family business? Avenge an old wrong?"

I couldn't answer.

"What's the plan?" A spark in her eyes. "What do we want from him? Money?"

I didn't answer, but something was communicated between us that she liked. She liked it very much.

My father had ended his phone call and was crossing the empty gallery space toward us. "The artist you're admiring is called Frederico," he told Monet.

Monet stifled a laugh. He'd said it so pompously, attempting to roll the final *r*. "Frederico what? What's his last name?"

Every painting in the gallery was by this same artist. They all had the lack of artistic skill, the flat slops of color, the nude subject with the blob of dark hair. Many featured the hideous couch. In fact, the artist was better at painting the couch than the human.

"Simply Frederico," my father said. "He prefers to go by only one name. He likes to conceal his signature—see, there, in the corner by her toe, where he signed? He's a master of the female form. *Artforum* called him the voice of—"

Monet broke in, making him stop. I figured she'd laugh in his face. Master? Voice of . . . what? But what she said next shocked me.

"I'm not here to see any paintings, Dad. Don't you know me? I'm here to see you." Then she stepped back and spread out her arms, as if to say, *Look! I'm your long-lost child you never bothered to send a single birthday card to! Embrace me!*

His expression went sideways with confusion. He coughed a guttural smoker's cough and said, "What now?"

"Dad, it's me. Your daughter. Bina. Don't you recognize me?"

She came in for the hug now—she was actually going so far as to touch him—and I felt myself turn into a mist in the shape of a person. Someone could walk straight through me, and I'd dissolve. I wasn't even there. Only two people were, and I was watching them reconnect. So this was how he would greet his estranged daughter.

He returned the hug, awkwardly, but when he pulled away he shook his head. "I don't remember your hair . . . like that," he said. That was all he said. After all these years, he had nothing more to say to me. He stood so stiffly. Not a millimeter of his face softened beneath the dark beard.

"So what next?" Monet said. "Want to take me to lunch?"

"Sabina?" he said. "Bina? It's you?"

The mist hardened to ice. Bina was something my mother had called me, from the beginning, before I even came out. Monet could have kept this going, but I didn't need her. Not for this.

"She's lying," I told him. "She's not Bina."

He seemed relieved. Then his face hardened—gazing at me anew. "What do you want?" he said. "Did your boyfriend knock you around or something?"

I touched my face. Makeup never seemed to hide it completely, no matter what I did. "I walked into a door," I said.

He didn't like that, not one bit. It was something my mother had been known to say. He changed the subject. "Did *she* send you? How is she?"

He wouldn't even call her by a name, but I knew who he meant: my mother.

Here was the man we left when I was nine years old. The man who threw the dishes, practically the whole set, until we had barely anything left to eat on. The man who called her terrible names, who did things to her she'd never told me, because it would hurt me to know, who made her walk into all those doors, here he was.

I would keep her safe, even now. "She's fine. She's doing *fantastic*."

"Why are you here then?" He wasn't smiling. He didn't seem at all happy to be reunited. "You're here for money. I can read you like I could her. That's what you want, right? Cash."

Heat buzzed in my ears. "I'm here for the summer, I'm staying at Catherine House, I—"

"I know the place. *She* stayed there. When she left me the first time."

I steeled my eyes at him.

"They tried to poison her to me. But it didn't work. She didn't stay long."

I knew that, too. Her city stories ended so abruptly, as if the sidewalk had dropped off and there was no one left to catch her but him. She went back to him, this stranger. Was it all because of me?

"I was the only one who visited her in the hospital," he was saying. "The *only* one. None of them came. Whole house full of chicks, and not one showed."

Monet watched him carefully. She was getting a clearer picture of him now. So was I.

"She was in the hospital?" This was the first I'd heard of it, and I'd heard most everything that went on that summer, or so I thought.

"After the accident." This new piece of information—*accident?*—stung me. "And you could be scamming me, coming here, pretending to be my kid. Don't think I don't know that." He paused. "Except you do look like her. That's the truth."

Usually I liked this said aloud and acknowledged. I needed to hear it, needed to remember. Because if I resembled her on the outside, where it was obvious, didn't we share so much more, on the inside, where only we could know and feel?

"You do look like your mother," he said. "Only chunkier."

I stepped back.

"But that doesn't mean I'm giving you money."

Monet spoke for me. "So that's it? You haven't seen your kid in years, and that's what you have to say?"

He refused to give me another word and stood there, quaking with rage. The familiarity of the moment squeezed my throat.

In an instant, Monet had his arm. For some reason, she had his arm and was leaning into his ear and sharing something, and he was nodding, visibly calmed, even subdued. It was eerie.

She turned now to me. "Let me talk to you for a sec. Alone."

"Wait," I said, because I was still at the edge of something, and it had nothing to do with his money. An accident. There'd been an accident I didn't know about. My mother's stories had swirled with forgotten street names and subway stops, clubs that used to be open but weren't anymore, defunct bands I'd never heard of, movies she watched in downtown theaters that had since shuttered, adventures she had in downtown parks, boots she wore that she bought on sale on the street where she said all boots used to live, the postcards she collected from

197

the shop on Christopher Street that was filled with old art prints and movie stills—enough murky and distracted detail to make a web. She'd left some things out, hadn't she? I was beginning to suspect that she'd distracted me with other things all so she could keep the most significant part of her summer to herself.

Monet pulled me across the gallery, and soon we were at the doorway. She wedged her arm in front of it so I couldn't open the door and leave.

"Get your face together," she said.

I'd been crying. That kept happening. I was facing the street, fully visible through the glass, and not a single person who walked past paused with any concern or even noticed. My mother always said people in the city minded their own business. She'd also once told me there was never another place where she felt so alone.

"What's the game plan here?" Monet said.

"Game? This isn't a game."

The last time I ever visited with him—the day I saw this gallery, and left empty-handed—I remembered my mother's hands in my hair, her warm body snug against mine as she pulled me close, and how safe I felt even though we were out in the noisy street surrounded by strangers. She apologized for taking me there. She should never have done it, she said. No amount of money was worth it, and we'd be fine without him, just fine.

Then she made me a promise. "You will never have to see that man ever again."

She never broke that promise. I did. All by myself, on this very day.

"What do you want to do?" Monet said, her voice pitched low. "He's not going to like *hand over* his credit cards . . . We could see how much he's got in his wallet if you want. Who should be the decoy?" She waggled her eyebrows.

"No, no," I said. I kept thinking about the accident he said she'd had. I kept thinking how *he* knew something about her that I didn't.

Monet pointed to one of the paintings on the wall, the largest, ugliest one, the one she'd called her favorite. "Go over there. By that poor girl's feet. Wait there. I'll take care of this." Then she was near my father again, and she was pulling him away. She said she needed to talk with him.

———

I might have followed, but something on the wall held me. The painting. That plaid couch. That very particular pattern on the couch. It tugged at me the way a vaguely recognizable face in a movie will tug, will spin your mind until you remember where you saw that person before, what role they used to play in some former costume.

What was coming to me was all texture. Nubby and rough against skin. Then the pattern and the distinct colors, the sour brown, the sickly tan, the urine-inspired yellow. I'd touched it, in real life, with my own hand.

That couch had lived in my father's house before we left him and most everything in it. It had been in his studio (the garage), and I wasn't allowed to sit on it. Now here it was, depicted in oil paint and hung in a Manhattan gallery far away from that garage, signed pretentiously, *Frederico*.

Maybe my father knew the artist, but that wouldn't explain the second thing.

The subject in the paintings. The girl.

In all the paintings, her hair was the same: a mess of curls hanging below her chin, brown squiggly lines, as if the artist didn't know how to properly render hair using a paintbrush. The same brown squiggles and face appeared on every canvas in the gallery. My hand lifted to my own head, where my hair was knotted and slick at the back of my neck, from summer humidity, but if I broke it free from the hair elastic it would have made my own mess of curls and flya-ways as usual. I had my mother's hair. When she'd stopped dyeing it, the brown grew back in, plain as tree bark. Same as mine.

Hair was only the beginning. We had the same hands and wrists, practically almost identical. Same big hips. Same big lips. He'd said we looked alike, didn't he?

This painting was of my mother. She was young again, rendered with globs and shaded body parts. The proportions were all off, but I saw the accusatory face of my mother. Full of secrets. Standing in the door of my basement bedroom, telling me she needed to send me away.

I had to go. Through the window, the street was dark now, as if a storm had barreled through the neighborhood, shrouding the block. I should have heard traffic noise and the buzz of activity outside, but I didn't. How long had we been here?

Moments later, Monet reappeared, tossing me a wallet. "How much you get?"

I caught it and held it close. It bulged with cards and sloppy lumps of cash, and I needed two hands to grasp it. "What'd you do to him?"

"I doubt Fred's coming back out here anytime soon," she said. "He's a little shaken, the pig. I saw him holding his chest when I left, like his heart couldn't take it. The shock might end up killing him." She was baiting me.

"What did you *do* to him?" I repeated.

She cocked her head.

"He's Frederico," I said.

She nodded, encouraging me.

"It's him," I said louder.

There was something about knowing that the man who made these things was my father. The trick he was pulling on the public by showing his own work and saying some artsy painter made them. The fact that he used my mother to do it for all these years.

A paint can sat on the bottom rung of a ladder nearby. I wish I could say I was the one who noticed it, that the idea came to me, but Monet crossed the gallery to the ladder. The paint was white, of course.

"He could come out at any second," Monet said, yet weren't her eyebrows raised? Didn't she point a finger at the paint can and say, "Hmm"?

I put the wallet down so my hands were free.

"Go on," she said. "Hurry up, before Daddy Dearest comes out."

She was so calm. At the same time, she was goading me. She'd done something to him, and now it was my turn.

It was a half gallon of white paint, not so heavy. A paintbrush was innocently set at its side. The lid popped right off, the paintbrush a loaded weapon, dripping everywhere.

I began with a splat, aimed it at the biggest canvas on the biggest wall. It took me over. It was all or nothing, and I wanted to destroy everything, every stolen scrap of my mother. I wanted to erase her from this place.

As I was spraying paint at the pictures, I changed. I turned powerful. Brutal. Brimming with rage.

Soon there was no more paint. There was no more artwork to ruin, except for one painting on the far wall. But I'd done enough, I'd made my mark, had my fill. My rage was spent.

I dropped the paintbrush. I kicked the paint can over. I marked the gray floor with white prints from my feet, and then I stood very still. I had paint in my hair, paint spattered over my bruises and ugly spots and mouth just like my mother's. I blinked, and all I saw was white. My mother felt so close to me; it was almost as if she were there with me in the gallery, softly saying, *That was beautiful, Bean*, in my paint-crusted ear.

True dark had fallen, thick now, and streetlights were on, but there were still people passing by, completely uninterested in what was going on inside. The only person bursting with emotion in this room was me.

I took the wallet and held it for a good moment. Then I dropped it in a pool of paint, where it would stick.

"Really?" Monet said.

"Really," I said.

She nodded with respect.

I grabbed the remaining painting—a small canvas tucked away in a corner—without a second thought. A couple of fresh white dots marred it, but apart from that it was an original Frederico in fine shape. I held it face-first against my chest and headed for the door.

Monet trailed after me.

"You could get arrested," she called.

Was it me, or did she sound amused?

"How many dollars' worth of damage would it have to be to become a felony?" she asked. "If it's art theft, do they have to call the FBI?" I could feel her behind me. This was still a game to her, one in which she felt not a single consequence, as if no one could catch her, no matter what she did. So reckless.

I sensed that same recklessness in me.

I was out the door, and so was she, and no one was yelling after us. I was across the street, and so was she, and all behind us was quiet.

Then we were around the corner, and the awning of a neighboring building made a safe haven where we could stop, and I did, my back against brick, letting myself go calm, leaning my mother against the wall for a moment, simply breathing.

Monet was only watching me now. She was perfectly silent, almost smiling.

After a few breaths, I was back to myself and I straightened. I lifted my mother in my arms again, the canvas slick with panic-sweat. "I'm okay. I'm okay now, I'm okay."

"You sure are," she said.

She registered the painting in my arms and, as she did, she happened to notice my hand.

"What's that you have on your finger?" she said.

I couldn't hide my hand. It was out in front of me, on display. I'd been wearing it with the stone facing in, but it must have gotten turned around in the excitement.

"It's nothing," I said.

"Nothing?" I could see all the things she wanted to say flash across her face, and she uttered none of them. Maybe she decided to put it away for later. Maybe something about that night made her, too, feel changed.

It was as we walked back to Catherine House that she bumped her shoulder into mine, a knock of appreciation. Her bare skin was cooler than it should have been in the heavy-hanging heat. She was so unbothered by everything, as if she knew already all the things that could be.

"What did you do to him?" I asked. She knew I meant that man I'd never have to see for the rest of my life, who I'd never again call my father. He hadn't come out of the back room, even with all the noise we must have made. For all I knew, she could have killed him.

"I told you to stop fighting," she said. "I told you you'd see some things, that they wouldn't make sense." She was setting off fireworks in my mind, bursts and pops in the wild field of my imagination. That was enough for now. More than enough.

It was something I hadn't even known I wanted, what each of us did forming one perfect whole.

She put her arm around me, jostling my mother in my embrace. I didn't mind the touch. The opal was near glowing. Monet could have stayed that way if she wanted, sidled up to me, the two of us against the world. Even though she'd stood by and watched me do all the destruction and then told me how much trouble I was in. It was almost as if she'd *wanted* me to get in trouble, was *hoping* he'd come out and catch me in the act. Even with that.

"You surprised me," she said. "I didn't know you had that in you."

I didn't know it, either.

DAWN

IT WAS A PHYSICAL SENSATION I COULDN'T PINPOINT IN MY BODY: knowing we were close to curfew and needing to be back inside—all of us there, safest together—before the clock turned.

We only just made it. A few minutes more, and the front gate would have been chained, and no one, certainly none of the tenants and not even Ms. Ballantine herself, who could not be bribed with cash or with favors, would come down to open it. The garden gate was locked, police tape cordoning it from entry, so we would have had to spend the night sleeping in a doorway down in the street. Anything could have happened.

Once we made it inside to the foyer, Monet stopped. "You're limping again. Is it your leg?"

I'd felt invincible in the gallery—still had, until she mentioned that. As soon as she put it to words, there was the dull throbbing in my ankle, the same ankle as the night in the woods, a thudding reminder. It wasn't sharp like a new injury—it was faint, a low pull.

But I kept walking. There was so much I didn't want to think about. When I was in this house, I wanted to close the curtains on all of that.

"Do you need to sit down?" Monet asked. "Here, let me take that."

She had her arms out to collect the portrait of my mother, but something in me—coarse, instinctual—would not let her have it. I clutched it to my chest, almost curling myself around it, and she backed off, arms up as if to defend herself.

"All right, all right," she said. "Keep it."

As we passed the front parlor, dim with only one gold-toned lamp left on, I had a sudden awareness that we had a witness. I'd been avoiding this room. For more than a week, I wouldn't dare look toward the parlor when I passed. But tonight was different. I was different. I lingered in view of the archway and let myself peer in.

I pretended at first, for protection. "Who's there?" I called, as if I might find Gretchen curled up on an armchair, fallen asleep with that book she was always lugging around. Or Anjali and Lacey, maybe, having a quiet conversation near the low-wattage lamp on the giant boat of a couch.

But I knew the room would be empty of tenants. Dust sifted and settled, charged and unable to take a seat. The long drapes hiding the street from view swayed ever so slightly along the gold carpet. The ceiling fan swept in circles. The grandfather clock ticked.

I approached, concealing my mother's face against my chest. Something told me I should. I walked closer, and Monet was right—I was favoring one leg.

As I came near, the portrait above the mantel shifted. Catherine was easing nearer to the front of the frame, where glass met open air. The mist crept in all around her, an erasure of white fog forming around her mouth. It wasn't mist at all—it was her warm breath contained in that cold tomb of glass.

"You come down here and talk to her, too?" Monet asked.

I started at her voice behind me.

I hadn't. Not once. After that first night—candlelight cupped in my hands, shimmer of blue light on the rooftop over our heads—I couldn't face it.

"Can you even imagine?" Monet said. She was beside me then. Catherine's black eyes were trained on her as much as they'd been trained on me.

"Imagine what?"

"What it must be like to *be* her, to watch us every day and every night from behind that glass and not be able to do anything."

Monet tucked a bright-blond lock behind her ear, and I found myself staring at the black hole there, tiny and deep, that burrowed its way into her head. The opal on my finger was growing warmer.

"Do you think she sees us?" I knew an answer to that question, if I let myself think it. Did Monet?

"You know she does. This was her house, and she's still in it, and now we're everywhere. Putting our dirty feet all over her furniture . . . getting our grubby paws on her stuff . . . talking about her like she's not here. That's what I think sometimes. But other times I wonder if maybe she doesn't want to be alone. Ever. So she makes sure."

We met eyes before the portrait, Monet and me. My hand was hot, and behind the painting pressed to my chest, my heart was thumping.

"We should talk," Monet said. "But not here." She gestured at the mantel. *Not in front of her.*

The portrait darkened, a tremor coming from behind the glass. It rippled through my body like a distant quake. We were upsetting her.

There was the distinct sense that she knew what Monet was about to tell me, and wanted me kept in the dark. It felt like someone was shoving me backward, into the dust and the dim, into the dark gold, down on the ground, and though I was softening and growing dizzy with a drugged sense of numbness and part of me almost wanted to let it have me, another part of me tore away and headed for the stairs.

I didn't feel like myself again until I had my hand on the banister.

We didn't pass any other tenants on the way up—everyone else in the house seemed to be tucked in behind closed doors, lights out for the night. But we weren't alone. Even after leaving the view of the front parlor, I still felt eyes at my back. Eyes on me from below, eyes from above. The portraits of the girls of Catherine House were awake as the tenants slept. The girls behind glass were gray-faced and murky-eyed. They were gazing at me in a way they hadn't before—now there was an awareness. Whatever I'd done tonight—whatever Monet had encouraged and nudged—and whatever we'd touched on while talking downstairs, it had caught their notice. They were wary of me.

I quickened my steps, though my ankle twinged.

On the landing below mine, Monet left for her room without a word. We'd shared something electric, a live wire exposed. But that had changed once curfew came and we'd reentered the house. "I thought you wanted to talk?" I called after her. She didn't answer.

As I turned the corner heading up to my floor, Gretchen came down, her shadow so towering and ceiling-bound, I almost didn't know who or what was coming.

What was she doing up there? Her room wasn't on the fifth floor.

As soon as she saw me, she grabbed my arm, pulled me close.

"Monet told me not to talk to you," she said, "but you're going to do it, right? You're going to help Catherine?"

I pulled my arm away. The one she'd grabbed was still

hurting from the night in the woods, but she also had jagged fingernails and a forceful grip. "Help with what?"

"We need to wake her again. She's trying to tell us something, and we don't know what. Her book doesn't say."

Something wasn't right about Gretchen, something in the eyes, urgent and blooming. It unnerved me.

"Were you upstairs in my room?" I asked.

"How could I be in your room? Your door was locked. Nobody locks their doors around here, I don't know why you do. What are you hiding? Why are you here?"

"What do you mean? I needed a room," I said simply. "I called, and they had a room for me."

"No one ever calls for a room."

But I had. It was almost as if I'd arrived here in the snap of two fingers. In the blink of an eye. A vacancy when I'd most needed it. And yet it was real—I could touch the walls on either side of me, I could feel the stairs under my feet.

"What's that?" Gretchen asked.

I was cradling the canvas in my arms, and I wasn't about to let her see it. When she pulled at it to turn it around, I kept it bound to me as if belted in place.

"It's like someone knocked you in the head and you don't know anything," Gretchen said.

"Excuse me?"

She was around the bend and thumping down the rest of the stairs before I could get an explanation.

I closed my door, locked it, and set my mother's portrait faceup on the bed. How was it that it could be a terrible rendition of her, the skill and detail not much better than a finger painting, and yet I felt her with me more than before? I felt her inside the canvas, and now I felt her inside this house. I was sure she was thinking of me, at that very moment, while I stared into the smudges meant to be her eyes. The smudges were grayish-greenish blue, a mash-up of colors that didn't claim one more than the other, which seemed right.

I found the largest item of clothing I owned—a hooded sweatshirt my mother had packed for me; it might have been hers once—and wrapped the portrait inside it. Then I slipped it between the box spring and the mattress, sandwiched it deeply in there, down where I'd put my feet.

It was when I let go that my phone started ringing.

The phone was in my bag somewhere, and I had to dig in there, searching, until I came up with its bright screen beaming with my mother's face.

Had she heard my thoughts, all the way across bridges and up the Thruway and along mountain roads, to know to call me this instant? We were that connected, rope frayed but holding even still?

Phone service was spotty. I had only one bar, but I still hoped to hear her voice when I answered. I didn't expect to get dead silence—static, faint and far-off, as if she were holding the phone up into the air to let me hear the wind blowing.

"Mom?" I shouted into the phone, but it was useless. The signal cut off. When I tried to return her call, voice mail again and again, no answer again and again, her phone unreachable as if she'd entered a tunnel.

She didn't call back.

I sat on the end of the bed, not thinking at first that I was sitting on her, and then I leaped up, feeling it all at once. She'd known to call me. Mother's intuition. She was aware I'd betrayed her by going to the gallery. That was all it was—she'd called simply to let me know she knew.

We'd had an understanding between us when it came to my father, and I'd broken it only once before, four years ago. After we'd visited the gallery, my mother made the promise that I'd never have to see him again, the promise she kept. Then she asked me to make a promise to her.

I was not to tell that man whose bed she slept in, or his girls, where we'd gone and who we saw there. I was to swallow this information and keep it where no one could ever get it out of me. I was her girl, hers more than anyone else could be, hers more than Charlotte was, hers more than Daniella was. She knew she could trust me. Couldn't she?

I nodded. I'd always been her secret-keeper. I was born into it.

After the gallery, the secret had kept its place while we rode the subway uptown and entered the museum, to meet them at the planned spot. She had to check the map to find it—*Water Lilies*, made in pieces and stretching like a giant muted smudge

213

over a long wall. The secret kept as we waited, as I stared at the thing, squinted, saw only smears of color, ridged and textured and begging for a finger to mess with it. The secret was not coming out when he emerged around the bend with his daughters. The secret stayed intact throughout the interweaving halls of the museum, up and down escalators, in and out of grand and airy rooms with masterpieces on display.

I thought I had a solid hold of it as I slept on the train headed to Poughkeepsie, the closest stop near home. That I had it stowed good and tight when we were back upstate and in the cheery yellow kitchen a dead woman had decorated.

Dinner was veggie burgers and tater tots, and I was cleaning my plate. The hunger overtook me, and I couldn't stop eating. I needed to stuff myself full of food, so nothing else would come out.

My mother's husband teased about how I could be so hungry if we'd had that big lunch downtown, my mother and I. Between mouthfuls, I said, "But we didn't get anything to eat." And there it went, the secret. It launched off my tongue and skidded across the table and dropped into his hands. Just like that, I had let the secret go.

"What do you mean you didn't have lunch?" he asked. Weren't we meeting her old friend from scene-study class? What was her name, Marina? Didn't we meet Marina downtown for lunch?

When the truth spilled out, it tasted like a lie. My stomach turned sour with it, and there was a burn in the back of my throat. The sisters' eyes batted back and forth, catching all of it. Worse was my mother's face across the table. Gray stone.

"Dawn?" he said. "What's she saying? You didn't meet Marina? You went to see *him*?"

I flattened a tot in my fingers.

"You know Bina and her wild imagination." These words of my mother's fell past me, littering the air in microscopic shards of hail. "Do you really think I'd make up a whole story about seeing Marina after all these years and go see him instead? What for?"

He was quiet. The girls were quiet. The energy between my mother and me was so loud.

"Sabina, why would you lie about something like that?" she said in a strange, stilted voice. She enunciated every word.

My own strange voice answered her. "I don't know. I'm sorry." We were performing now—like a scene to be studied in her old class. Was that what she wanted from me? To make it better? To fix it with pretend?

"Why are you trying to drive a wedge between us? This is our family now. You know this. I would never lie like that. Explain yourself."

I wasn't as good at calling up the dialogue, and I wasn't sure how I was supposed to explain. I'd said out loud that we went to see my father at his gallery. I wasn't sure what would erase those words now. My mind went a panicked white. I did the only thing I could think to do, my face burning, my stomach coiling, my mother playacting across from me, proving her worth as an actress. I put my head down on the table and closed my eyes. The darkness behind my closed lids was absolute at first, like a soft, thick blackout curtain.

I heard my mother through the darkness.

"Sabina, stand up."

I heard her but didn't respond.

"I said get up."

When I opened my eyes, I saw that the girls were delighted. Charlotte clapped her hands and kicked Daniella under the table so she'd clap hers. I saw my mother blazing with light.

"Dawn," I heard him say, his voice low. "That's enough. She's upset. She knows she was wrong. Let her be." He was so forgiving. He wasn't a bad man, and maybe I should have met his eyes when I spoke to him or called him by his name sometime.

"Get up, Sabina. You're done with dinner now. Now go."

I didn't make it to my bedroom. There was a spot in the garage where my mother stored an old crate of our unneeded things from our last house, and sometimes I went there, simply to perch on it and feel it under me. I would touch the objects inside, but I never took them out where the girls might see them. The small covered garage smelled damp, like mildew and like the oil that puddled under the minivan. It was dark, without any windows to the outside. The corner with the crate was a cocoon, and I folded myself up there, confused and trying to cry without sound.

It might have been hours later when she came to me and apologized. She was so ashamed. I was so ashamed. We'd both done awful things, and to each other, and we wouldn't accept being forgiven so soon. She wrapped her arms around me in the dark corner, and I stopped shaking so much and calmed. She sounded like herself again.

"Why do you spend so much time in here?" she said. "It smells."

"Why did we go see him anyway?" I said back. "Was it really for money?"

"He owes it to us. And I was ready . . . to ask."

I pressed my face into her shoulder, soaking her shirt. "Where would we have gone with it?" That money wouldn't have been used to buy a car or a new pair of boots. It wouldn't have landed in a savings account to earn interest. It wasn't my future college fund or a vacation to Niagara Falls. She didn't say it, but I knew.

The secret my mother wanted to hide wasn't that we visited the gallery and asked her ex-husband for money. It was what she would have done with that money. Depending on how much he gave, we could have gone anywhere, or stayed in-state and chosen a borough. The city—the sidewalks all around us, heading in every direction, river to river, bridge to bridge—had been in our reach. Now it was lost again.

She held me, and I held her. She begged me to forgive her, and I said I would. The smell of oil tinged with gasoline filled the garage.

A rattling at my window startled me.

A head appeared. Monet again, now on the fire escape, leaning on the black-barred cage between air and brick to stretch her legs. Only her face and one bare elbow entered my window. The rest of her body seemed suspended over the city, ethereal.

"Hey," she said, acting casual, like she hadn't left for her room before without a goodbye and wasn't showing up now without an invitation.

"Why can't you use the stairs?"

"Here," she said. In her extended hand was a twenty-dollar bill. "I think you won the bet about Fred, or I did. Either way, here. Yours."

I didn't want to take money from her, but when she placed it inside, on the windowsill, I didn't push it away. For a second, the air smelled like gasoline and I thought of my mother. She had another secret, one she hadn't told me, about an accident that had happened in this house. If she knew I was here, she might come running and show up at the door, and then what would I do? Go home with her? Pretend to be gone and have everyone cover for me, forcing her to lug crates of old towels and unwanted sweaters to the street to complete the charade?

Monet was eyeing the closet. Maybe she thought I'd stowed the portrait of my mother in there, for safekeeping, since it wasn't hanging plainly on the wall. I couldn't understand why she wanted to see it, why she couldn't let it be only mine.

The night had tied us up together. She knew something about me now, something I'd thought was unknowable. At the same time, I didn't know a single thing about her, or at least nothing I could say for sure was true.

"I heard you with Gretchen on the stairs," she said.

I rolled my eyes. "She's intense."

But Monet wasn't smiling or making fun. The seriousness in her face skewed me. "Your mom really never told you about her accident, did she?"

"You know about that?"

She nodded as if she knew every last thing.

"I'm going up," she said. "C'mon."

She lifted her chin at what was above us. I knew she meant the rooftop, even though it was forbidden. I paused, and she leaned in. "Don't you want to see the view?"

I did. I wanted to see the skyline from up there. I wanted to know for certain if it was how my mother had described it, the way it made a pulsing electric beat in her toes, the way her eyes were marked by it, as if burned through, until she could see the city dancing on the backs of her eyelids for hours afterward, a drawing pinned up while she slept. I'd always believed that had I not come into the picture, she would have embraced these lights forever and committed to becoming one of them. She would have stayed.

I didn't move.

Something was telling me that Monet meant another kind of view. She meant the thing I'd awakened, unwittingly, by coming here, by finding that opal, by being my mother's daughter. It was all anyone seemed to care about, but how could I explain I didn't want or need to know so much, unless it involved my mother?

"It's sturdy," she said. "Watch." She jumped up and down to show it would catch her weight.

I shook my head. The fire escape had only open air beneath it. It seemed to defy gravity and was so fragile, tacked on to the front of the house, and I didn't understand how it stayed wedged into the brick. I imagined taking a step out onto it, and then the fall.

"No?" she said.

"No," I said.

Monet didn't fight me or force me or taunt me for my fear. She didn't even ask if I was sure, because I wasn't, as it seemed she was about to tell me something important and I'd miss it. She didn't give me the chance—she was up the ladder beyond my reach in no time, seeing the buildings from here to the end of the island, whatever that looked like.

I got ready for bed, washing all the makeup off my face to reveal the still-livid bruises. Shouldn't they have faded by now? Shouldn't I have recovered? The mirror showed only the worst of me, as if I'd never be over it.

Back in my room, I curled up close to the window, where I could at least feel a touch of air in the stifling heat. I thought about my mother, about whatever sent her to the hospital when she lived in this house and about whether Monet was only pretending to know so she could lure me up the fire escape.

There was no other way up to the roof—the stairs in the center of the house didn't go any higher than my floor, and I didn't know of another staircase except for the one behind my wall, bricked off.

The small door was painted white, even the knob whited out. Everything in the gallery had been painted this same white. It was the color of trying to hide something. Of putting one over on you. Of lies.

Lacey had said this door led to a closet, but that was a lie. This time I took my phone for a flashlight—even without a signal, it worked for that at least—and I was up the stairs and around the bend in no time. As before, the corridor was narrow and tight, and there was no door, only the hastily built wall of bricks. I could see more clearly this time the towering stack that filled the doorframe, rough-edged and red.

I put a hand to the bricks. So cold.

And quiet. I found the crack in the bricks where I remembered, a crevice through which to see. This had to be the way to the roof, and maybe I'd be able to spy Monet on the other side, but when I pressed my eye in, straining with all my might, all that reflected back was darkness. It was a darkness that held nothing and no one, apart from memories that had been stowed away where almost nobody could find them, walled in brick by brick by brick.

My eyes open.

"I'm right here." That's me. That's my voice. I'm yelling into the woods. "Where'd you go? I'm right here." I'm shouting it, but to no one, because they're all gone now, they've given up on me and didn't bother chasing me all the way out of the woods, to the road. My throat is ragged, my body filling with hot rushes of pain. There's something wrong with one of my legs, and there's something wrong with one of my eyes, so I'm crooked as I walk, like a suitcase with a broken wheel.

I hear wind in the trees, and that's all.

Then I sense the vehicle approaching. Two headlights, brighter than exploding stars, and I'm waving my arms. *Stop, I'm trying to tell them. Help me. Stop.*

It doesn't stop.

A van roars past, giant and bright blue, with a smoking tailpipe and screeching tires. There are stickers all over the bumper—unreadable as they blur past—and something blocking the windows so there's no way to see who's inside. I'm okay. I've lurched out of the way just in time.

But I'm confused, turned around. I must have jumped too far into the trees, because when I stand again, I'm not clear on which way to go. My flashlight isn't in my hand anymore, and I can't remember the last time I held it. I start walking, or trying to. I'm pushing branches out of the way, stepping wrong on a path that isn't a path at all. I keep going, and what I mean is to head home, but in the dark I can't see which way is out and which way is deeper in, where trails stop and no parties are held. Back there are wild acres of wooded forest, hilltops and climbing cliffsides and thick tangles of trees. And the ravine.

I stretch my arms out in front of me, aiming for stray branches, slapping them away, as if that might help me navigate the darkness. The road is right here. I'll be home in no time—or I would be, if only my ankle weren't screaming every time I took a step. If only I could see better, through the swollen pinhole of one of my eyes. If only my head wasn't sending thunder strikes all through my skull, trying to crack me open.

I might be walking in circles. At some point, I stop, but when I look ahead, there's only darkness. It's like the ground falls off and the whole rest of the world is down there, where I can't see but could be a part of it, if only I take the first step in.

———

I came awake at the bottom of the closet stairs, a hammer pounding inside my head. It was so hot, too hot, so I pushed back into my room. The small space was in disarray, the bed tipped over so the extra door could open, the dresser drawers knocked onto the floor and bursting with spills, a picture of my mother splayed out on the floor. I set the mattress back and got in the bed, but, now, here was the window. The fire escape I couldn't climb. The view I never did see for myself. All the things I'd never done and wanted to do.

I took hold of the windowsill, bracing myself, gulping air, and slithered out. I did it before I could change my mind.

If anyone had been watching from down below on the side-walk, or from one of the town houses across the way, if anyone had seen me slide out on my stomach, trying to keep a foot heel-locked onto the window frame, trying not to look down, accidentally looking down, then the vertigo, then my head spinning, then having to close my eyes and lie there with my arms slack and prickling, if anyone had seen this, they would have laughed. Monet would have collided into a wall with laughter. She would have shaken with it, but not as I was shaking out on the fire escape from having the ground so far away and, up above, all that endless night sky.

Then again it was as my mother said it would be, to feel the city out there above and around me, in all pulsing frequencies and on all sides. It was everything.

The warm breeze in my hair, the sweat on my skin cooling. Monet was still up there, and I was down here, and I told myself I'd stay out for a touch longer. At some point I forgot to be afraid, because I closed my eyes to sleep.

I must have remained on the fire escape, only the upper half of my body, until dawn. If she ever climbed back down the ladder to spend the night inside, in her bed the way ordinary people did, I didn't feel her pass by.

When I jolted awake, it was light out, and the view made me catch myself for a fall that wasn't happening. I was pro-tected, held in place by the sturdy black cage. The hand gripping it was still wearing the opal—I'd been sloppy, and I went out of the house with it, slept in it, and wore it in open air, where it could have slipped off and dropped five stories and gotten picked up by some lucky stranger in the street.

But was it lucky?

With my eyes closed and my ears plugged, I could play pretend. I could tell myself everyone was happy, as I was. I could ignore Gretchen's confusing desperation and Lacey's attempt to leave. I could forget Anjali's note. And I made every effort to, for days. Even Monet on the roof, acting like she wanted to tell me something, I never made it up there to hear her out, to see. It was cold of me to ignore them all, so maybe the person I was lying to the most was myself.

And yet, I did feel lucky. To be in this city. In this house. In this room, away from everything that had fallen to pieces at home. It was a fantasy come true, a wishful thought dug up from piles of brick and concrete and set to lights. If that wasn't luck, what should I call it?

PART FOUR

EXCAVATIONS

A DAY LATER, MONET PULLED ME ASIDE, AWAY FROM THE OTH-
ers. She said she knew a little French place nearby where we
could have lunch and talk. "I promise it's on steady ground,"
she said, and I wasn't sure if she was joking, or getting in a dig
at me. It wasn't too far down the block, in a storefront below
street level, where we were seated at a wobbly table by a window. "This is on me," she said. With a tiny burst of shame, but
also a sense of delight because it was the two of us, I said okay.

We were the only customers in the small restaurant. The
waiter poured tap water, and then Monet got something fizzy
and lemony, and asked for a second one for me. From the
menu, she ordered up a feast. The food was the kind a child
might choose: fries, which were called *frites*, and pastries and
dessert. I didn't have the heart to tell her I wasn't that hungry.

I'd gone with every intention of asking *her* questions. I
wanted to know what information she had on my mother. I

wanted to ask more about Catherine. But with her in front of me, so much else fell away, as if there were no room on the screen but for her face. Her hair today was rainbow-tinted. I was beginning to wonder if she had something against the natural hair that grew out of her head, because she kept trying to disguise it, which in a way was disguising herself. Deftly, with obvious skill, she turned the conversation to center on me.

It became apparent that she expected to learn everything about me, as much as could be contained in one lunch conversation. She started with my father, bored of that in an instant, then asked about my mother. Did I share things with my mother? Did I have the kind of relationship that girls long for, where we wore each other's clothes and drank each other's iced coffees, where we shared secrets, me with her but especially her with me? Monet liked knowing I did have that, once, but she also seemed alarmed to know I'd barely spoken to my mother since I moved to Catherine House, that when I got her on the phone, she hung up on me.

"And she never told you why she went home," she said, as if to be rock-solid on that. "Or how," she added.

"What she told me was a lie," I said.

"And she doesn't know you're here, right now, staying in this house." It wasn't a question. She was sure of that, and I couldn't remember if it was something I'd mentioned.

"I was going to tell her, but she hasn't called me back."

Monet sucked in a sip of her fizzy lemon water, swirling the bubbles around in her mouth with concentration. I found myself softening, relaxing in the chair. When was the last time I could trust someone? I couldn't remember. I'd told things to girls I thought were my friends, who'd turned around and told someone else. I'd told things that then got distorted, taunted into other shapes, twisted, erased. I'd told lies that became truths, and when I'd told the truth, everyone said I was lying. But that was back home. Here, I could be new.

The more we sat together in that empty, dim-lit restaurant, the more I talked. Not about the party. Not about that, not yet. But about everything else.

"Mostly what I remember is the next morning and hitchhiking here," I heard myself say, felt it starting to spill. How my mother was the one who taught me how to flag down a ride, the two of us on the side of the road, thumbs out, waiting for a car to stop, when I was just a kid. About that time I confronted my mother in the basement of the new house when she was doing laundry and accused her of being miserable and cowardly and pathetic, because she stayed married to him without even a glance at the road—and it only occurred to me as I shaped the story that the bad guy wasn't my mother full of excuses who'd forgotten how to hitch rides and dream big dreams. It was me; I was the one who'd decided she should leave. As I discovered this, I said so to Monet. I said a lot of things.

The sheen in Monet's cheeks brightened as she consumed my words and the food on our table. She devoured from the plates indiscriminately. She mixed frites with bites of pear tart, and chocolate croissants with cheese and onion soup. She licked crumbs off porcelain. She slurped. As she ate, I kept talking. It was as if I'd been hypnotized.

I told her I used to hate my father, though I'd barely known him, and how uncomplicated it used to be, when I could hate a man I might not have recognized on a street corner. I told her I'd wanted to wreck my mother's marriage with a sledge-hammer, if only she hadn't seemed so content to hold on.

I told her about my first crush on a boy, in the first grade, how he jumped off the diving board at the pool with the wings of his pockets out. The splash he made.

I told her about my first crush on a girl, last year, in the tenth grade, when she stood at the front of English class and read song lyrics instead of a poem. The words she said.

I told her how the first time I stole something, a glow-in-the-dark keychain from the hardware store, I gripped it so hard it almost cut my palm open. All the pleasure it gave.

I told her my mistakes. That I didn't mean to mess with Daniella's boyfriend, but it was only the once and before I knew it, they were back together. That I didn't mean to crash my mother's car, and that I'd only been drinking a little. That when I had the bottle of hydrocodone in my hands, I knew what it was. I'd done my research. And it was true I was think-ing of what it would be like to disappear, and how to do it gently. But then I thought of other ways one might go about disappearing—physical places that exist in the world, with street signs and subway stops and rooms for rent. There were places where a girl could go, and disappear another way, and keep on living.

So many of the things that had been said about me around town, in school, were lies. But when there's one speck of truth in the lie, no matter how tiny, it can make all of it seem real. It wasn't true what my stepsisters told my mother to get me kicked out of the house, but she believed what she thought she knew.

That was what I told Monet.

Throughout my storytelling, she stuffed her face. With each new chapter, it seemed she needed more and more to chew. I didn't think she'd ever get her fill.

By the time I was finished and took a breath, there were too many empty plates to count, nothing but empty plates, and I was so tired. I leaned up against the window and went silent.

Monet's eyes were shining, her cheeks filled with life.

When I didn't say anything more, her face shifted, turning more serious. "Now I'll tell you a story," she said. She leaned forward, closer to me, and put her hands on the table.

"Your mother jumped off the roof. That was the accident eighteen years ago she never told you about. She was trying to escape, and no one thought she could. She made Catherine angry, because she stole something that wasn't hers, and she left with it, and took it with her, and, really, no one has seen it since." She said this last bit so pointedly.

I shook my head. "Why would my mother . . . *jump*?" Unspoken was the question: Did she know, at that point, she was pregnant with me?

This story wasn't like Monet's other stories. There were no wild embellishments, no curving rivers or helicopters dipping low from the sky. The story of Catherine House was supposed to end with my mother on the fire escape and my father at the gate. She walked down the stairs to meet him; she didn't fly through the sky. It was a sad story, but it was what I knew, what I'd heard all my life. She gave up on her dreams and went down to meet him at the gate. Didn't she?

Monet switched gears. "So what about that thing I saw you wearing? That thing I heard you say was your mom's . . . Where'd you ever come across *that*?"

The opal. Yes. She'd been well aware during lunch that it wasn't on my hand.

"When did I tell you it was my mom's?" Had I? Did I? I was sure I hadn't. And yet she knew so many things. So much. She'd even known where to find me when I first arrived in the city, before I landed at the house. She'd been waiting at the intersection of Waverly and Waverly, situated as it was between the subway and our block, knowing I'd pause in confusion when I was walking by.

I covered my bare hand, and then, to be safe, I put both hands under the table.

"Maybe it was one of the girls who told me," she answered, and I recognized it sharply as a lie. "Gretchen, maybe. Anjali? Does it matter?"

"Someone gave it to my mom a really long time ago. And

she gave it to me." Another partial truth with a soft bit of deception attached, my specialty.

"Really," she said.

I held myself still. It was what my mother had told me, but I wasn't sure what to believe in anymore.

Monet signaled to the waiter for more water and asked for the check. But it was as she did this, as she lowered her arm, that I noticed the change in her face. A strange settling that erased the shine in her warm brown eyes, that flattened her expression.

"I'll be right back," she said. "Finish off that tart if you want."

She slipped into the back of the restaurant, headed for the bathrooms. I gazed out the window, waiting, until I realized I'd been waiting for a while.

I stood. The bill was on our table, on a small silver platter, unpaid. There were no customers at the other tables. Was this restaurant even open anymore? I went to the back hallway, passing an empty bar and the doorway of an empty kitchen, and poked into the bathrooms. There were two, unisex, as small as broom closets, gray with faucet leaks, deserted. When I returned to the main room, no one was there, not even our waiter.

Monet had taken her bag with her to the bathroom—I'd idly noticed it slung over her shoulder—and she'd ordered so much I didn't have enough money to pay.

I stood beside the table for a moment, trying to steady my panic. A streak of feet passed by the window, sunken below the street so I couldn't see above the knees. I took my own bag, pushed my chair in, and rushed out to join them.

On my walk back to the house, I noticed that the blue van was gone. Someone had moved it away, maybe for good, and it filled me with relief. I continued quickly past the spot, still headed for the house, but somehow I'd taken the long way around and was coming from the opposite end of the street, across from where I usually walked. Here, the cat lady from across the street was outside again, but this time she was sunning herself from inside an iron cage.

I did a double take. I hadn't yet gotten used to the proper way to act around all the odd activity on the streets of New York, which was to lower your eyes, shut your heart, step away. I edged closer.

It wasn't exactly a cage. Her ground-floor apartment had security bars over a box of a yard, set on concrete, right outside a door that peeked into a slovenly kitchen. It was just large enough for a lawn chair and her cats. She had many cats. Cats climbing the bars, climbing on her, dozing in the wedge of sunlight that reached into the cage, poking out from between her ankles. The cage kept the cats from running off into the street, where they'd be flattened by traffic, but the sun could still come in. And she could still people-watch and keep an eye on her neighbors. I remembered seeing her outside the garden the morning I thought I saw Lacey.

A flyer pasted on the outside of the cage caught my attention.

MISSING CAT
VINCENT
Big with gray stripes.
White belly and white mittens.
Likes to climb. Always hungry.

The woman stood from her chair and shuffled over to the wall of the cage that faced the street. "You seen my Vinny? This ring any bells? Gray stripes? Big?"

"I haven't seen a cat," I said.

Her eyes were clouded with distrust. "You live around here? You sure you haven't seen him?"

"I haven't. I live over there—"

I stopped, and a bolt of worry shot through me.

My arm was out and pointing at the building across the street. The garden gate beside it was open, and a large truck was parked outside, back gaping. A group of men blocked it from view. Parked in front of the truck was a police cruiser, and standing in obvious dismay beside it was Ms. Ballantine.

"What's going on over there?" I asked, and when I turned to the woman in the cage, she grinned. Her teeth gleamed with pearly, artificial light. Dentures.

"They've gone and done it," she said. "You live there? You know about that?"

She swept her arm to indicate what was going on across the street, what was making Ms. Ballantine grab the bars of the garden gate with her fists, what was causing the commotion inside the garden, what was making the windows of the house pool with darkness, even though it wasn't night yet. I didn't know, but remembering what had been buried in there—*who* had been buried—I could guess.

"They can't have a body in there," the woman said. "I heard some of them talking. There's zoning laws." She seemed delighted about this. She could have opened the door and spoken to me face-to-face without bars between, but she didn't. "You're in the house with all the girls? That's where you are?"

"It's a boardinghouse," I said distractedly. "I rent a room there." My eyes were intent on the garden. It seemed—and I couldn't be sure—that they'd lugged some digging equipment inside. Were there really laws that would make them have to suddenly dig a body out of a grave? And what would that do to Catherine? A shudder overtook me. "I'm sorry, but really, I haven't seen any cats around here." I said that as if the conversation was closed, but still I hovered and made no move to cross the street. I couldn't go yet. *I'd* done this.

"I've lived in this apartment seventy years," the woman said, raising her voice so I couldn't ignore her. "Seven-oh. I was a girl. It was my parents' apartment before me."

"That's nice," I said, unsure why she was telling me. Ms.

Ballantine, speaking with a police officer, noticed me from across the narrow street. She shaded her eyes in my direction. She lifted her arm. Time turned slow, and I felt sure she was about to extend her arm and point, point right at me, and then the officer would turn and he would see me.

But instead Ms. Ballantine shifted and blocked his view of me.

The old woman noticed none of this.

"You think I don't remember," she was saying.

I took a few steps away. I was thankful for the cage now, for the barrier.

"I know you," she said. "I told you about my Vinny already. Why're you pretending like I didn't tell you? You said you would look for him after your acting class. I remember now. You said you would look for my cat, but you didn't."

"I never said that."

With great effort, the old woman stood and came as close to the bars as she could manage. She had her hand on her chest, where she wore a gold cross necklace.

She touched it to her fingers, as if to reassure herself. What kind of monster did she think I was, because I denied talking to her about her missing cat? I couldn't help it—I laughed.

"I knew it was you," she said. "You don't forget a laugh like that."

Ms. Ballantine had drifted away now, and it appeared the police officer was leaving. I waited for the car to pull away before I crossed the street.

"You give him back!" the old woman called, and I froze in the middle of the street, where I could get run over. I slowly turned around.

"My cat," she called. "I know you've got him. You bring him here to me."

I kept walking.

She continued calling after me, but her voice faded.

I was near the garden now. I was prodded forward by the quiet in there, by the green. When I pushed open the gate, it creaked like an animal crying. And when I followed the path to the grave, I saw that the plants were mashed down, crushed by numerous feet. The path led me right to the monument, the headstone, but beneath it was a gaping hole in the dirt. A hole where a coffin would be buried.

"What are you doing in here?" a man said.

I bent down and picked up something that had fallen off the headstone—a miniature Eiffel Tower.

"What's she doing? She can't be in here."

They led me out, but not before I gleaned what I could: There'd been a complaint about the garden that belonged to Catherine House. This land near a home was not approved for a gravesite.

All of this would have mattered and possibly caused an incident, and great trouble, if they'd opened up the grave of Catherine de Barra and lifted her century-old skeleton out in its box. If they'd disturbed her for reasons of zoning and taken her away from this house. I could imagine a thunderous darkening over the block. Tree branches whipping in the furious wind. The cat lady across the street maybe needing her cross of protection then, for whatever curses and wishes of destruction might be on the way.

I could imagine all of that, but there was no need.

Because there was no body buried inside that grave. We all had been told that Catherine de Barra's remains were here, marked by that stone. All girls in the house were told this. But if her remains had ever been there, they were somewhere else now. Gone.

———

When I entered the house, it was to a hush. The others now knew. Some girls had been watching from the windows, and Ms. Ballantine was making an announcement to a group gathered in the parlor. We would clean traces of intruders from the garden later, she explained. We would fill the hole with dirt. We would place the offered items back on the headstone. All this, even if there was no body. We would go on as we were, because this was our home and would always be, and Catherine deserved this from us.

Always? The weight of that word hung low. The others whispered, faces close together, furious. No one opened the circle and offered me a space to listen. Some even edged away from me, making sure I couldn't overhear.

I was about to slip upstairs to see if I could find Monet when Gretchen stepped into the outer room and marched over to me. "All this is because of you," she said. "You called the cops on us." She gripped my wrist as she spoke, and she was stronger than I was. This was what it felt like, to be the one held down.

I started to say I was sorry, to try to explain, but she wasn't finished.

"You and your mother." She spit out that last word: *mother*. "It's because of the two of you. She was the one who was supposed to free Catherine, she was the last tenant, in the last room, she came at the right time, we were all waiting, and then she left and never came back. She's why none of us can leave now."

Gretchen had just told me more than anyone else would. But she was also accusing and insulting my mother. Another girl had come up now, freckles like puncture wounds, eyes twitching. She stared at me, and I wished she would stop. She wore a washed-out dress with old-fashioned buttons climbing up to her throat.

Gretchen let go of my arm but wasn't finished. "I told her she was thinking only of herself, but she *didn't* listen. She *never* listened. Just like you don't listen."

She was talking about my mother.

"What do you even mean?" I said. "You never met my mom."

Gretchen snickered, then shook her head. "Linda," she said, to the girl buttoned to her throat. "Can you believe this girl? What's the point of her?"

All of it was nonsense. The mist may as well have escaped the picture and engulfed everyone in the room. I felt the same sense of impossibility and confusion as if it already had.

Yet all the while, a screw inside me was turning. A tight, boxed-up part of me was coming loose, a crack of light seeping in. What was this place, and how had I been fooled?

I imagined them ganging up on me on the gold carpet. All of the tenants coming at me, the drop to the floor, the names spit down, the inevitable kicks from all their shoes. Ms. Ballantine in the circle and the stab of her heels.

I started up the stairs again, and Gretchen called after me.

"The police were after you, but Ms. B protected you! She wouldn't even let them up to see your room!"

I kept going.

"Something about an art gallery!" Gretchen called. "What did you do? What did you steal?"

I hurried up the stairs, fast, six flights, three landings, and made a swift turn onto the fourth floor, my fist pounding on the door to Room 10. No one answered, and the knob was stiff, surely locked, but when I jiggled it hard enough, the door just pushed in.

I entered Monet's room. There was no one inside, and the window was pushed all the way up, without a screen, obscenely open, so anyone looking could see everything.

In all the years I'd pictured the room my mother had lived in, and hoped I would one day stand inside, I didn't think about how oppressively hot it would be. How very small it might be. How dingy. How sad. How the fire escape marred the view.

How the floorboards creaked, how the bed was so tiny, how there wasn't room for anything worth having at all. I had the exact replica of this room, one floor up, but my mother's stories had made hers seem so different, so special.

Monet wasn't in the room or on the fire escape.

This time, I did the climb myself, as she would have. I could have barely told us apart, except she had longer legs. I was feeling outside myself, reckless, the way I felt when I'd been drinking, as if I had nothing to lose, apart from the fact that I kept losing, over and over again, and in whole new ways.

My own window was wide open, also pushed up as high as it would go, which wasn't how I'd left it. Usually, when I went out, I kept my window open a crack.

I slipped in off the fire escape onto my bed.

My door—the one that led out into the common room, the ordinary door—was swinging. I was positive I'd locked it before I left, because I always locked my door, so the only way in would have been through the window.

I sensed something had been taken, but I forced myself to be hopeful. I closed my door, locked it, moved the dresser to hide the view, crouched down, and checked behind the radiator. My hand was back there, reaching, worming around. I could feel pointy objects and soft ones, carved items and souvenirs made of shell and glass and stone, all pieces of my collection. There was a moment when I couldn't find the sock I'd had to use instead of my mother's blue schmatte, when it seemed that the space contained only air, but then, before I could panic, my fingers found the opal wedged in deep where I'd kept it, still secure.

I pulled out my arm in relief and dropped flat on my back, on the hardwood floor.

The rest of my room had her prints all over it. I knew she'd gone searching again, that she'd sifted through the contents of my drawers and my closet and every surface, and yet she hadn't found it. My hiding spot was too good.

But, still, something wasn't right. My head pounded as if a ferocious thing had taken up residence deep inside my bad ear.

My eyes lifted, slowly, to the opposite wall—it wasn't bare the way it had been before.

The painting of my mother was there now. Monet had removed it from where it had been sandwiched between my mattress and box spring, and she'd hung it openly, so I would have to see it, on a leftover nail.

FIRE ESCAPES

WE DIDN'T SPEAK OF WHAT HAPPENED IN THE FRENCH RESTAUrant. Not that night, and not in the days that followed. I was almost embarrassed about all I'd told Monet, how bare I'd stripped myself, all the clumsy, honest bits I'd revealed. It made me wish I had a dark garage to hide in until the shame passed.

I'd taken to sleeping near the window so I could leave a part of myself dangling out on the fire escape. A forearm. A hunk of hair. My bad ankle, attached to my foot. It was slightly cooler there, where the breeze began, and I was getting used to the height. I could imagine myself as someone else, until I happened to pass a mirror and see who I was. Purple eye and lip, the pair of them apparently a part of me now. Sweat-frizzed hair. Eyes gray today, or green, or maybe blue, depending on the shirt I had on. Partly my mother's face, but mostly mine.

My life in the city wasn't turning into what I'd hoped. The bookstore on the corner denied me a job stocking shelves and ringing up customers, and my cell phone stopped connecting, the account suspended into dead air. In my mind, where I could keep avoiding truth, I denied the inevitable end to my stay in Catherine House. Money was running out. The thirty-first was coming swift and soon.

When I closed my eyes at night, I could feel myself sinking. The bed turned softer, too yielding, and I drifted lower, until I hit hard ground. Sometimes I woke to the smell of smoke, the crackle of kindling, and I bolted upward, thinking we needed to evacuate, but it was only the faint scent of my memories. That campfire was from another life, almost a different body. Once, I woke with a leaf in my hair, small and summer green, as if from a dream. It must have blown in from off the street somewhere, that's all.

If I could, I would have told my mother about Monet. "Have you ever met a girl like that?" I would have asked. Practically a new color of hair every day. Sewn up with secrets, but whole other worlds flashing in her eyes. And then there were her stories. Sometimes she said she was from a one-stoplight town out West where the sky was so enormous you might believe nothing was left on the planet but it. Other times she said she grew up breathing coal mines, or at the craggy edge of the ocean, or that she learned to drive in a city where the streets were carved from cow paths and confused all manner of cars. Some days she was one person, and other days, from a different angle, she was someone else. My mother, an actress, a chameleon, might have been able to figure her out. She would have told me if I could trust her, if she was or had ever been a true friend.

Toward the end of the month, we gathered for the photograph. Ms. Ballantine told us to meet in the parlor, gold-bottomed and decorated in more sneeze-inducing gold, the mythic Catherine lording over us all. In the minutes before, there was a flurry of commotion at the bathroom mirrors, freshening lipstick and checking nose shine. I felt a part of things in a way that made my heart fizz up, my cheeks go pink against the usual purple. Harper helped with my concealer. Ana Sofía attempted to help with my hair.

Downstairs, everyone crowded before the fireplace to find a spot. This was where the pictures of the Catherine House girls were always taken. Sit in the middle, they said to me. Let Bina have a chair, they said. Someone told Monet to move to the back because she was tall, and she took the spot behind me, directly beneath the portrait of Catherine, having to stand on her own two legs. Her hair that day was maroon. The others, my housemates, pressed in around me in rows below and above, crammed in close, eyes forward to lock with the lens.

Ms. Ballantine stood before us with an old camera so heavy she kept it supported with a strap around her thin neck. "Five, four, three . . ." she began.

I couldn't keep still. Something was gnawing at me, shadowy-soft.

"Smile, Bina," someone hissed beside me—Linda, the tenant with the dark spatter of freckles. She'd been staying here forever, she'd told me, so long she'd forgotten what for. Muriel had been here for quite a while, too—she acted like she didn't know what year it was beyond the gate. This was a boardinghouse, meant to be temporary, but something about appearing in the photograph with these girls was permanent in a way that made me uneasy, as if once snapped it would feel like living inside that cage of cats on the street.

Time to smile. I let my mouth open, though my head was pounding and my ears had that hum. Maybe thirty-one days here was enough, though I'd hoped to stay the whole summer. I'd done it. I'd proven I could leave home and be on my own. Wasn't that enough?

I couldn't know what Monet's face was showing in the picture, because she was behind me, but I know what my face did when the shutter opened and we were captured.

I showed my teeth and played pretend.

I was coming down the stairs the next day when I spotted them there at the door.

Two police officers, both men, suited up and small-eyed, pistols bragging from their holsters. They were speaking with

Ms. Ballantine. It was an opportunity, a twist of fate I could keep twisting. I considered letting them see me, letting them know I was underage and probably flagged in a database of runaways, so they could sound the alarm and call home. But something wouldn't let me. I backed up and kept to the top of the landing, concealed by the shadows. I edged an ear and an eye out, attempting to listen and see.

Ms. Ballantine's narrow body blocked their way. Her arm stretched across the doorway, her yellow hair catching the light and throwing it in their faces. She may have been slight, but she wasn't budging an inch. Even if I'd wanted them to find me, she wouldn't have let them.

I couldn't hear what they said—if they asked for me by name, what they knew—but I could imagine. A couple of girls were near the decorative vase, eavesdropping in better range. One of them—June (long, lonely face; never spoke of home)—turned toward the staircase. She pointed up at me and gave a slight nod. *Yes. You.*

Message received.

From where I stood, from what I could decipher, the officers wanted to enter, but Ms. Ballantine kept them outside, in the punishing heat. I may have been the careless girl who called the city's attention to the garden, which called their attention to me, but I was one of hers and still had her loyalty, even if I wasn't sure I wanted it. Besides, the officers were men, and Ms. Ballantine had a healthy distrust of men, uniformed or otherwise. They'd never be allowed up to my room to spy the stolen art I now had hanging, openly, frameless, on the otherwise blank wall, thanks to Monet.

Still, I strained to hear. I realized my father must have sent them after me. He wanted me apprehended, cuffed and charged, jailed and spending my nights on a cold metal bunk. I'd have to tell my mother all about this during my one phone call. Assuming she'd answer.

In my mind, I'd already spent a decade behind bars and was able to bench 140 pounds when I heard Ms. Ballantine answering them extra-loudly, as if to carry the words up through the foyer and along the staircase to where I lurked.

There was no tenant here by the name of Sabina Tremper, Ms. Ballantine said. She'd never heard of such a girl. And if they could not provide a search warrant, they should see themselves down the stairs.

The two cops left soon after, in defeat. The chandelier glass high over the room tinkled, as if with antiauthoritarian glee.

Once the door was closed, I came safely down and watched them through the windows. I saw them exit the iron gate from my perch behind the heavy velvet curtains, deep-breathing in the mildew, wondering if they'd turn around.

If they did and happened to see me, would I stay put so they could have an unobstructed view of my face? Would I tell them my name? What would I do?

Ms. Ballantine was suddenly behind me, an ice-cold hand on my shoulder. Her jewelry had such deliberate weight. "There's nothing to worry about," she said. "Getting the proper search warrant for this house—*if* they do—will take days. And when they come back, I'll tell them the same thing I told them today." She smirked.

I believed it. To any parent or friend or the NYPD, she would lie and deflect to keep us here, safe. Maybe my father *did* bang on the front gate and yell for my mother to come out eighteen years ago. Maybe Ms. Ballantine told him there was no tenant here by the name of Dawn Tremper, even if she was there, hiding behind these same curtains that probably hadn't been washed since that day.

June eyed me, as did the girl with her, as did another girl from the chaise.

I watched Ms. Ballantine take the stairs up, finished with our discarded visitors, to her room on the second floor. I followed and soon was in a hallway separate from the tenants' quarters, where the walls turned more decorative, wallpapered and not so dingy, with colorful glass wall sconces instead of overhead fixtures, nice moldings, smooth and clean. If other staff members were housed here, I never saw any. Ms. Ballantine's room was at the end of the hallway, and the door was open. A cavernous space stretched toward a bank of windows. She had four, all to herself. Brocade curtains, deep mauve, hung to the floor, and a four-poster bed, high up on oiled oak legs, marked the center of the room. Bright, abundant light cast in from the garden.

But most noticeable was the way the temperature dropped as I drifted in the open doorway. She had air-conditioning.

"Miss Tremper," she said.

Not a question, and not a command to leave. The cool air was so refreshing that I stood in its reach, letting it touch me.

"Didn't you hear me tell you all is well, and it's very likely they won't return?"

Part of me wanted to apologize. For the police visit, for the desecration of the grave, even though it wasn't a grave, for being trouble, as I so often was. But something was bothering me. Something was clicking inside my head.

"I usually don't allow the tenants in here," she said. "We've had issues with *thievery*."

Someone who liked a small, significant object to hold in her hand, to worry it smooth in her palm, to hold it fisted under her pillow, to stow it away in the hollow behind her radiator, would know from a quick casing of the room where the best collectibles would be found. In this particular room, the vanity. A gold satin jewelry box on top.

"Yes," Ms. Ballantine said. "That was our Catherine's." She self-consciously stroked the bracelets on her bony wrists, her rings. She saw my eyes drift to a rocking chair by the window, to its blue satin cushion. The only blue in the room. "And, yes, that as well. In fact, all of this was. The furniture, the tapestries, some of the items in the chest and in the closet . . . I've kept it intact, as she would have wanted. She appreciates it, I know. It helps make all of this easier."

She was living in a dead person's room. How old *was* Ms. Ballantine? How long had she been caretaker of this house? A chill crept up my arms and swirled around me.

"What did you come here to ask?" she said.

I swallowed. "I was thinking about my lease . . ."

Her face went oddly blank.

"I only paid through the thirty-first," I reminded her, though if she didn't remember when my lease was up, maybe I shouldn't have mentioned it. "That's Sunday," I added. I wanted to punch myself, but it was done.

"Yes," she echoed. "Sunday."

"The thing is, I don't have enough for next month." Truth: I had a handful of dollars above zero, plus some change. I had no extra beyond that, nothing saved. Besides, if someone had called to hire me for a job, they couldn't have reached me once my cell phone got shut off. "And so I think it's time . . . I guess . . . for me to go home."

How difficult it was for me to say that, but once it was in the air, spoken aloud in this grand room, I turned clearer and more conscious. Ready.

Only, Ms. Ballantine wasn't responding. She was watching me intently, taking her time.

I started to add something, but she stopped me.

"Miss Tremper, I need to tell you: This conversation is completely unnecessary. And a little troublesome." She turned to a corner of her room, there where the rocking chair stood. She gave a quick nod to the chair, as if someone in it had offered a suggestion. "Miss Tremper, the dates on the rental agreements are a formality. You weren't clear on this?"

I shook my head.

"This keeps happening," she said. "I'm not sure why the confusion."

None of it made sense. How did she expect me to get the money for another month? Was she saying I could stay for free? She had to be. Days ago, I might have been relieved. I wasn't anymore.

"Now, if that's all . . ." she said, waving me toward the door.

I could have left then. I almost did, was turning for the door and everything, when the chill cycloned around me. The question came right out from nowhere.

"Do you remember my mom's accident?"

Her neck cracked. It made a brittle sound. "I was waiting for you to ask. I thought it would be long before today."

"Oh. I guess I didn't know if you'd tell me."

Her face darkened. "If you're here to confront me about why we didn't go to the hospital, why we left her out there . . . if that's why you're here, I want you to know we felt bad about it, but there was nothing we could do. Not for her. Not anymore."

"Nothing you could do?"

"It was after curfew," she said. "And it was a far fall." She paused. "Such a tragedy she broke her leg."

So that was it? How my mother's story in the city ended? I wanted to sit down with this news. The daring, delicious magic of her time in the city was fizzling.

"She didn't come back after," Ms. Ballantine said. "What we heard, and I believe it's genuine, is that when she was at the hospital she discovered she was having *you*."

The math added up—if she'd left my father and spent two exhilarating months here in this house, they could have been the months she was pregnant. Which meant I was here, once before, when she was.

"I expected you to ask," Ms. Ballantine said. "In fact, I brought it up from storage for you." She went to the closet and returned with a cardboard box, taped on top. Marked on the outside was the name Dawn Tremper, the dates she was here, the year.

I must have made a sound as I took it in my arms. I was trying so hard not to.

"Your mother's things. Her papers, her souvenirs. She had a collection of photos of herself, glossies, the same picture, dozens of them."

"Her headshots. For when she went on auditions."

She sniffed. "Your mother paid on time. She met curfew. There were so few infractions, until that night. Our problem was the screaming."

"The what?"

"For her audition. That was the one role she did get, as I remember. Dozens of auditions, and one role."

The movie was a slasher film, a black-and-white short. In it, my mother said she screamed so much she lost her voice. This box contained that experience and more. The sound of her. Her plans. Her budding dreams. Yet the box wasn't heavy at all. So much hope, sitting in storage all those years, and it hardly weighed a thing.

There was a creak of floorboards in the hallway, and we both turned at the same time to see who'd come, but it was no one and nothing. Empty doorway, empty hall.

When I swiveled back, Ms. Ballantine's face had changed. There was a different light in her eyes. "Is she here?" she breathed. "Is she in the room with us right now?" Her voice was high and hopeful, like a little girl's.

I turned again, but no one was there.

Ms. Ballantine stepped nearer to me. There was plush carpet under her black heels, nothing threadbare, not in this room.

"I've never seen her outside of that picture," she confessed. "Not in all these years. But I sense her. I feel her near me. Sometimes I think I hear her voice"—she tapped her temple—"in here."

She was ramrod straight, alerted to any movement at the doorway, but all it showed was the hallway floor and the hallway wall. Both were brightly lit, not a shadow.

"Is she angry?" Her eyes blinking fast. A hitch of fear in her voice.

"I . . ."

"She reached out to you," Ms. Ballantine said. "She woke when you arrived. It's you. As it was your mother before you. Please, what do you see?" She'd believe anything I told her.

As I contemplated the endless cruelties I might inflict with the power she'd granted me, I happened to glance to the other wall.

Shadows aren't solid or built of hard lines, but in this one a texture of skin could be made out. Ridged with fur, as if she'd been growing mold for more than a hundred years.

A sick, cold feeling pulled from inside my own body, telling me we had a connection—that thing in the rocking chair and me.

I started backing away, careful to keep her in my sight.

We shared something. I didn't want to know what, couldn't let myself see what. Except she smelled like my last night in the woods had smelled, like fresh, sour-wet dirt when my face was mashed into it and I didn't think I had the strength to get up. She fell a long way, and they say she never landed, but I can imagine what she might have found at the bottom if she had. I knew what it tasted like. The grit on my tongue.

Ms. Ballantine had been right about us not being alone in the room, but her sense of direction was off. She was standing in the doorway, far across the room, to be close to what she thought was Catherine. All the while, the rocking chair by the window rocked back and forth, back and forth, silently moving. The shadow in it swallowed the garden light.

There was a thing people used to say to me, at home: *You look so much like your mother.* Catherine didn't say it out loud—she couldn't without a mouth, could she? But she was thinking it again. She did whenever she saw me. Her thought wormed its way into my ear.

"I have to go," I told Ms. Ballantine, rushing for the door. "I have to get this box upstairs." I took off, pushing past the cold spot in the room. It was only an ordinary vent in the wall, blasting out cooled air for the living, and I was still able to feel it.

———

I was on the stairs. I had my mother's box, still sealed, at my feet and the group portrait containing my mother close up to my nose. I'd wiped the dusty glass as clean as I could with the hem of my shirt, but it still wasn't clear enough or close enough to see her true expression in the frame.

I registered Monet behind me but didn't turn to greet her.

"Where have you been?" she said, at my back.

"Right here," I said. "Around."

She hovered. I was so aware of her proximity, her bare arms, her long legs, the way she slipped off her shoe and crunched her naked purple-painted toes to the floorboards, the way her lungs took in air as she breathed. Somehow, knowing she was there calmed and centered me after what I'd witnessed in the rocking chair. Even my mother behind glass hadn't done that.

Finally I tore my eyes away and turned. She was a redhead today.

"You okay?" she said. I said I was. "You sure?" She grabbed my hand, but I didn't know what she was really doing until she shook it, as if we were two gentlemen meeting during a stroll on an old-time cobblestone street. Her smile was so smooth. But there was nothing on my hand for her to take.

"If you're still looking for it, it's not on me," I said.

"Whatever do you mean? Looking for what?"

She knew what I meant, and I knew she knew, and yet we kept the words off our lips.

"You're keeping secrets," she said. No judgment, simply an observation.

"You told me to on the day we met," I shot back.

She nodded. "That I did."

It made me think how she'd been completely unapologetic about leaving me with the bill at the restaurant—in fact, she never brought it up. After our lunch alone together in the dark quiet of the low-ceilinged space, tucked away under the street, a dot of chocolate from a croissant melting at the corner of her mouth, after all the secrets I'd given her and not one in return, after all that, she wouldn't be real with me.

"I *know* you've been in my room," I said. "Don't deny it."

"When? How? I'm just coming upstairs now."

"The fire escape. You crawled in my window, you were looking for my hiding spot, but you didn't find it . . ."

Once I said this out loud—the slip of mentioning the hiding spot, acknowledging that in fact I did have one, and it was inside my room, still to be discovered—I shut myself up.

Her eyes had come alive, and that should have concerned me, but something else caught my attention. As it did, a chill started creeping up from my ankles.

A crease of concern in Monet's forehead. Her voice so loud. "Are you really all right, Bina? Are you having one of those episodes again? You know you don't look so hot, right? I think you need to sit down."

An *episode*. The last person who'd said that to me was Ms. Ballantine herself, my first afternoon in the dusty coffin of her office. And my head did hurt, but it was an ache I was getting used to, an uncomfortable hum in the background, always with me, more so when I slept.

This wasn't anything to do with that.

It was my mother. My young mother captured in the frame of the group portrait. She'd changed, the same way the portrait downstairs liked to change. Now, from out of nowhere, she wore a fierce, urgent stare aimed out at the viewer—me. She stood in the topmost row, directly under the frame containing Catherine de Barra, packed in tight among the other girls, with her mouth gaping as if to say something important, her arms caught in a frantic wave.

She was shouting something at the camera. Waving at *me*. Warning me.

I swore she hadn't been doing that before.

I went up close to it. "Mom?" The image became blurrier the closer I got. I tore it off the wall, but her figure clouded, a textured series of dots up close, unidentifiable as anything other than a field of black and white and gray.

Monet was peering around wildly. The stairwell twisted above and below us, with shadows leaking from the walls, but no one else was there to witness this. I dropped the frame on the floor—maybe it shattered, I don't know—picked up the box instead, and tore off upstairs. I heard her calling after me and her footfalls on the stairs behind me, but I was inside my room with the dead bolt turned, sitting on the floor with my back against the door, before she could get through. I was always the one curious about her, wanting to follow and eavesdrop, to soak in, to understand.

Now she was the one chasing after me.

She went away after a while. She left me in peace. So I got up off the floor and told myself it was time.

What my mother must have wanted was for me to open the box. I had the weight of everything she had to say in my arms, all the answers.

Except at first I didn't understand. Inside the ordinary brown box was another: a shoebox large enough for a pair of knee-high boots, though it contained no boots. There were no headshots, either. Instead, I found the very things I'd been admiring all my life, the items pinned on the bulletinboardovermymother'sdresserathome.Somehowthey were here.

I spread them out all over the floor of my room. The photographs weren't the kind she would have used for auditions. They were candid, soft-focus, a carnival of color. Her hair in different shades and lengths, her face forming different smiles, some sweet and small, some midlaugh, with a view of her tonsils. I'd seen these pictures already—but now I circled them in a new light, trying to understand. Her arms slung around the shoulders of girls who were so familiar, mugging with them on a fire escape, posing with a wriggling gray-striped cat in her arms.

I held up the last photo, trying to get a closer view of the cat. White belly. White mittens. The cat was identical to the one on the old lady's flyer.

There was also her collection of ticket stubs from clubs, movies, plays. I knew every story. At the bottom of the box, a four-leaf clover preserved in a tiny plastic baggie. I remembered how she told me she found this lucky four-leaf clover in Central Park. She'd been so mystified at having come across one in her lifetime, spotted as if by magic in the giant expanse of green grass. Now it was magic, or something much worse, that transported it here.

Every time I tried to invent a solid explanation in my head, that same creeping chill came over my body, a high-pitched notion from toes to fingers to ears to the top of the head telling me no.

No.

There was a rustling sound on the fire escape—not a mourning dove that had made a nest, not wind, but something more shadowy, and deliberate. But I couldn't care about it. My emotions got the best of me, and I couldn't stand to have all these impossible things in front of me anymore and to be forced to connect the dots. I shoved my dresser aside and went for the hole, squeezing as much of my body in the slim space behind the radiator to shove the old Dawn inside, where I couldn't see what I'd been avoiding. She'd been trying to follow Catherine's footsteps in escaping, and she had, she'd made it. She'd been brave all along, and for some reason she never wanted me here.

When I tunneled my hand in, it felt like there might be another hand reaching from way back in her top dresser drawer off Blue Mountain Road, all the way down here, for me.

———

It was dark, night already, when I made it out to the street. Ms. Ballantine's office was locked, so I couldn't use the landline in there, and I didn't want to ask one of the others if I could borrow her phone.

I didn't expect it would be easy to find a pay phone. But a few turns away, there was one on a corner, an ancient, stickered, sticky contraption shielded from weather in a silver booth. I lifted the receiver and miraculously heard a dial tone. There was a slot to put actual coins in, and it said local calls were twenty-five cents, a quarter each, which was how much they were when my mother lived here.

But my call wasn't local. To be safe, I shoved all four of the quarters I had into the machine, punched in the digits, then let it ring.

My mother never answered a call from an unfamiliar number on her cell phone, but I thought someone in the house might answer the line hooked up in the yellow kitchen. I was right. Daniella—the one least likely to hang up—was the one who said hello. I'd gotten lucky.

"Let me talk to my mom," I told her. "Give her the phone."

There was some scrambling on the other end as she realized—that I was calling from this fuzzy, unknown number, that it was me, really me. So much static.

When she came back on the line, her voice was so serious, and it was still her, not my mother. "*How* are you calling?" she said. "I don't understand."

"I'm on a pay phone."

"Oh my god," she said. "Char, come here. She says she's Bina. Calling from . . . I don't even know where. She wants to talk to Mom."

"Don't give Mom the phone, you freak."

"Hello?" I said.

I heard Charlotte in the background. "If it's really her, tell her to go away."

"I can't just tell her that."

"Tell her to go away and stay away forever."

Daniella returned. She hesitated and said it in a mouse voice, but she said it. "Stay away," she said, through a haze of static. "Forever."

She hung up. I had no more quarters, but the static kept hissing.

I'd lost track of time. It was a weeknight, which meant an early curfew, and I should have been inside, in my room, not out here, aching, on the street. I should have—

"Miss," someone said. "Do you need help?"

No one had ever taken much notice of me on the street before, not enough to offer to help me. This wasn't what the city was supposed to be like. It wasn't what my mother told me.

I pushed past them—a woman in black, another two women in black; everyone wore black here like they hoped the night would make them disappear. Then it did for a moment. Then I was alone. I wasn't myself. Dizzy by a lamppost. Needing to catch my balance. Sitting with my feet in a sewer grate on the curb. I couldn't remember which way Catherine House was, which turns I'd taken, which corners, which crosswalks, how many stop signs, what I was doing, where I put my keys.

"Hey, girl, can I call someone for you?" A manicured hand was holding a bejeweled phone right in my face. I wanted to grab the phone and run, outright snatch it like a thief and go flying, but I also needed to lie down on the sidewalk, because my ankle was aching, wouldn't work anymore, my legs wouldn't either, and all I could see was through a pinhole in my one good eye.

A curtain of darkness drew itself closed around me, and then, with the sound of a train coming, it all went white like a blank wall in a bare room.

———

I burst through, falling backward. Someone had me by the arms, holding my weight, and then let me go so I was crumpled on the small patch of concrete on the other side of the gate. This was the familiar front space of Catherine House, a city yard without any grass, and I was inside it somehow, the hulking iron gate shielding me from the street.

Some of the others had gathered around me. Gretchen. Lacey. Anjali. More.

Their voices filtered down.

"She tried to stay out."

"She learned her lesson."

"Leave her alone." It was Anjali, bending over me, eyes fierce. "You shouldn't have done that," she said to me.

"Where am I?" I asked.

"Home," she said quietly. "Where you belong."

Now that I was safe inside the locked gate and whatever commotion I'd caused was over, the other girls lost interest and started up the stoop. There wasn't really anywhere for me to go—up against the iron fence to hold the bars and feel the wind coursing through, or up the stairs with them, behind the sleek black door and behind the curtains, inside. I would, but not yet.

In time I noticed I was alone out there but for one set of feet.

Purple-painted toes.

One foot nudged me, gently, not to hurt, and then the long legs bent and the face leaned in so close. Her hair was fire tonight, every shade of flame.

"I'm leaving Sunday night," she said. She paused. The city screamed all around us, and I wasn't allowed back into it; I'd have to wait for morning. "Maybe you could come with me."

I tried to read her face. My eyesight was coming clear again, both eyes working now that I was behind the gate. "How?" I asked.

She scratched her nose. As she did, I saw it. The opal set on the simple silver band. She wore it facing out so it made a dancing pattern all over her hand. It fit her so perfectly, but appearances didn't matter. Intentions did. Purpose.

The rustling on the fire escape had been her. I hadn't been careful enough when I went for the hiding spot. I hadn't been thinking, and as soon as I'd left the house she found it and made it hers. There was some small part of me, still kicking, still thinking the link to my mother mattered, that ached to grab her arm before she knew what was coming and wrestle it out of her hand. But I didn't have the strength to confront her, and besides . . . it looked so right where it was. A person like me shouldn't be allowed to have something like that. I'd ruin it.

"Your mom knew the secret," she said. "I don't know how she found out. But I'm going to try. My lease is up Sunday. Isn't yours?" Monday was the first of August, a month I never thought I'd be allowed to have in this house. Now I saw I couldn't escape. My mother was trying to tell me that. The other girls had tried to tell me that. And Monet knew it all along.

I reached up for her hand, but only so I could get on my feet and make it up the front stoop.

Maybe it was the opal twinkling on her finger. Maybe it was actually believing something she'd told me for the first time.

"Meet me on the roof right before midnight," she said. "Sunday."

She started climbing the stoop before I could answer, yes or no, or did it have to be the roof, and why and how, and are you sure I can come with you? I didn't ask her, but it wouldn't have mattered. In the month I'd known her, Monet Mathis had shown me how much she loved avoiding the truth. If I wanted to trust her, I'd have to connect the dots and bridge the pieces myself.

I followed her inside and closed the door.

THE EDGE

SUNDAY NIGHT, THE LAST NIGHT OF JULY, I BRAVED THE LADDER at the topmost level of the fire escape and climbed up to the roof. I came empty-handed, alone, and not entirely sure what to make of all this. But I had to come.

The rooftop was smaller than I expected, the bottom sticky and smudged, like flypaper at my feet. The air and everything around me was dim, a murky warmth that was golden in some places but mostly gray, and the view was of a sweep of lights, outlines of rooftops stretching into the distance, uncountable. Then there was the constant hum, coming from boxy structures housed on roofs and buildings nearby, from all around us, above and below. I didn't go close enough to the edge to look down—I couldn't—but I knew the street was on one side and the private garden on another. A crack of darkness showed the thin vertical space between buildings, and I kept my distance.

Monet appeared from behind a chimney.

"You're here," she said. She seemed surprised, which made me feel small. Then she leaped over and took me by the hand to show me her private area and her own personal vista of the city, and a thumping started in my chest. She'd asked me to leave with her. I almost, in that moment, believed she knew a way out and was about to show me.

On the tar-covered expanse, Monet had set up a lawn chair, a crate on which to rest her feet, and a gold-velvet couch pillow borrowed from the parlor furniture downstairs. Scattered on a low wall were a toy-army pair of binoculars, old snack wrappers, and a few grimy green goblets from the dining room. She'd spent lots of time here. On the roof below the wall was a bowl with cat food in it: dry kibble.

There wasn't another chair for me, so we stood in her den and peered out. No other human beings could be seen on rooftops in any direction, and for a moment it seemed we had come to a forgotten part of New York and had the city all to ourselves.

"Is this what you wanted to show me?" I finally asked. If we were planning our escape from up here, I wondered if it might involve a rescue from a helicopter, her long-lost spy of a mother at the controls, reaching our arms up into whipping wind. I wondered if it involved a story she had yet to tell me, one featuring a walk across a tightrope between buildings or scaling down the side of the garden wall with mountain gear, carefully creeping past Ms. Ballantine's wide wall of windows.

I was hopeful, and open to anything, but she didn't offer a story yet.

"Yeah," was all she said. "Everyone's always asking where I go at night. Where else could I go? *You* know what happens after curfew."

I did know—and I didn't. There was a blank spot in my memory over how I got back that night. I was at the curb near the phone booth, and then I was on our side of the gate. Next I checked, the lock was secured, the chain intact, and all I knew was there was no way back through it.

"But what about my first night? Where'd you go then?"

"I *tried* to stay out," she said. "But I couldn't make it past the garden."

A warm feeling came over me: She'd let me in on something. She'd told me a true secret.

"I just thought you should hear it from me before I go," she said.

Before I go. Hadn't she just admitted it was impossible to leave Catherine House?

She walked away from me and sat in her lawn chair. She had her seat aimed toward the dense blocks of Midtown, where the Empire State Building glowed white that night amid the other tall towers. A chimney top protruded behind her; she could tilt back in her chair and not fall, and the spires and less romantic things, like water tanks and bulbous knots of electrical wires from other surrounding rooftops, faded into the low light.

She seemed to be waiting for something—but what? Was it me?

Her eyes could have been any color in the night—it was too dim to tell. She had her ordinary hair showing, nothing different to disguise herself with tonight. My mother might have been on this very rooftop when she'd had her accident, and she never returned after. She never spoke of what happened, not even to me. That was when I knew. It was happening again.

"It's almost midnight," she said. "That's when I have to do it. Don't look at me like that. I know I'll make it." She was crossing to the far edge of the building. It was where we saw the blue light we all told ourselves was Catherine de Barra. She stepped toward it with such determination. It made my knees feel loose, my stomach shake.

"But—" I started.

She turned and cut me short. "Curfew is a lie," she said.

I remembered the legend about Catherine. How the air had her. How the night took her. But how the hard ground never came. The pavement never met her. The night never let her body go, as if it wanted her entirely for itself. That was the story Monet had told me my first morning in the house.

I shook my head.

"I'll make it," she said. "Come." It sounded like a promise. She leaned over to see what was down there, but I couldn't meet her. There wasn't a railing; there was only a narrow ledge. The air was too boundless and uncontained where she wanted to go.

She shielded her eyes with her hand and looked down. She still had it on. Surely she hadn't taken it off since she found where I'd kept it hidden.

The opal there on her finger. The low light of the rooftop liked its deep darkness, but now I could see the colors swirling inside. Red and gold, blue and green, all tumbled around inside the black stone, moving faster than I'd ever seen before. The opal had come alive. The black was warm and flushed. It showed the universe above and around us, the galaxy of uncountable, unreachable stars. It wanted her to do it; it was telling her it was time.

She was smiling, but so sadly. Was that pity on her face? The dark was hiding so much of her expression.

"What's the first thing you remember about this city?" she said. "Quick. Don't think too hard. From the day you got here."

I wanted to say *her*, bumping into her in the fork of a double-named road. But I picked something else and pretended it was what came to me first. "The train," I said. "Going through the tunnels."

"Grand Central?" she said. "I remember that, too."

It wasn't what I expected. I'd always imagined her coming here from far away—arriving on a plane that swooped down from the sky, pulling up to the house in a speeding taxi or, better, a glossy black SUV, bare legs sliding out from the back seat. There could have been mystical ways to arrive, too, foggy in origin, lacking in explanation, simply appearing like a dot

274

of color in the night sky. But she'd arrived on a commuter train. Same as me.

"I hope I get to see you again, Sabina Tremper from nowhere interesting," she said, softening the blow. "If you make it, if you wake up and you get yourself out, that's where you'll find me. Just after midnight by the clock. I'll be looking for you."

"What are you saying?" I started, but it was too late. I'd gotten scared, and she'd seen what I was made of. I'd ruined one more thing.

She backed up.

"Wait, what day?" I said. "Midnight when? Tomorrow? Next week?"

She didn't answer so mundane a question. She circled, only once.

"Wait," I said. "What if you don't make it?"

I sensed her right behind me, her breath on the back of my neck for a tense second, her muscles coiled, ready. Then she ran to gain momentum, and all I can say is there wasn't a way to stop her. It was almost like she flew.

It was midnight and the light in the air was blue and it was already happening, and I wasn't a part of it. My hesitation had cost me. I'd held back too long.

I probably could have told the story a hundred different ways, depending on who was listening, but the truth was this:

She dangled in the beautiful black for a moment, and I swore her eyes were wide open, and I swore that this was a moment that lasted long enough for me to remember it always, to feel it in my own body, to know it in my bones. The part of the story I didn't tell any of the other girls, and wouldn't ever, happened when she lifted her hand.

My mother once did the very same thing, but her arm was raised for the sun, to try to flag down passing cars. Monet's arm was curled, her hand in a fist, and I swore it was aimed at me. A pop of light came, blazing and burning a perfect circle in my retinas. I was dizzied and stumbled back, shielding my eyes, and I heard it drop somewhere close to me, somewhere so close, with a *ping*.

When I opened my eyes again, there was no girl in the sky anymore. There was no burst of brightness. She'd been a ball of legs and light and amazing stories and perfect secrets, but she wasn't there anymore. She had disappeared from view.

The wind carried the smell of burning wood. A siren wailed somewhere across the city for someone else. I pulled myself to my feet. And I made myself start walking. And I did what I knew she wanted, because there wasn't anything more I could do. I went to the edge, and I looked down to search for her in the street.

―――――――――

It was only in the hours after, once I was sure she was gone, that I went looking. I searched and searched to see what had dropped from the night, what I suspected she'd thrown to me, but there was nothing on the sticky tarred surface of the rooftop, nothing I could find in the darkness. I had to climb back down the ladder by myself. I had to sit alone in my hot room and wonder if it would forever be this stifling. I was facing the fact that I had missed my chance. I might not ever see Monet, might not ever see my mother again.

The night was empty, and I'd ruined it for myself. I'd ruined everything. When I saw that she'd successfully cleared the gate, when I saw her stand up, illuminated in the glow of the streetlamps, where I couldn't reach, when I saw her grab her suitcase and drive off in that taxi, I knew it would take such a long time to get over this.

I'd never met a better liar, or a girl I admired more.

I hoped that she might turn the taxicab around and come back for us, help get the rest of us out, ram that gate and knock it over and set us all loose into the streets, where any terrible thing could happen but it would be our choice, our risk, our running feet. I hoped for it all night, but it never came.

LOOKING AT THE SKY

MONET MATHIS MADE IT OVER THE GATE EASILY. I FIGURED SHE knew this night was coming and always knew she'd make it. Maybe even since the first day I met her and she met me, she knew.

By Monday morning, she was still gone, but I was unsure if any of it had even happened. All I knew for sure was that I was awake—and she wasn't in the house anymore. She wasn't in the room beneath my room, but out there, somewhere, without me. I could have gone with her, but I'd been afraid.

As soon as the gate was open, I went out into the street to search for the opal ring. I'd been sure for a single moment in all the confusion that she'd tried to toss it to me, but I'd combed the rooftop for anything remotely shiny, anything at all, and all I found were some bottle caps, foil gum wrappers, and one marble, a weathered cat's-eye that had probably been up there near a hundred years.

Still in my pajamas, I checked outside in front of the house. The streets had been cleaned and the trash picked up. I noted a shattered crack in the sidewalk that hadn't been there before. Nothing else marked what had happened only hours ago in the night, what I'd witnessed from up on the rooftop, and what strangers and passersby had witnessed from down in the street. The rules of the world bent to fit Catherine House for one striking moment, and then the world righted itself, and people tried to make sense of what it was on ground. Even I had done that. I was still doing it now.

Not too far away was the crossing where I first saw Monet, at Waverly and Waverly, one street that became two, or two streets that became one—maps didn't explain it. It was where I'd stumbled into her, which could have been simple coincidence. Sidewalks filled with too many people on any given day, and you're bound to run into someone you'll see again later. That's all.

I returned to my room and locked myself in.

As the sun continued to rise, I remained where I was. There was barely any air in my small room, but I didn't go out on the fire escape to try to catch a breeze. I sat on the edge of my narrow bed facing my exposed brick wall. Between the bed and the slim desk was that microscopic floor space, identical to the space between her bed and her desk, enough to lie down lengthwise, skull skimming the wall and toes pointing at the door, where I'd spent some hours listening to her. A cloud of dust rose up as I dropped down to my familiar cool spot on the creaking floorboards. My ear to the modest patch of space between bed and desk, I took in the stillness below, the airlessness, the emptiness she left behind. She really wasn't there. I closed my eyes. I let my limbs go slack, my weight sink. If she decided to come back, this was where she'd find me.

Morning turned to afternoon; I didn't know when. I only knew the floor had turned hot and I didn't understand anything and I was alone.

When the door to the room beneath mine banged open—easily, she hadn't left it locked—I was startled into sitting up. Some girls had gone in to ransack her room, and they were banging around down there, rummaging through her stuff. The noise carried up through the floorboards.

One of my legs was asleep, all pins and needles from having been on the floor so long. My head felt the same. But I leaned hard on the banister and made it down one flight and to the doorway of Room 10 in time to find a few of them left: Gretchen was at the closet, checking the top shelf. Ana Sofía and Linda were searching Monet's desk drawer and under her bed.

They'd been in the room not much more than a minute, but the damage was done. Her bed was stripped, sheets balled up at the bottom. Her dresser drawers were gaping, her hangers scattered across the mattress and floor. But they were too late, and they must have realized. Monet had packed what she wanted already. What was left behind were only the things she didn't care about anymore.

Colorful heads of hair were piled on the mattress. Monet had emptied out her room when no one was paying attention, but she'd left her wigs behind. Every last one.

Linda grabbed a few (the lavender one, a blond one, the peppery-blue) and left.

Gretchen closed the closet. "Most everything's gone," she said to me. "When did she get it all out? I didn't see her do any of this. Did you?"

I shook my head.

Ana Sofía slipped out, and then it was Gretchen and me, the two of us, alone. She towered over me. I could see the taut tendons in her throat.

"Did she tell you where she was going?"

"No."

Gretchen dropped down on the bed with a thump and hunched her shoulders. Her usual defiant commitment to wearing black—thick black rims around the eyes; black from head to toe—would have been terrifying to her family before people knew what a goth was. She'd scared the twins, she'd said. But now she seemed like a shadow. A sad bra strap hung down her arm, washed-out pink, the worst color of all.

"But *how*?" she said in a tiny voice. "How'd she get out?" For the first time, it occurred to me that even Gretchen might have wanted to leave or stay the night somewhere else at one time or another. I didn't want to ask how long she'd been living here. I didn't want to know how old the twins were now.

"I don't know yet," I said. I sat at the edge of the bare mattress. How could one girl leap over and stay out, and another get thrown back in? Would any of us ever have a chance like that again?

"I never trusted her," Gretchen said, her voice hard again. "I never thought she was really one of us." She stood to her full height, almost knocking me over. Then she kicked at the desk chair until it toppled against the wall.

In the commotion, the gold-bound book she always carried and kept close fell out of the long folds of her skirt. It skittered and landed, faceup and wedged open, on the floor between us. I got to it first, so she had to watch as I lifted it up and found a random page. We met eyes. I flipped through some more, scanning the pages at the beginning, the pages at the back. They were blank, every one. Gretchen removed the book from my hands. She lowered her head so her bangs hid her eyes, and left the room.

Now I reached out to close the door and seal myself in, to take a moment in private. I righted the chair and sat down. If Monet had left something important here, I didn't want anyone else to find it.

The girls who lived in this house didn't really have Monet's back, not like I did. There was a point at which you threw your lot in with someone. There was a point when you were all in, and there was no scrambling out of it when you got scared, or found morals, or wanted to save your own skin.

I would tell Monet all of this, if only I could get to her.

As I sat trying to make sense of what had happened, I heard a sound outside the window. There was the flash of a tail on the windowsill and a meow. A gray cat stepped into the frame and assessed me. When I reached out to gather it in my arms, it snarled and batted me with a jagged, white-furred claw.

"Hey," I said, "Vinny, come here." He hissed and wouldn't get any closer—I may have been in her window, but he knew I wasn't her. "Did she forget to feed you?" I asked, though it occurred to me that maybe the food bowl had been left up on the roof with the crumbs of kibble for me to take over. But it didn't matter—the cat was too fast for me, for anyone. With one leap, he was down on a lower level of fire escape, and then on the fence and then into the narrow alley.

I was crawling back in when I spotted it. She'd tied a polka-dot scarf to the ladder, one I had a passing memory of seeing tied around her artificial hair. Cupped inside the scarf was a folded postcard, muted colors peeking out.

Water lilies.

"Funny," I said.

No one was there to agree.

Monet's message on the blank side was difficult to decipher in her horrendous handwriting, and it took some squinting and a fair amount of interpretation to make it come to life:

If you don't have it back already, check the body.

She didn't have to sign her name. I knew.

The card was crushed in my hand. I knew immediately that she meant the opal, and I knew from those spare sloppily scrawled words that she'd always meant to give it back to me. By the body, she meant Catherine de Barra's empty grave.

All of that as impeccably clear as if she had her mouth to my ear.

But another part came more slowly. The why.

When I'd peered down on her from the edge of the rooftop, down and down after she defied physics and proved she had another life still to live, she'd been looking up right at me. It was as if she'd expected something, as if she were waiting. As if she were waiting for *me*.

I'd never named what I felt for her, because something this amorphous, something this tangled, couldn't find itself a name. Maybe it was only that I wished I could be like her—so reckless, and at the same time, so sure.

I had to sit down, fast. The heat was all up in my head. My mouth was so dry, and the tiny room was steaming, with not just my confusion but the first-day-of-August heat. My shirt was damp against my neck. I was having trouble breathing.

This had been my mother's room for a short time. Before I came to be, the girl who would become my mother slept inside these four walls, dreaming her dreams. I was beginning to understand I was one of them.

I rushed out and dove for the bathroom off the fourth-floor common area—it was closer than mine upstairs. I had to climb over a scattering of shoes. A chunky purple heel caught in the bathroom door before I closed it and secured it with the dead bolt.

One of Monet's floormates was banging on the door. "This isn't even your bathroom!" she shouted. "C'mon, you know you're not supposed to be in there."

"I just need some water," I shouted back.

She pounded on the door, but I didn't open it. I let the faucet run and leaned over the sink, letting it cool my arms up to my elbows.

My mother used to tell me how she'd get into character before an audition, before her big role in that small movie. She'd close herself into a bathroom with a mirror—the smaller the room, the better. She'd lock the door. She'd stare into the glass. And she'd tell herself who she was. If she had to scream it, she'd scream. She'd look into her own face, and she'd do so much as shout it at herself until she believed. Eventually, no matter how long it took, she would emerge from the bathroom as that character, that person, an invention that real.

"But what if the mirror didn't work?" I'd asked her. "What if you didn't believe?"

"Then I'd never be able to come out, would I?" she'd said.

The mirror showed my face, and what it showed me was something I hadn't wanted to see for thirty-one days. It seemed like someone had punched me hours before, the bruises and scrapes fresh and searing.

The girl in the common area continued banging, rattling the door in its frame, but with the dead bolt in place, there was no way to open it. Soon it sounded like she was joined by a second girl. They both needed the bathroom. I opened the door, and they almost tumbled in on top of me.

"It's all yours," I said. Then I went for the stairs.

Outside, I made it to the gate that led to the garden. The chains had been loosened. Someone had been inside since the excavation. The green ivy poking through the bars in the tall fence bristled with energy, as if someone—something—were still in there.

I fumbled with the key and swept the yellow police tape aside, letting it drift away in the wind. The gate opened outward, showing the lush green inside. When I closed it, the whole city went quiet.

I pushed through, all the way to the back, where the dirt was freshly packed near the headstone, and a slab of granite had been placed overtop, as if to make whatever was down there stay down. The offerings—the coins and stones and pieces of glass, the souvenirs and tchotchkes, the carvings and weathered creations—had been returned to where they'd lived all these years, before the city disturbed the ground here. In the shaggy grass, the cherry-tomato plants were trampled, red fruits smashed, nothing edible remaining.

I orbited the grave, empty but for our pretending, walking around and around, trying to figure out what Monet had meant by her note. Did she nestle it safely under some leaves? Did she dig into the dirt beneath the monument and shove it in as deep as it would go, and should I have brought a shovel?

But when? I'd witnessed almost every movement she'd made between the rooftop and the taxi, apart from when she disappeared. There hadn't been time to go to the garden and hide it, for me or for herself.

It occurred to me that I only thought I knew her. Only thought I had ahold of what went tumbling through her mind, her outlandish plans, her best intentions. I didn't know the girl, or anything substantial about her. I hardly even knew myself.

That was when I spotted it.

There on the top of the headstone, where I swore I'd checked already, a gleaming spot of all imaginable colors in a bed of bright black called to me. There it was, like an illusion.

It had come loose from the setting—the silver band was separate, and bent, as if it had fallen a long way and gotten crushed in the process. But the opal was there, almost the way I remembered it. A crack now showed deep in its center, with a small chip apparent at the surface. Otherwise it was intact. And solid enough to take in my hand.

I closed it up in my fist just to squeeze it, and then let it sit on my open palm and catch the light of the garden.

The opal had the dark multicolored sheen I remembered, dancing with possibility. It wasn't all black; that was the magic of it. It was blue, like a sapphire, and red, like a ruby. It was green, like an emerald. It was purple, like an amethyst. Orange, like fire. It was dangerous to be so many things at once.

Maybe, before it was a piece of jewelry, it simply came up out of the ground like this, otherworldly and ominous, beautiful and brutal, but most of all mysterious, like a life unlived. I still didn't know how my mother had gotten hold of it eighteen years ago. When I'd asked if a boyfriend had given it to her, and if that boyfriend had been my father, she had laughed and said, "Oh no, something this important would never come from a boyfriend. You could only get something like this for yourself."

She'd said it saved her life. Now, I considered, it might have had a hand in saving Monet's.

And Monet had made sure it found its way back to me.

When I reentered the house, there was a heated gathering downstairs. My first reaction was to hang back, but then I saw what had their attention. It wasn't me. No one said hello or seemed to notice I'd gone outside. No one asked if I'd been trying to find her. Monet's name didn't even come up.

The mob of girls was in the parlor, all turned toward the fireplace, talking over one another, craning their necks and shoving, trying to push one another aside to see for themselves.

Ms. Ballantine was among them, crowded up close to the front, able to touch the portrait with her bare hands, though she didn't, as if she would mar it with fingerprints.

I couldn't see with them all in the way, but I could feel the way the air in the room had changed. It was thinner. My breath was shallower in my lungs.

I coughed, and Anjali turned to me. She was at the back of the crowd, wringing her hands. She spoke in a muted voice. "I just want to go home," she said.

I pushed past Gretchen, tall enough to block most anyone behind her from seeing what was happening on the wall. Tears streaked down her face.

Near her some other girls, Lacey and Ana Sofía and more, were shaking.

Harper was at Ms. Ballantine's shoulder, gripping the spindly bones of her arm. "Who did this?" Harper was saying. Ms. Ballantine didn't even have her voice to chime in. Harper whipped around, facing us all, and the energy in her eyes was disturbed, the tendons in her neck grotesque. "Who. Did. This."

Once Harper moved, accusing everyone around her, she created an opening, and it was then that I could fully see. The black-and-white photograph was in place in its frame on the wall, but nothing was moving behind glass.

The chair was empty.

The photograph had always been centered around that chair—young Catherine de Barra posed in it, hands turned into a knot on her lap, face aimed at the camera and shel-lacked in a silver haze. She was always observing and keeping track. Her eyes—solid as midnight—followed us wherever we went in the room, until we were out of reach, outside the perimeter or up the stairs.

Yet, now, no one was looking. No one was in the chair.

That was the first thing. The second was the crack in the glass frame.

I rushed for it. I pushed through. Harper jumped aside, and even Ms. Ballantine let me get close, her bony shoulder pressed into mine. I got as near as I could. I needed to be sure. I even had to feel it with my fingers, get my hands on it, so I'd know it all the way through. In truth I should have known already, as soon as I saw what happened to the opal.

The crack in the glass was the same shape as what I'd seen worn deep into the center of the opal. And there, in the place where her face had been, the glass was chipped. The crack shot outward from there.

Catherine de Barra was no longer posed inside her own photograph. She wasn't in the picture, and she wasn't a shift-ing shadow in any corners of the room. She wasn't shrinking back behind the long drapes. She wasn't stretched out on gold-velvet furniture, flickering in our eye line, then gone. She wasn't assembling and disassembling in particles of dust. She, like Monet, had abandoned us to our own devices, turned her back on us all.

"She's gone, isn't she?" Lacey asked.

She was.

Ms. Ballantine went for the closest piece of furniture—a footstool, gold and no longer grand—and dropped her weight onto it. Her head was in her hands, and I saw the white of her scalp and the gray roots growing out behind the faded yellow dye. Her fingers seemed so much bonier now, her skin almost translucent.

She looked so old. If she'd been around when this place first became a boardinghouse, as I suspected, she would be far older than a century. Which was impossible, of course.

"What are we going to do?" Harper said.

I kept to the edge of the crowd now, studying them all and seeing how quickly it had fallen apart. Everything was crumbling, and Ms. Ballantine was a shadow of herself. Had Monet done all of this, even let Catherine loose? Or did I have something to do with it, since I was the one who'd found the opal in the first place? Did I ruin one more thing? Yet here I was, my feet planted on the gold carpet, threadbare in more spots than I'd wanted to see, holding fast.

With heavy footsteps, the girls separated, some edging to other parts of the parlor, some drifting to the communal fridge to forage, some making their way upstairs, to their rooms. No one knew how living here would be different tomorrow, and none could put it to words. All we knew was that we were still here.

I, too, ended up in my room. I tried to close off all thoughts of Monet. She wanted me to meet her at midnight, but I didn't know how I'd get out—if I ever would. The cracks between the floorboards were soundless and smelled of dust and wood. The fire escape was empty and so quiet.

There was something left unanswered. It had been there above my head all these weeks. I tipped my mattress over, stood it and the box spring up against the other wall. I shifted the dresser aside. The small door in the wall was never locked to me, and opened as easily as ever. The lightbulb clicked on. The stairs barely groaned under my feet, the brick casing I climbed through as narrow as before but holding me in place, making me feel safe.

At the top, where the bricks were stacked and the exit to the rooftop sealed off, I pressed my cheek to the rough surface. Up at the top of the passage, it was all darkness, but on the other side of this wall, on the roof, I knew there had to be a door.

———

The woods at home hold a certain scent that's sharper and fresher than anything that grows in the city. Pine needles and tree bark, the running water of the brook that stretches through the forest, crisscrossed by highway and fallen trees. It seeps into your skin, especially if you've spent a whole night deep inside, where the tree covering is thick, the ground damp, and every turn or attempt to get out a trick meant to keep you circling.

I am back here again, in the woods the night of the party. I've never left.

The dark drops forward at my feet, and I am at the edge, not sure if I should take a step. I'm right here, poised at this edge, at the moment that changes everything. The wind catches, and tangles through my hair. Pain buckles my knees, and I need something to hold on to, but there is no railing here. There are no lights here—no windows, no ledges to catch my feet, no strangers to crowd around me on the sidewalk and find my body.

A sound from behind me—the crack of a branch, a howl of wind that to my mind sounds like it might be coming from an animal or, worse, a girl.

With my last burst of energy, I start to run, and then it happens. When I fall, it feels like a mile between me and anything else. Maybe it is. I start kicking, but that only speeds things up.

The sight of all the stars doesn't make a difference. They streak past, and I can't hold on.

Then I'm at the bottom. My ears are ringing. I'm holding my phone, and the light in the forest is pale blue, an otherworldly glow. On its face is another face: my mother's. She's calling me. She's calling me, she's been calling me. I try to pick up, and I hear her shouting my name over and over into what sounds like a highway full of rushing wind.

When the phone goes dark, it takes my sight with it, and I

lie there, at the bottom of the ravine, with the blue light at the edge of my eye line gone and not coming back.

A sound close to my ears rattles me. It's heavy, and choking.

It's me. It's the sound of my own breathing, slower and more ragged as the night goes on.

———

Silence sifts into my ears and makes its way deep into my head. It rustles like leaves, and then it cracks.

I'm still here.

Light blares, and my eyes blink open, trying to adjust. I'm warm now, though not much of me can move.

I see a pair of brown work boots squared before me. They crunch branches underneath as they edge closer, and that's how I understand what that is. The cracking sound. Those are the dead arms of trees.

The light now is far too bright, until it separates into many lights. The face is the only thing that blots out the sun.

The boots stay put, but the face turns away. "I found her," a deep voice shouts.

The sound of others coming closer, feet crunching through brush. The sight of wild coils of weeds high up above, as if I'm far away from anything green. Whistles blow, piercing the air as if to communicate with one another, which causes my ears to ring. I'm unable to turn my head or close my eyes or open them or move any part of me or make any sound. I'm unable. Even if I try, I can't do it. I'm a part of the dirt on the ground. A whistle is the last thing I hear.

"I found her," a panicked voice said. Light was casting down at me, circling me and shocking me, and I was putting my arms up to cover my face. Anjali was there, trying to get me to stand up and come out.

I wasn't at the top of the stairs anymore, but somehow down at the bottom. When I scrabbled out of Anjali's grasp and craned around to even see the stairs, to see how dark they were around the bend, there were none. No stairs. The small white door in my wall *was* open, but to a closet. I was inside a low-ceilinged compartment in the wall that didn't lead up, or out, or anywhere.

"What were you doing?" Anjali asked.

Lacey drifted in the doorway, acting concerned. "You were making noises."

"Weird crying, howling noises," Anjali added.

"We thought you had an animal in your room," Lacey said.

They watched me for a long time, both wary, though they helped me close the unnecessary door and set my bed to rights. They put the dresser back where it was, and picked up my desk chair, which had fallen.

They seemed resigned to our lives here, resigned to

another night inside, and when I said I didn't want to join them for dinner, because I couldn't afford the money they were all pooling for takeout, they let me be.

———

I didn't want to come out again until deep in the night.

It was late enough and at the same time early enough that the other girls on my floor were still sleeping. I could have the shower to myself for as long as I wanted. When I cleared the fog from the bathroom mirror, opening a streak with my hand where my face could be made out, it was different. Something had changed. The mirror was mounted over the sink for a taller person, and so I had to strain to my highest height, on my toes, the very tips, in order to see my whole head.

Steam from the shower was leaking out of the air-shaft window, unclouding the glass. My black eye was fading. The purple that had seemed to never go away was fainter. The scab on my lip was closing. And it was once I saw myself that I realized: The constant pulsing pain at the back of my head that I'd gotten used to over the course of the month wasn't there. My bruises were healing. My head ... it was almost clear.

Back in my room, it came over me, the desire to start over, to try my hand at being a new kind of person. Carefully I crept down the stairs with a pillowcase full of the things I'd taken over the past four weeks. I'd cleaned out the hollow behind my radiator, whatever I could reach, so if I missed anything it was because it was rammed in too deep. I'd put my mother's things aside and took the rest, all of it, every last piece. The last thing to go in was the portrait of my mother, lifted from the nail on my wall.

Outside girls' doors, I left the items from my collection, offerings, the way the people in Catherine de Barra's life had left them for her. I returned the strand of silver beads. I returned the library card. I returned the lipstick, the pocket-knife, the ribbon. I returned every pen. I may have gotten some of the rooms wrong, but my best intentions were there.

Two things were left. One was the stone.

It was slick with sweat now, crushed into the deep center of my closed fist. I could feel the chip. The gouge went deep, a crack that seemed to want to split it in uneven halves, and I kept myself from digging in with a finger and breaking it entirely apart.

I could have kept it, I could have sold it, I could have saved it for the moment I met someone worthy and given it away. But it didn't belong to me. It didn't belong even to my mother, and she'd kept it near her all these years.

I needed to let it go. Maybe that was what made me climb out on the fire escape and hold it up to the night. When I opened my fist, it was shaking and unable to stay still, as if I were releasing a living thing.

With force, I tossed it high, willing it above the roofline, across the garden, and beyond the fence.

I followed it with my eyes, singular and bright like a shoot-ing star. Then it broke apart, it shattered, and the pieces went in every direction. The sky went from gray to purple. It went from blue to green to pink to beyond all colors that had names, perfectly black and every color contained in the color black, and for just a moment the sky over Catherine House was opalescent, alive with the shards of the broken stone, magnified and multiplied, and the most beautiful and devastating thing I'd ever seen.

Then it was done.

I grabbed the railing to steady myself. My fingers were stained purple and blue and black and green.

When I peered down, the tall iron gate that separated the house's small front yard from the wild, uncontained city was swinging. It was always locked at this hour, from inside and outside, held fast with a chain. But now a faint breeze moved it back and forth, back and forth.

I needed to be sure. I climbed back inside and went down all the stairs.

In the foyer, I looked through the tall window beside the front door, the stained glass mashed up against my face. No one was out there.

At this hour, the street beyond our gate was like an abandoned set from a movie—no one around and no cameras rolling. A ghost town.

I unlocked the front door. The gate was still open. I could still see it swinging. Its chain had fallen to the pavement.

I took the stairs down and stood in the opening for a single moment.

Then I pushed it wider. And walked through.

I didn't latch the gate when I left. I let it swing so its creaking would call to the others, and then I pressed the buzzer nested in the gate. I jammed my finger in, and its electrified screech carried up the stairs. No one was awake to answer the door, but they'd hear the buzzer from their beds. The girls in the lower rooms would hear it more clearly, the sound puncturing their dreams, entering their small rooms and finding their ears on their sweat-drenched pillows. I wanted to go back and wake Anjali, and Lacey, and even Gretchen and the others, but they would hear it. They'd hear it ring and ring, and then they'd find the gate swinging.

Even now, as I paused at the corner and let myself look back, I saw a light come on in one of the rooms. Lacey's room. I saw another light, in another room two floors up. If I waited long enough, I was sure I'd see the front door open and one of the girls—I hoped Anjali—slip out in bare feet, curious.

Me, I needed to start walking. I could have chosen any direction. Uptown or downtown, east side or west side, Bleecker Street or Sixth Avenue or all the ways Waverly went winding.

I aimed myself at the heart of the city. My feet were on ground, and there were so many blocks to go, but for the first time ever I felt like I belonged here. My legs felt so long. I almost felt like I could reach up and touch the sky.

PART FIVE

Sometime After

THROUGH GLASS

THERE IS NOW ONE LAST THING TO DO, AND IT IS NOT AN EASY thing.

I am at the window, on the dark side of the glass, watching my mother inside my stepfather's house. There's a motion sensor over the back lawn, but it won't find me. I'm safe. The neighbor's dog, chained out front, can't hear me. When the wind picks up, I almost float.

My mother doesn't know I've come back. That I'm here at this particular window near the ragged embankment of trees, to see how she's faring in his house, with me gone.

She's alone tonight. He has a work dinner again—I spotted him heading for the driveway in his tie—and the girls left minutes ago, talking of a party at someone's house, contained to a gated backyard. From what I hear, no one wants to party in the woods after a body's been found, and they think it's ruined summer. Still, there has to be some kind of party, with the same eternal argument over who would buy beer.

The house hushes, as if a cloud moves to cover it. Inside, my mother has awakened and started moving about the rooms.

I still think of this split-level ranch, painted moss green and showing the beginnings of a termite infestation, as *his* house, always will, no matter how many years she stays married to him and shares the bedroom. It never stopped being his house, from furniture to what hangs on the walls to cups in the cupboard. The only place ever truly hers was the room she rented, tiny and dusty with the narrow bed and the one window, that summer she lived in the city. That's what I used to tell myself when I thought I knew what she wanted.

I haven't been able to go inside the house, and so I stay to the periphery, outside the walls, peering in where I can. Sometimes, some nights since I've come here to look in on her, I find my mother in the rocking chair he makes her keep in the hallway. She nursed me in it, the story goes. We found it at the end of the driveway, with the garbage bags on trash day, soon after the new family moved into our old house. My mother stopped the car, got out, and sat in it for a while, rocking over the gravel. It crunched. "This should be yours one day," she said. In a fit of strength, she carried it over her head to the trunk, but it didn't fit, so she wedged it into the back seat, with two of the legs pointing out the window. When she brought it back to the house, there wasn't room in the bedroom she shared with him. There wasn't room in the living room or the den, either—it didn't match the furniture—and so here it lives, at the end of the corridor, near the tall window facing the back bend of trees. The seat cushion is blue.

On this visit, the rocking chair is empty.

So is what I can see of the kitchen.

The plush sofa in the den has the remote on it and nothing else.

I wait for many minutes to see her cross the floor of her bedroom and make her way to her dresser, which is just in view. She opens her top drawer and digs in the back, as she used to, deep in, but she doesn't pull anything out. It's not in there, if that's what she's searching for. I see her at her dresser as if she's been keeping something precious in there, but it's gone and not coming back, no matter how much she hopes to find it. I've let it go. The next thing to let go of is her.

She takes her hands out of the dresser, empty.

She gazes at the pictures pinned over her bureau. There are so many of me now. When she looks at them, I wonder what she believes and remembers, what stories she tells herself.

Now she's closing the drawer. She's walking past the suitcase, the one she'd packed for me that night. She hasn't moved it from the space beside her dresser in all this time. I imagine that inside it, my clothes are still rolled into compact balls, and there are at least ten sets of clean underwear. She made sure.

She's leaving the bedroom and heading down the hallway, coming closer.

I want her to.

Once she sits in the rocking chair and pulls the string for the light, I get that sweet, singing feeling I always do when she's near and has come closer to the glass. She's barefoot, and her hair is slightly longer. Her back is to me, and I can make out the whorl in the center of her ear.

She lifts a book from where she stowed it on the side table, but she doesn't part its pages. She rubs her bare arms as if she's caught a chill, though it's still summer. I noticed the month on the kitchen calendar. Some years she'd go with a Degas or an O'Keeffe or even a Dalí, but this time it's the impressionists again. She shivers as if she's cold, as if she's forgotten it's summer and that everything starts and ends in summer. Summer is the time for reinvention and release. Summer is when the electricity is most charged, the night has the most potential, the roads lead in every direction, and the skies are mostly clear.

She's in one of those moods again—the set of her face tells me. She has stopped tending the small garden patch beside the driveway. I think she's stopped going to yoga. Sometimes she sits with a book in her lap, without lifting it to read, for hours at a time. Whenever the phone rings, she jolts and shoots a glance at it, then deflates before answering, as if she knows the person she wants to be calling won't ever be on the line.

I want to make her understand.

I want to communicate with her, somehow, the way we used to.

All she needs to do is glance over her shoulder. My breath might leave behind the hint of a face, and she's my mother, so she'd recognize it. Who else would? I wish my knuckles could make a sound on the glass, that they could hit so hard it'd shatter. But maybe it's better this way. I don't want to scare her.

It's taken me enough visits, but the time is right. I may not be able to come back, after tonight.

I am not sure where to leave it to keep it safe from the elements, and I don't have anything to wrap it in. Insignificant things I once owned, like my old hoodie, are long gone.

It's as ugly as I remember. As terrible as it was the first time I saw it, in my father's possession. But maybe when someone who's hurt you has stolen something from you, and kept it from you and priced it for sale on his wall, you can't rest until it's returned to your hands. Even if you didn't know it existed, wouldn't you want control over it, if you knew? She might tear it apart with scissors, or douse it in gasoline and light it up in the pit in the backyard. She might bury it in garbage at the dump, or scratch the canvas clean away to bald white. Or she might not see herself in it at all.

But I want her to know she can trust me, even now, to protect her heart.

I know she tried to protect me.

I leave it propped up against the glass. Just as I touch it—warm and cold at once—I feel the electricity where I used to feel my fingers, and I have to move back. I'm fighting the wind to stay even this close.

She's standing. Her eyes have gone wide. I swear it. This time she sees me. This time we have a dark moment together, across time and space, through glass.

She's reaching for the door. She's breathing so fast. I'm not.

But once she opens it, she doesn't look into my eyes or anywhere near where I am. She doesn't say hello or invite me in. She bends down and reaches out. Her hand is like my hand— same fingers, same fingernails—or at least it used to be.

She finds it and lifts it into her arms. She knows what it is. How could she not? I'm just not sure if she knows who brought it here.

She checks the backyard. She puts a hand over her eyes, searching.

I know she wants to call out to me, but she doesn't. She's not yet ready to admit it out loud, to say my name.

Behind the house are only trees, but she spends a long moment scanning the fringe, as if I could be out there somehow and might have climbed all the way to the top.

She grasps the painting closer in her arms, and shuts the door to the night. She fiddles with the lightbulb, but it's dead, so she heads to the kitchen. From there she heads to the living room. She never looks to be sure again, and she never lets it go.

I could watch her from the window for the whole rest of the night if I wanted. I could wonder what's running through her mind, what pieces are connected from rooftop to rooftop until they meet here, where she lives.

I do wonder what she's thinking now as much as I wonder what she was thinking then, standing on the topmost point of Catherine House, her toes curled at the edge. Did she believe the stories about Catherine? Did she know the opal would help her get back home? Did she expect a whole other future to catch hold of her in the air, one that might hurt, talons on her back, carting her away? Or did she just fall, an accident, a mistake . . . one that led to today?

I'll always wonder.

I hold steady in the glass for a long moment, longer than I should, seeing straight through to the inside rooms, because there's no reflection. Then, when I'm ready, I let the wind tug me away.

PASSENGERS

A STREAK OF WHITE LIGHT AND THE ECHO OF A VOICE IN MY EAR:
Wake up.

I'm awake. The late train rolls into the station, lights flickering, wheels cranking, passengers in the seats around me animated, alive. There's no intercom announcement to tell us we're here, only the passing underground platforms to show that the heart of Grand Central Terminal is within reach. The shadows in the tunnels are so clear now. When I press up against the glass, they ripple with attention. As the train rolls past, their heads lift, their forms drift closer, as if I'm burning the brightest of candles in this window, from this particular blue vinyl seat, and they need to acknowledge I've come.

The train reaches the end of the track and pulls into the station. It might be the same platform from that summer afternoon thirty-two days ago or a thousand, I've lost count. People crowd the aisle and plunge toward the doors at either end of the car, aching to get out. There are fewer passengers at night, but they're louder. Their anticipation leaks.

A girl sitting near me is slower, and all alone. She has a small suitcase she needs to get down from the rack and a pink sleep crease on her face. Whoever she is, she steps on me while pulling the suitcase down, and doesn't say sorry. Then she's gone.

On the platform, bodies surge past, a stampede that sets me reeling and keeps me back. I wait for them to leave, wait for the conductor to vacate the train; then I listen. The mouth of the tunnel is quiet and filled with folds of velvety black. Nothing is coming after me.

I slip out into the main concourse, where tickets are sold and where hundreds of thousands of people cross within a single day. There, under a tall domed ceiling containing a dizzying mural of the constellations, there in the center of the grand room, is a circular information kiosk. And its pinnacle, its centermost point, is a tall four-faced clock, glossy brass and golden in the light. There can't be any other.

Just after midnight by the clock, she'd said. *I'll be looking for you.*

I'm early. Only ordinary people drift near the kiosk now. They ask questions, they plan trips. Their feet are on ground, and not one of them is the girl I've come to meet.

The air is gold-tinged, shimmering with the smallest particles of dust. Soot and grime cling to the edges of the room. Still, the clock's faces shine—legend says each face is made of pure opal—and they're telling me I still have time. Once midnight is here and gone, I'll know for sure if I've missed her, but until then I can't keep still. I circle. I have no luggage and nothing to hold me down anymore, and I might be moving faster than I should, disturbing people gathered to wait for a coming train. Sometimes they stare after me, wondering. I'm a blur at the corner of their eyes. A moving shadow, gone when they blink.

To get a better view, I rise to the platform where the two staircases meet. I see others like me on the concourse, slipping by, hoping when maybe they shouldn't still hang on to hope, and we recognize one another well enough to keep to ourselves. I suspect that on any given day, Grand Central is teeming with us. We're another kind of passenger.

It's the rest of the people I search, to see if she's among them. I pause on faces and certain bodies as I pass. Sometimes they appear as familiar as a living memory, vivid with color and taste and surges of light, but only for a moment, and only because I'm making an effort. None of them are the girl I'm seeking. Once, I think I see a face I don't want to see, walking forward with her meager mouth pinched, her daggered eyes on the downstairs gates. But if that's her, free after near a hundred years in the house she is said to have died in, she's not here for me. I tell myself it could be any other angry young woman traveling through this city. There must be so many.

When I return my gaze to the center of the concourse, the clock shows it's a minute past midnight. Then another, and one more.

She's not coming. I took too long, and she didn't wait.

Just then I feel a tug, and I look to a shining face of the clock one more time. The glass is milky and shifting in tone in the station light.

Then I see her.

It might be her. It could be.

She's a shadow near the kiosk, a slippery form out of the corner of the eye, same as me. We are the same, and maybe always have been.

She has her back to me, and there's a moment when I question myself, when her movements make her seem like someone else, and then in the next moment, it's clearly her, it can't be anyone else, just as I'm now someone new, with a clean slate and a second chance. Outside the house, neither of us wears a mask.

How many nights has she come here? She said she'd be looking for me, but for how long?

I've reached the bottom of the stairs. I'm crossing the floor now, getting closer. The details of her don't matter. Hair color. Shoes on her feet. A dress that's black or blue or something else entirely. Even with her back to me, I notice the cowlick sticking up in her hair, her long legs and the way she leans, and it's infinitely what I remember.

I'm at the clock now. She's turned away from me, facing the information screen, as if she might reach out and finger a timetable, or cause some trouble and knock a stack of them over for fun to watch them spill.

I hold back. Is she only at the information desk to make a plan to go somewhere else? Will she take the Hudson Line away from here, or another train away from here, or will she head out to the street to hail a taxi? Have I only caught her when she's leaving, once again? I used to wonder what might happen, after. I never expected it to be a train station, littered with strangers, coiled with noise. So much had come before this moment: All the anticipation and questioning if she'd be here, and the darkness between, when the trees stood sentry over my body and the whistling rang through the vacant space between my ears. All the wondering before the flash of light took me over and put me back on the train.

Before the woods that night, I didn't know anything about her. Now she's real.

I tap her bare shoulder. Her skin is warm like smoke and cool like air, the exact temperature of the room. She doesn't seem to feel me.

I shift until I'm in her sight, if only she would stop busying herself with the train schedules and turn her head, just a little.

"Monet?" My voice cracks from disuse, but it makes sound. I hear myself as if the noise bounces off the celestial ceiling straight down to where we are. Even if it's only a whisper.

Does she hear?

She turns. A stack of timetables falls from the container in a rippling cascade. Neither of us moves to try to retrieve them. I make out her eyes from the shadows: deep brown with flecks of amber. Mine, I can't say.

After all this time, she's right in front of me, and it's a few minutes after midnight, as she'd promised. I don't know how long it's been since she dropped from the sky outside the gate and walked away without a scratch on her. But this is her, isn't it? I'd know her anywhere.

I only hope she knows it's me.

ACKNOWLEDGMENTS

THIS BOOK WENT THROUGH A NUMBER OF TRANSFORMATIONS as I tried to dig out its heart and uncover its true face. It wasn't easy. I will never forget the insightful, lightbulb-blazing question my editor, Elise Howard, asked me when we met at a café on Bleecker Street to talk about one of the many foggy drafts of this book. Without her, I never would have found my way out of the fog. My agent, Michael Bourret, assured me, again and again, that there was a light at the end of this tunnel of rewriting and revising and he never once let me forget it. Without his unwavering confidence in me and his wise guidance, I would never have made it this far in my career.

Thank you to the whole Algonquin Young Readers team, my publishing home, especially: Sarah Alpert, Kristen Bianco, Jacquelynn Burke, Jodie Cohen, Caitlin Humphrey,

ACKNOWLEDGMENTS

Krestyna Lypen, Ashley Mason, Michael McKenzie, Craig Popelars, Caitlin Rubinstein, Travis Smith, Carla Weise, and Laura Williams. Thank you to Kieryn Ziegler, Lauren Abramo, the team at Dystel, Goderich & Bourret, and Dana Spector at Paradigm Agency. Thank you for the sharp copy-edits of Elizabeth Johnson and proofreading by Dan Janeck, and the gorgeous art and cover design by Sarah J. Coleman.

Thank you to the Corporation of Yaddo, who may recognize the furniture. I'll admit that the seeds of this story were found during a residency in West House. Significant pieces of this book were also written at the Writers Room in New York City, Think Coffee on Mercer Street, the Merchant Hotel in Salem, Massachusetts, and the Highlights Foundation.

These people gave me moments of light when I needed it, and I hope I can do the same for them: Will Alexander, Elana K. Arnold, Bree Barton, Gerry Bello, Libba Bray, Phillip Brigham, Martha Brockenbrough, Amy Rose Capetta, Jess Capelle, Alison Cherry, Kara Lee Corthron, Marie Miranda Cruz, Echo Eggebrecht, Rebekah Faubion, Stephanie Feldstein, Melissa Fisher, Stephanie Garber, David Macinnis Gill, Alex Grizinski, Michelle Hodkin, Holly Hughes, Trevor Ingerson, Kelly Jensen, Varian Johnson, Jeanne Kay, Margot Knight, Uma Krishnaswami, Stephanie Kuehnert, Justine Larbalestier, Eileen Lawrence, Christine H. Lee, Jacqui Lipton, Samantha Mabry, Kekla Magoon, Cori McCarthy, Diana Mikhail, Phoebe North, Jilana Ordman, Micol Ostow, Emily X.R. Pan, Lilliam Rivera, Laura Ruby, Selah Saterstrom, Liz Garton

Scanlon, Cynthia Leitich Smith, Cristin Stickles, Erin Swan, Mandy Sue, Courtney Summers, Linda Urban, Daiana Vargas, and Aaron Zimmerman and the Tuesday Night Workshop. Thanks to my VCFA advisees, my fellow VCFA faculty, the program staff at Djerassi and my beloved Djerassi writers, especially those of you still with me from the beginning.

Thank you to my family, always unwavering in their support: Laurel Rose and Dan; Josh and Kristin; Shawnee; Marc; and most of all, my incredible mother, Arlene Seymour, who used to wander the streets of New York with hair to her waist and suede boots to her knees.

At the center of the writing storm, and during my foggiest and most lost, there's been my lifelong love, Erik, who shared the past twenty-one years in New York City with me, all because I refused to live anywhere else. I may have cried the day we let go of the keys to our tiny Village shoebox and said good-bye to the city only months after finishing this book, but with him at my side, I know that wherever we end up, it will be home.

Get lost in another tale of ghostly
suspense by Nova Ren Suma in

———

THE WALLS AROUND US

———

Read on for a preview.

Amber:

———

WE WENT WILD

———

WE WENT WILD that hot night. We howled, we raged, we screamed. We were girls—some of us fourteen and fifteen; some sixteen, seventeen—but when the locks came undone, the doors of our cells gaping open and no one to shove us back in, we made the noise of savage animals, of men.

We flooded the corridors, crowding together in the clammy, cooped-up dark. We abandoned our assigned colors—green for most of us, yellow for those of us in segregation, traffic-cone orange for anyone unlucky enough to be new. We left behind our jumpsuit skins. We showed off our angry, wobbly tattoos.

When outside the thunder crashed, we overtook A-wing and B-wing. When lightning flashed, we mobbed C-wing.

We even took our chances in D-wing, which held Suicide Watch and Solitary.

We were gasoline rushing for a lit match. We were bared teeth. Balled fists. A stampede of slick feet. We went wild, like anyone would. We lost our fool heads.

Just try to understand. After the crimes that had put us inside, after all the hideous things we were accused of and convicted of, the things some of us had done without apology and the things some of us had sworn we were innocent of doing (sworn on our mothers if we had mothers, sworn on our pets if we ever had a puppy dog or a scrawny cat, sworn on our own measly lives if we had nobody), after all that time behind bars, on this night we were free we were free we were free.

Some of us found that terrifying.

On this night, the first Saturday of that now-infamous August, there were forty-one girls locked up in the Aurora Hills Secure Juvenile Detention Center in the far northern reaches of the state, which meant we were one shy of full capacity. We weren't yet forty-two.

To our surprise, to our wide-eyed delight, the cells of B-wing and C-wing, of A-wing and even D-wing, had come open, and there we stood, a thunder of thudding hearts in the darkness. We stood outside our cages. We stood outside.

We looked to the guards' stations: They were unmanned.

We looked to the sliding gates at the end of our corridors: They were wide-open.

We looked to the floodlights ringing the high ceiling: The bulbs had gone dim.

We looked (or we tried to look; it was the way our bodies pulled) through the window slits and into the storm pounding outside, all across the compound. If only we could see past the triple-fenced perimeter, over and beyond the coils of barbed wire. Past the guards' tower. Past the steep road that plunged downhill to the tall iron gate at the bottom. We remembered, from when the blue-painted short bus from the county jail had carried us up here. We remembered we weren't so far from the public road.

That was when it hit us—how little time we were sure to have before the corrections officers returned to their posts. Maybe we should have been sensible about our sudden freedom, cautious. We weren't. We didn't stop to question the open locks. Not then. We didn't pause to wonder why the emergency lights hadn't blinked on, why the alarms didn't blare. We didn't think, either, about the COs who were supposed to be on night duty—where they could have gone, why their booths were empty, their chairs bare.

We scattered. We spread out. We pushed through barriers that were always locked to us before. We ran.

The night burst open the way a good riot tends to, when it takes over the yard and no one knows who started what, or cares. The shouts and screams, the whoops and wails. Forty-one of the worst female juvenile offenders in the state set loose without warning or reason or armed guards to take us down. It was beautiful and it was powerful, like lightning in our hands.

Some of us weren't thinking and only wanted to kick in the glass fronts of the vending machines in the canteen for snacks or pillage pills from the clinic to get a fix. Some of us wanted to pound a face in and jump someone, jump anyone; it didn't matter who. A couple of us simply wanted to slip out back under the murky cloud covering and shoot some hoops in the rain.

Then there were those of us, the ones with brains, who took a breath. And considered. Because, with no COs coming at us with clubs out, no alarms bleating or intercoms crackling commands to herd us back to our cells, the night really was ours, for the first time in days. Weeks. Months. Years.

And what's a girl to do with her first free night in years?

The most violent among us—the daddy killers, the slitters of strangers' throats, the point-blank shooters of pleading gas-station attendants—would later admit to finding a sense of peace in the plush darkness, a kind of justice not offered by the juvenile courts.

Sure, some of us knew we didn't deserve this reprieve. Not one of us was truly innocent, not when we were made to stand in the light, our bits and cavities and cavity fillings exposed. When we faced this truth inside ourselves, it somehow felt more ugly than the day we witnessed the judge say "guilty" and heard the courtroom cheer.

That was why a few of us hung back. Didn't leave our cells, where we kept our drawings and our love letters. Where we stowed our one good comb and stashed all our Reese's Peanut Butter Cups, which were like gold doubloons up in Aurora Hills, since we didn't have access to cash. Some of us stayed put in the place we knew.

Because what was out there? Who would keep us safe, on the outside?

Where, really, would a girl from Aurora Hills, who'd disappointed her family and scared off English teachers and social workers and public defenders and anyone who tried to help her, a girl who'd terrorized her neighborhood, who was as good as garbage (she'd been told), who was probably best left forgotten (she'd read this in letters from home), where would a girl like that go?

A lot of us did try to run—even if it was only habit. Some of us had been running all our lives. We ran because we could and because we couldn't not. We ran for our lives. We still thought they were worth running for.

Most of us didn't get far. We got distracted. Overexcited. Overcome. A couple of us came to a stop somewhere in one of the hallways outside our designated wing and sank to the cracked and pitted floor in gratitude, as if we'd been acquitted of all our crimes, our records expunged.

This felt like everything we'd dared let ourselves dream up, when the taunting fantasies slipped in between the bars. Wishes for fast getaway cars or Rapunzel ropes to climb out the narrow window openings. Pleas for forgiveness, for vengeance, for glittery new lives on some far-off riviera where we'd never again have to face hate or law or pain. It was happening. To us. We never did believe it could happen to kids like us.

Some of us cried.

There we were, set loose on the defenseless night, instantly wanting everything we could imagine: To thumb a ride at the nearest freeway. To call an old boyfriend and get laid. To have a never-ending breadstick feast at the Olive Garden. To sleep under fluffy covers in a large, soft bed.

That August marked my third summer at Aurora Hills. I'd been locked up here since I was fourteen (manslaughter; I pled innocent; I stuffed myself into a skirt and sheer hose for trial; my mother turned her face away when I was found guilty and hasn't looked my way since). But it's not my arrival I find myself thinking about, now that we have so much time to sit here thinking. It's not the judge's ruling and the deafening years of my sentence and how I landed here because not one person believed me when I said I didn't do it. I let go of all that a long time ago.

It's this one night that I keep coming back to. That first Saturday in August, when the locks couldn't hold us. That brief gift of freedom we'd take to our graves.

I get hung up on it sometimes, on what if things had gone another way. If I'd made it past the gates and gotten out. If I'd run.

Maybe I would have made it over the three sets of fencing and down the hill to the free patch of road and my part in this story would be over. Maybe all that was about to come tumbling at us after this, someone else would have to bear witness to. Someone else would have to do the remembering.

Because that was the night we went wild. I remember how we fought and we cried and we hid and we flung ourselves through windows and we pumped our legs with everything we had and we went running as far as we could make it, which wasn't far.

On that night, we felt emotions we hadn't had a taste of for six months, twelve months, eleven and a half weeks, nine hundred and nine days.

We were alive. I remember it that way. We were still alive, and we couldn't make heads or tails of the darkness, so we couldn't see how close we were to the end.

ALISON CHERRY

Nova Ren Suma is the author of the #1 *New York Times* bestselling *The Walls Around Us*, which was an Edgar Award finalist. She also wrote *Imaginary Girls* and *17 & Gone* and is co-creator of *FORESHADOW: A Serial YA Anthology.* She has an MFA in fiction from Columbia University and teaches at Vermont College of Fine Arts. Originally from the Hudson Valley, she spent most of her adult life in New York City and now lives in Philadelphia.